A
Long
Day's
Journey
Into
Death

Published by Long Midnight Publishing, 2023

copyright © 2023 Douglas Lindsay

ISBN: 979-8852033420

By Douglas Lindsay

The DI Buchan Series:

Buchan
Painted In Blood
The Lonely And The Dead
A Long Day's Journey Into Death

The DS Hutton Series

The Barney Thomson Series

DCI Jericho

The DI Westphall Trilogy

Pereira & Bain

Others:

Lost in Juarez
Being For The Benefit Of Mr Kite!
A Room With No Natural Light
Ballad In Blue
These Are The Stories We Tell
Alice On The Shore

A
LONG
DAY'S
JOURNEY
INTO
DEATH

DOUGLAS
LINDSAY

LMP

1

05:59

Buchan stared at himself in the mirror. He'd been standing in the same spot, naked, in his bathroom for three minutes, leaning on the rim of the sink. He'd showered, shaved, brushed his teeth. He was looking into his own eyes, thinking through the day ahead. But the day ahead did not promise much, and he couldn't focus. As soon as he thought of Davie Bancroft, and the paperwork, and the interview game they would both play, his mind forcibly pulled him in another direction. Any direction.

He saw nothing when he looked into his own eyes. Did that mean there was nothing to see, or was that normal? Did anyone see anything when staring into their own eyes? Was it a whim of romantic or literary fiction to think otherwise? Was it one of those notions people were gaslit into thinking they should believe?

The eyes, thought Buchan, well my eyes at any rate, say nothing.

The alarm on his phone beside the bed started going off. Buchan turned away from the mirror and walked into the bedroom. The curtains were open, the day already set fair and bright.

*

When he walked through to the open-plan kitchen/diner/sitting room Detective Constable Roth was in her usual position, sitting in one of the comfortable chairs by the window, her legs curled up on the seat, a MacBook open in her lap. The room smelled of coffee.

Edelman, the cat, was sleeping in the chair opposite.

Just over three months previously Roth had arrived one evening at Buchan's house needing someone to talk to, as she began the slow recovery from seventy-two hours of kidnap, torture and sexual assault. She'd stayed in his apartment, sleeping in the spare room, every night since. One morning she'd made him breakfast, and he'd asked her not to do it again. 'How about coffee?' she'd said, and Buchan had said, 'Coffee would be nice,' and so the coffee was waiting for him every morning, regardless of how early he appeared in the kitchen.

Sometimes she cooked them dinner.

Since the kidnap, Roth had not slept for more than two hours at a time. She wore comfortable lounge pants, and a baggy, San Francisco 49ers T-shirt. A month earlier she'd had her hair cut short, so that it was now its natural auburn. Buchan, like everyone else at the station, had never seen Roth with anything other than pink hair.

Buchan poured himself a coffee from the percolator, warm milk from a small pot on the hob, a glass of water from the bottle in the fridge, then came and stood by the window. Edelman did not stir. It was apparent that the cat liked having Roth around. Buchan wondered if he would go with her when she left.

On the low table between the two chairs, there was a beautiful, ornamental chess set, figures of hand-carved wood. He'd bought it so that Roth could use it when playing chess against the app on her phone. He hadn't bought it for her, as such, not so that she would take it with her when she left. He'd thought of it as art, and worth the several thousand pounds he'd paid.

Regardless of what he told himself, he also knew he'd insist she take it with her. And if she refused, there it would sit, a melancholic remembrance of her time here.

'Didn't sleep well again?' he said. He wasn't looking at her.

'Not too bad.'

The Clyde, four floors below them, was flowing with one of those beautiful, iridescent flat calms that Buchan could stare at all day. The window was open, the sounds of the city waking up coming into the apartment. The sounds were distant though, and this part of the river felt like the laziest of Sunday mornings, the lazy river that Hoagy Carmichael sang about.

Yet, there was something about looking at a river, not unlike staring into his own eyes in the mirror. He always felt there was something missing, as though the river should be providing a philosophical insight that always eluded him.

'What have you got on today?' she asked, although it might have been a while later. Buchan and Roth had found they were both comfortable with silence.

'Speaking to Davie Bancroft,' said Buchan.

'Oh.'

Buchan nodded. Everyone knew Bancroft, the great escapologist. So many people had been due to testify against him over the years, and so many people had withdrawn the evidence, or had left town, or had taken the blame themselves. And there was nothing cunning about him. He was brutal and unpleasant, and every single time the police spoke to him, it was ugly and unforgiving.

'Have we got anything that's going to stick?' she asked.

'We have a witness. Runs a small newsagent in the Gallowgate. Says she's been paying him monthly protection money for over five years. She's got it fully documented. Has audio, though we haven't verified it yet. In March she was one-week overdue with her money. One of Bancroft's people raped her as payment.'

'Jesus. You think she'll follow through?'

'No,' said Buchan.

He took a drink of coffee, another, and then tipped the mug and finished it off. Drank the water, and then finally turned and looked at Roth for the first time since he'd come to stand at the window.

'You're seeing Jan today?'

Jan was Roth's therapist. Roth nodded.

'Ten-thirty.'

'Got anything else on?'

'Meeting mum for lunch at one.'

Buchan never asked why Roth didn't go and stay with her mother.

He held her gaze for a moment, was going to say that it would be nice if she made dinner for them that evening, and then decided he would leave it to see how the day was going, and then he nodded, and turned away from the window.

'See you later,' he said.

'Boss,' said Roth.

2

Buchan was sitting in the Jigsaw Man's café, with another cup of coffee, another glass of water, and a pain aux raisin. Sometime after he'd said to Roth that he didn't want her to make breakfast, he'd told her it had become part of his routine to eat in the café by the river, the Stand Alone, in between his apartment and the Serious Crime Unit building. He'd felt strangely awkward telling her, as though there was some element of betrayal in it. 'OK,' she'd said.

The Jigsaw Man's table was empty. He was rarely here this early. Over time Buchan had worked out that he generally appeared in the café sometime around ten, and would sit in position at his table at the back, drinking coffee and occasionally eating, while doing a jigsaw on a table for four. Sometimes customers sat with him. Buchan got the impression he was some kind of local sage. He had never spoken to him.

He flicked through the news on the BBC website on his phone. Nine days previously he'd had no idea who Claire Avercamp was. That was when she'd first been reported missing. He'd seen a report on her disappearance at work, he'd at least become aware of who she was, and the films she'd directed, and he'd judged it not really a matter for the police. Certainly not for the SCU. It had been quite some time since she'd made a movie, and the promise of her early twenties, two BAFTA nominations and the award of *Un Certain Regard* at Cannes, had been flushed away on drink and drugs and self-destructive relationships. It was not the first time she'd gone missing, and even her mother who'd reported the disappearance to the police, had said she presumed she was likely lying dead in some squalid bedsit somewhere.

There barely seemed to be any story worth telling, but it hadn't stopped the newspapers reporting it every day for the previous nine days, though it had slowly been moving down through the pages.

'Slow news month,' Buchan said to himself, flicking the screen onto the next story.

3

Buchan's mornings were conducted in three stages along the river. His apartment, the café, and the office. And now he was standing at the window, looking down on the seemingly still water, the traffic beginning to pick up on the opposite bank, along Clyde Street into the Broomielaw.

The only other person in the office was DC Ellie Dawkins, who'd nodded at Buchan as he'd entered, and then had lowered her head to her keyboard and continued writing whatever report it was she was working on. Buchan couldn't remember.

Dawkins had taken over most of Roth's duties during her prolonged sick leave. She was good, well-organised, but lacked Roth's spark. Or, at least, the spark the old Roth had had.

'Boss,' said DS Kane, appearing from nowhere, joining Buchan at the window.

'Sam.'

She indicated the coffee in her hand and said, 'Sure I can't get you one?'

She'd noticed Buchan's habits had changed, but didn't know why. No one else at SCU knew that Roth had been staying with Buchan all this time.

'I'm good,' said Buchan. 'Maybe later.'

Together they looked down on the river, one of those days when it was impossible to tell which way it flowed, or whether the tide was coming or going.

'We all set for Bancroft?' asked Kane, after a few moments. She wasn't as comfortable with the silences as Roth had become.

'Nope,' said Buchan.

She turned and looked at him, a little surprised.

'Really?'

He took a moment, long enough that she gave up waiting for an immediate answer, and turned back to the view.

'We have what we have,' said Buchan, eventually, 'but I don't know that it's any more than we've ever had before. Strike that. We know it's not. It's a game, and he's better at it than us.

He's a poundshop, I don't know, Blofeld maybe, or a poundshop Vito Corleone, and we have nothing with which to pierce the armour. And what are we doing today? Where is it getting us?'

'We have a witness.'

'We've had witnesses before.'

'I've got a good feeling about this one.'

Buchan turned and gave Kane a rueful smile.

'Sure, Sam,' he said.

Another short silence was ended by Kane asking, 'What did you do last night?'

Buchan had worked until eight-thirty, he'd sat in the Winter Moon for fifteen minutes and two drinks, he hadn't spoken to Janey, and had had no more than a brief discussion on Claire Avercamp with Duncan the Pakistani priest, and then he'd gone home, where he and Roth had largely sat in silence listening to Oscar Peterson and Chet Baker, while Roth had lost a game of chess against her phone in fifty-seven moves.

'Usual,' he said. 'You?'

'Watched *The Sound of Music* again,' said Kane.

'Are you sixty?' asked Buchan, and Kane tapped him on the arm.

'Bugger off, boss,' she said, laughing, and she turned away from the window and sat down at her desk to begin the day.

4

Davie Bancroft was supposed to report to SCU at seven-forty-five a.m. He had a reputation for scrupulous timekeeping. Indeed, everything that the police asked of him, he would happily do to the letter. 'I'm unimpeachable,' he'd said to Buchan more than once, usually accompanied by a shrug or a smirk.

He had not arrived by seven-forty-five a.m.

'What d'you think?' Kane said to Buchan, at seven-forty-six.

'It's unusual for him, but let's not get carried away. We have to give him until eight before we start asking, and at least quarter-past before we start cooking up a storm.'

His phone rang.

'Maybe this is it,' said Kane, referring to Bancroft's late arrival, rather than the ringing phone. 'Maybe this is him not showing up because he's in trouble, because he doesn't have all his ducks in a row.'

'Or maybe his alarm didn't go off or he got held up in traffic. Let's…,' and he finished the sentence with a *remain calm for the moment* gesture.

'Buchan,' he said, lifting the phone.

'Inspector, have you got a minute?'

Chief Inspector Liddell. Buchan nodded down the phone.

'You want me to come up?'

'Please.'

He hung up, he lifted his suit jacket off the back of the chair and shrugged it on over his shoulders, and then indicated the upper floor with a small head movement.

'Won't be long,' he said.

'I'll let you know if he shows,' said Kane.

Buchan left the office, and walked quickly up the stairs to the seventh floor.

5

Chief Inspector Liddell was sitting at her desk, wearing a familiar maroon top, twirling a familiar unlit cigarette around her fingers.

'Inspector,' said Liddell, 'thanks for coming up.'

Buchan nodded, and stood before her desk. There was something in her manner to imply that whatever she was about to share might be a little different to the norm. He didn't ask, however. The story, such as it was, would come.

'You'll have read in the news about the disappearance of the film director, Claire Avercamp?' said Liddell, after a few moments.

Buchan nodded. That was why that name had come into his head when he'd walked up the stairs. A premonition, not just a random memory dump from an hour earlier.

Liddell smiled grimly and said, 'I've rather been fearing this would happen for the last nine days.'

She put the cigarette in her mouth, did not light it, and then returned to twirling it around her fingers.

'I feel this will end badly,' she continued, 'but here we are. Claire's father and I were old university friends. There was a thing that happened… well, I'm not going to go into what that was.' She stopped, held Buchan's gaze.

'I don't need to know,' said Buchan.

'I owe him, that's all. Thirty-three years I've owed him. I knew it would come some day and, to be honest, I don't grudge him it. I wouldn't be here now without him. I wouldn't be anywhere.

'So, this is obviously exactly what a parent would say, but he says the stories in the press the last week, the drinking and drug-taking and her bouts of depression, inevitably leading to… well, you're nodding, you've seen what it's led to. He says that yes, there were drugs and there was alcohol, but she was a young woman on the celebrity circuit. The press took one or two incidents and made them career-defining. She'd been treated for depression, but he says that all of that was behind her. Although, he was honest enough to admit that her mother would disagree.'

'Nevertheless, her father is sure she hasn't just gone off on a massive bender somewhere.'

'Correct. For the last six months Claire's been working on a documentary feature on the theft and trafficking of antique books. I don't know if you recall the robbery out at Eurocentral at the end of October?' Buchan nodded. 'This was her hook. Who stole the books, why'd they steal them, where have they gone?'

'And her dad's convinced her disappearance now is related to the work she was doing?'

'He's more measured than that, but he at least thinks it more likely than Claire falling off the wagon and vanishing into a bottle.'

They stared at each other across the desk. Something to be said, but typically Buchan thought it obvious and so wasn't saying it, waiting instead for Liddell to accept its obviousness, and to answer the point.

'I know what you're thinking. What about the local station investigating her disappearance, and what about the unit at Dalmarnock that are investigating the book theft?'

'You're right,' said Buchan. 'You do know what I'm thinking.'

'I've spoken to the locals and, as you might expect, they are swamped with the everyday bullshit of a station. Robbery, rape, assault, and on and on. They don't have the time to investigate the disappearance of a known alcoholic. That was the station chief's line, and I can't blame her. She also said, go ahead, it's yours if you want it. So, we don't need to worry about anyone sniping at our backs.'

'What about Dalmarnock and the Eurocentral investigation?'

'Good question. We don't know if Claire spoke to anyone there yet, we don't know how involved she was with them. If they even knew what she was doing. You will need to speak to them.'

'What about Avercamp being pictured drunk in Edinburgh three weeks ago,' said Buchan, hating that he was bringing tabloid gossip to the table. But it was something he'd read in the news, and its currency as a story was one of the main drivers for the assumption that whatever had happened to her, was likely self-inflicted.

'She told her parents that her drinks were spiked, but people don't want to believe that, particularly when they claim she was an alcoholic in the first place.'

'So, where was she in the process?' asked Buchan.

'How do you mean?'

'In the process of making the film. Was she filming as she went along? Is there a cinematographer attached? A writer? Producers? Does the film have a name, does it have a distributor?'

Liddell was waving self-consciously long before he'd finished the rapid-fire questioning, and he slowed and didn't complete the final question.

'I think you know a lot more about film production than I do, inspector. I have the name of someone she was working with on the project, if you wouldn't mind taking it on. You can familiarise yourself with the story, then speak to this colleague of Claire's.'

Buchan had nothing to say. He didn't need the chief telling him how to handle the case, such as it was. All he needed to know was that she wanted him to do it.

'You're due to speak to Davie Bancroft today?' said Liddell.

'Yes.'

'You got anything else on?'

Buchan looked at the time, then took his phone out and checked if Kane had been in touch. A minute earlier she'd sent the message: *No sign of him yet.*

'Might not even have that,' said Buchan. 'He's late.'

'You don't mind spending a day or two on this?'

'It's fine,' said Buchan. 'You sure I won't be stepping on toes?'

'Doesn't look like it, but perhaps you'll find some along the way.'

'You know who's been investigating the Eurocentral raid?'

'DI Savage.'

'Rose,' said Buchan, nodding. 'I know her.'

He paused, he thought about how it would go when he had to speak to her. He realised he didn't know her well enough to have any idea.

'You happy?' said Liddell, a familiar small smile on her lips, enjoying the question.

'Oh, I'm all in, boss,' said Buchan.

—

10

'Good. For now, the chat with Savage aside, I'd rather it was just you,' said Liddell. 'I think we're OK taking this on, but you never know. So I'd rather be light touch. If, on the off-chance you turn up anything useful and need to expand, then speak to me and maybe we'll bring in the others. First off, see what you can dig up yourself.'

'What does your old friend do now?' asked Buchan, as the case seemed to have been addressed as much as it was likely to be.

'He was always a little fly-by-night, going from one thing to another. We never really stayed in touch. Seems he's just started a distillery outside Largs. Firth of Clyde Gin. He promised to send me a bottle.'

She made the appropriate whatever gesture.

Buchan stared to the side for a moment, processing the information, and if there was anything else he needed to ask, then he said, 'OK, chief. I'll speak to this contact he's given us, and let you know how it goes.'

He checked the time again, then added, with more than a hint of sardonicism, 'I'll give it until ten-thirty.'

Liddell smiled and shook her head, indicating for him to leave.

6

Buchan sat in his 1959 Facel Vega HK500, having left the office just in time to hit the morning traffic head on. He wasn't going far, due to meet Harriet Blake at her house in Shawlands before the day really got going. He'd had a quick look at the police files on the case before he'd left, realising that Avercamp's father might have had a point. There had been very little interest shown in the investigation by the locals in Bridgeton. The story's prominence in the press had made little difference.

Nevertheless, while the police could always claim manpower issues, and as an excuse it was tired and old and obvious, it was also, as Buchan well knew, true.

'Hey,' he said, his phone on speaker.

'What's up?' asked Roth.

'You still at home?'

'Sure.'

'You got time to look at something for me?'

'Sure.'

'I'm spending the day on the Claire Avercamp story,' he said, her, 'Really?' cutting across him as he continued, 'And I was wondering if you could just immerse yourself in her career and life, and everything there is about her online. Put something together.'

'Is there new information?'

'No,' said Buchan. He wondered how much he should say. The boss had, after all, asked him not to involve any of the others. But Roth was not on duty, so this felt a little like working to the letter, if not the spirit of the request. Everything about his dealings with Roth at the moment would be considered inappropriate, or at the very least *odd*, but he completely trusted her, and in this instance it was hardly a massive breach of protocol.

'Her father is an old university buddy of the chief's.'

'Ah, one of those.'

He could see her smile.

'That's where we are. I'm just going to take a look, see if

there's anything showing up beyond what the press are saying. Apparently she was working on an exposé about the antique book raid at Eurocentral last autumn.'

'I haven't seen anything about that,' said Roth. 'I remember the break-in, but that's been, like, completely dead for months now. And there's never been anything about it in connection with Claire Avercamp.'

'That's pretty much all I've got. I'm on my way to speak to someone she was working with. I'll call afterwards. Can you just have a trawl through the mire, see if there's anything that leaps out at you? Plus, sorry, I wouldn't mind a potted life story, as I'd barely heard of the woman before last week.'

'On it, boss,' said Roth.

7

There was music playing from a radio in the corner of the kitchen. One of the modern, digital Roberts radios, designed to look like a nineteen-sixties classic. A strange, haunting tune. She saw him looking at the speaker, and smiled.

'No idea what it is,' she said. 'Radio 3, they play all sorts.'

Harriet Blake laid the tea in front of him, and then sat down on the other side of the kitchen table.

'You haven't had anyone from the police speak to you in the past week?' asked Buchan.

'Wasn't expecting it, to be honest. Look where we are. You wait fifteen hours for an ambulance, you can't get a GP's appointment any more than you can get the council to come and repair the giant sinkhole on the road outside your house, and if the police turn up to investigate a crime, you can consider yourself bloody lucky.' She waved the comment away. 'I'm not criticising, inspector, not one bit. All the public services have been run to the bone.'

She made another extravagant gesture, as if to expel that part of the conversation.

'You're here now,' she said.

She was forty, her hair designer untidy, a light summer dress to meet the forecast warm, early May day head on.

'You're working with Claire on a documentary about stolen antique books?'

'One way of putting it, but yes, I guess we've started down the road.'

'What's the other way of putting it?'

She smiled, she took a drink of tea, she winced at its heat.

'I don't know why I'm drinking tea, I'm already hot.'

She blew over her face, ruffling the loose hairs of her fringe. It reminded Buchan of Janey.

'Claire has this idea for a movie. You know, they're pretty in vogue at the moment, those kind of, you know, they're not docu-dramas, but they're decent budget, high-end, cinematic documentaries. She thinks that'll work for her. She's quite caught up in the story. Not sure why, she's just got the bug. She's been putting ideas together, she's been speaking to people. One of your lot, actually. Detective Inspector Savage.'

'What did DI Savage have to say about her making the film?'

'Unimpressed. Told her not to interfere with police business. Promised her a world of cooperation once they've built their case and have their suspects behind bars, but way more hostile regarding any interest prior to that.'

'And what's your part in it?'

'I'll produce the movie, should it ever happen. But at the moment, there's not much of a movie to produce.'

'You haven't started filming?'

'No. Very early days. The idea of the film's still formulating.'

'Claire doesn't have a partner?'

'You mean a working partner in the project, or a pillow talk partner?'

'I meant the latter, but either.'

'No men, or women, currently in her life, no. And as for working with Claire... I don't know if you know about her career,' and Buchan shook his head, 'but her last project was an absolute car crash. I mean, holy shit. She was in such a bad place while she was making it.'

'What was it called?'

'*This Joy Is Called Sadness.*'

'I don't know it,' said Buchan.

'Well, no, you wouldn't, because it didn't come close to getting finished. Her previous couple of movies were pretty poor. I mean, she'd really fallen off the cliff, to be honest. Should have taken a break. But she had this idea for, you know, this piece of existentialist whatever. Arthouse, but... well, she called it mainstream arthouse. Managed to get American money to make the movie. I think she had to shag a couple of people, but it wasn't like she wasn't happy to do that. God, there's so much content getting made these days, so much shit getting thrown at the wall. But she got her budget, and somehow she managed to shag her way to writing, producing *and* directing.'

'And it was a car crash.'

'Yes. Too much alcohol, too many drugs, too much wild abandon. She was four weeks behind schedule after four weeks. A couple of the leads walked. The cinematographer walked. By the time the studio pulled the plug she'd spent most of the budget. It was, frankly, *never work again* territory.'

'When was that?'

'Three years ago. Took her a couple of years to sort her shit out. She got there in the end, I really think she did.'

'You're persuaded enough to be happy to produce this new movie?'

Harriet Blake smiled.

'I'm not going to say it's a no-lose situation. There's always the capacity to lose in this business. But Claire and I go back a long way. I felt I owed her this much, that's all.' She paused, considered her words. 'And, like I said, Claire can be very persuasive with the sex. Nevertheless, no one is putting any money up front here. No one, me included, has so far committed anything to this, and no one will until Claire has a solid package for us. A beginning, a middle and an end. With a positive result in the investigation too, I should add.'

'Is she a trained journalist?'

'Oh, yes. That's what she... you know, she didn't study film, she studied journalism, but then, she wrote that first script, and boom! Life took off in a different direction.'

'So this is her returning to her roots.'

'Going back to basics,' said Blake, nodding.

'Are you in the loop?'

Another drink of tea, this one to the accompaniment of her shaking head.

'Not especially. We spoke on the phone a few weeks ago, you know, after the... you read about the incident in Edinburgh?'

'Yes.'

'I was worried about her. Well, to be honest, I thought, that's it, it's over, and I did not, I'm afraid, particularly believe her when she said her drinks had been spiked.'

'What about now?'

'Now... I don't know. Either way, it ties in. Either she'd started drinking again, and so she falls into the abyss and out of sight. Or someone was out to ruin her, possibly to get her to stop the investigation, they pushed her off the wagon, and when she forced herself to get back on it, they took more drastic action. Or, of course, she was pushed off the wagon and she's lost herself as a result.'

'Which do you think?'

For the first time Blake showed the worry she must have been feeling, and she laid down her mug of tea, leaning into the table a little.

'I don't know,' she said. 'I don't… I don't know how she could currently be OK, I don't know how this ends well. If she's just done this to herself, well, it's such a waste, but we've all seen it coming. But, my God, if someone has kidnapped her or… if someone's killed her just as she was getting her life back together, just as she was getting somewhere…'

She shivered, she was lost for a moment.

'You've had no sight of anything that Claire was working on?' asked Buchan. 'Any names, anywhere she'd been?'

'Daniel Maplethorpe,' said Blake.

'Daniel Maplethorpe?'

'It's a name I remember. She'd mentioned a few people, but really, I was trying to make sure I didn't get sucked in. I didn't want to know names, I didn't want to know too much. I was trying to encourage her, but without getting my hopes up.'

'Maplethorpe?'

'Yeah, I just remember that one because it kind of stood out. Not a name you hear, I suppose. I think she'd spoken to him a couple of times. I didn't ask anything specific, I didn't look the guy up.' A pause, and then, 'I can't imagine there are too many Daniel Maplethorpes in the world.'

'No other names? Really, take your time.'

'I've been waiting for the police to come for nine days,' she said. 'I've had all the time I need, and this is all I've got.' Another beat or two, and then she said, 'Maplethorpe,' with a shrug.

8

Buchan was back in the car, on the phone to Roth.

'Getting anywhere?' asked Roth.

'I'm heading round to Avercamp's apartment,' said Buchan. 'Likely need to call Apple, see if I can get a look at her iCloud.'

'This year?'

'I know people,' said Buchan, and he could see Roth smiling on the other end of the phone. 'What have we got on Avercamp?'

'Thirty-six,' said Roth, getting on with it, and Buchan recognised the straightforward business voice he hadn't heard from Roth since she'd been in the office. 'Studied journalism at St Andrews, but never worked in the field. In her final year she wrote the script, *Two Falls Meadow*, it got picked up straight away, movie came out a couple of years later. She got a BAFTA nomination for best original screenplay. She then had two hit movies she both wrote and directed. *Rattlesnake* and *A Cry In The Light*.'

'I don't know them,' said Buchan.

'Let's call them arthouse hit movies. The kind of thing the critics love, they do well at festivals, Netflix and Amazon love to have them on their slate, but ultimately the audience, compared to *Mission Impossible A Hundred*, is pretty titch.' A pause, then she resumed the narrative, and Buchan reminded himself to let her get to the end without interruption. 'By this time, though, there were stories of alcohol, and a couple of shitty relationships. Oh, there was also one where she accused an executive of abuse, and that got into Me Too territory. She was drunk when she told a reporter the story, then she withdrew it. Classically sad tale, unfortunately. She was the victim, and she so botched the telling of it, the other side managed to make her look like the bad guy. And her next movie was a flop. Whether that was as a reaction to the sexual assault story, it's hard to tell. Maybe the business just decided she wasn't one of them anymore, and needed taken down a peg or two. Either she was too big for her boots, she was messing things up with substance abuse, or the other thing: vindictive men coming for her because she'd let the audience see behind the curtain.

'So, that was *My Cousin Martha*, then there was *We, The Malcontent*, which again bombed. Second movie in a row, critics didn't like it, no awards, no nominations, not many festivals, no money, no audience. To be fair, with a title like that, she wasn't going to get very far. Then she still had enough of a reputation to get the money to make a show for MoviePlay, got a decent cast involved, and she blew it.'

'Her producer's just been telling me about it. *This Joy Is Called Sadness*.'

'Yep. That sounds like it was a disaster. There's a lot written about it, but it's all unverified gossip. The actual people involved all seem quite tight-lipped. However it actually played out, it was ugly, she got kicked off, they gave it another few days, then decided to shut the whole thing down. Meanwhile, Claire retreated to her safe space. Lots of drink, lots of drugs, a score of shitty relationships, all well-documented in the media, with men *and* women. Lots of rumours, presumably a lot of falsehoods in amongst them all, but that's where we are. Then, there's no knight in shining armour, she just kind of vanishes. She stopped hitting the town, I guess. There are a few stories asking what happened, a kind of even split between suggestions she's holed up in some squalid crack den, or she's gone off to get cleaned up somewhere. But, basically, until she appeared drunk in Edinburgh a few weeks ago, she'd fallen off the radar.'

'No mention of her putting another project together?'

'Nothing.'

'Any mention of rare or antique books?'

'Not so far.'

'Any hint of where she might actually have been since she vanished?'

'No one seems to know. Or, you know, no one in press terms. There may be plenty of people who knew, just none who spoke to the gutters.'

'OK, thanks.'

He checked the time. Still early, well before nine, felt like he was flying quickly through the start of the day, even if he hadn't actually got anywhere yet.

'You got time before seeing the doc to look at another couple of people?'

'Ages yet,' said Roth. 'Shoot.'

*

Before moving on to Buchan's next request, Roth re-watched a short clip of Avercamp being interviewed for a podcast. Avercamp was ostensibly there to talk about *We, The Malcontent*, but the interviewer wasn't particularly interested in the movie, and the questions were much more focussed on the arc of Avercamp's career.

Hair dyed fluorescent pink, a nose ring, a lip ring, tattoos on one forearm, another on her neck, head down, she reacted badly to every question. She wanted to talk about the film. She wanted, more than anything, to speak the truth, thought Roth. But she can't. The film business doesn't like truth. No business likes truth.

What was it about her? What was it that spoke to her? Was it just the obvious? The pink hair, the piercing? (Albeit, Roth now had neither.) The struggle to recover from abuse? Roth's work colleagues had, at least, been far more understanding than anyone Avercamp had had to deal with. Nevertheless, the woman was speaking to her. Her fear, her discomfort, the sense that she was lost.

That's it, thought Roth. Avercamp was lost, just as she herself was lost. And while Avercamp turned to drink and alcohol and ruinous relationships, Roth was dealing with her feelings of being utterly adrift by hiding away in the house of her detective inspector.

'Pick your poison,' she said quietly, and then she managed to click off the video of Avercamp, filled with a familiar melancholy, and began to address the next request on Buchan's list.

9

Buchan let himself into Claire Avercamp's apartment, a ground-floor studio flat in Bridgeton. Late seventies build, just around the corner from the Cross.

On the face of it, the flat gave up no secrets. It was bland. A cipher that said nothing about the person who lived there. Buchan assumed she likely rented the place already furnished, doing nothing to put her own stamp on it. The kind of place you'd come to live anonymously, having brought nothing of yourself from your previous existence.

His phone rang. He was sitting at the dining table, looking at the main room. A folded-out sofa bed, a duvet smoothed out over it. There was no phone and no laptop, no electronic equipment of any sort, bar the small television on a small unit, an Apple Box and a router beside it. The router was still switched on. An orange and blue rug on a neutral, beige carpet. On the walls, three black and white prints of old Manhattan: the Empire State, Central Park in winter, a llama sticking its head and neck out of the window of a taxi on Fifth Avenue.

'Sam,' he said, putting the phone on speaker.

'I'm at Bancroft's house,' said Kane. 'Janet says he left here at seven-fifteen, plenty of time to get in.'

'And we've no word of him after that?'

'Nope.'

Buchan looked at the picture of the llama, which was staring at him from the opposite wall.

'You've called him?'

'His phone's switched off.'

'Dammit,' muttered Buchan.

He leaned into the table, lowered his gaze away from the llama's steady stare.

'I'll check back in when I can,' said Buchan, 'you all right to lead on this for now?'

'Of course. You happy for me to raise the stakes?'

'You have the con, Sam, do what you think's best. And, just for clarity, yes, happy for you to raise the stakes, if that's what you need to do.'

'Boss.'

They hung up.

Buchan stared at his phone. He had another call to make, tapping his right index finger on the table while he thought it through.

He had a contact at Apple who owed him. He had the guy's personal number, he was pretty certain he'd get what he needed when he asked. But these things, these favours people owed the police, they weren't indefinite and endless, they wouldn't result in favours being repaid in perpetuity. This would be a one-off, and then it would be done. If he made the call now, the favour would have been repaid. The chances were, however, that Buchan would want to ask him something else next week.

How many times had he thought about it in the last couple of years, and had decided to save it for another day? To park a potential request in favour of a slower, more formal approach to Apple for information?

'Bugger it,' he muttered. Leave it long enough and his contact would have moved on, and the chance for anything would be gone.

He found the number, pressed call and waited.

10

Savage had been looking askance at Buchan since he'd sat down opposite her. They were in a small office at Police HQ in Dalmarnock. The room was bright, the river glinting in the sun behind Savage's left shoulder. Buchan wasn't going to apologise for having turned up, but he understood her position.

'I'm surprised SCU could be bothered,' she said.

'Why?'

She kind of shrugged, straightening her shoulders.

'You know who Tom Brady is?'

Buchan shook his head.

'Played American football. When he came into the league he was a nobody. For every player in the league you get cards, you know, collectors' cards. Every player, every season. Kids collect them, adults too, if they've got nothing better to do. Tom Brady arrives, there's a card. He's a nobody, so hardly any cards are produced, and hardly anyone bothers keeping the ones that are. Twenty-something years later he's a phenomenon. One of those cards, and we're talking, the kind of card you'll buy in a pack of six at Tesco for a pound-fifty, a Tom Brady, rookie season card, goes at auction for two-point-four million dollars.'

She looked at him, eyebrows raised, kind of asking the question if he was keeping up, and so he nodded.

'One month later, one month, although not that it matters, a 1566, second edition of Copernicus's *De Revolutionibus*, so you know, this is near as dammit *a piece of history*, gets sold at auction in Paris for just over four hundred and fifty thousand euros.'

She left it at that for a moment, then made a *that's about the size of it* gesture.

'Plenty of people are still going to think a four hundred thousand pound book is worth stealing,' said Buchan.

'Sure, but everything in perspective. There's a market for it, and there are criminal gangs making a living out of it, but there's a reason this one's on my desk, and not on the desk of someone at SCU. It may be *something*, but compared to all sorts of other things, this is small potatoes.'

Buchan was nodding. He'd wondered, and he'd already thought it through, and he'd decided that more than likely this was the issue. Just as market forces dictated that a player's sports card was more valuable than original, early modern science, so would the police allocate their resources.

'How's the investigation going?'

Savage looked at her computer screen, turning back to Buchan with another shrug.

'You want me to send you the file?'

'How big is it?' he asked bluntly, and Savage laughed.

'Big enough. You want the synopsis?'

'Please. But yes, also send it, I'll get one of my people to have a look through, if that's OK.'

'Of course. So, we had the break-in at a warehouse at Eurocentral along the M8. There was a stock of books being sent from eastern Europe – Tallinn, Riga, Warsaw, Vilnius mainly – so the Baltic states and Poland, to the US. They transited in the UK for cataloguing with the European HQ of the auction house that was going to sell them in New York.

'This was a big warehouse, there were all sorts of things in there to be stolen. The only things that were taken, were the books. Someone knew the books were there, they broke in, they left behind the shoes and the watches and the dehumidifiers and the whatever else was in there, and they made off with the books. We've had some people over from Poland, and they're not happy.'

'I don't even remember that break-in being on the news,' said Buchan.

'It was right in the middle of the Truss prime ministerial psychodrama. No one was talking about anything else. I'm sure it wasn't the only thing that slipped beneath the radar. Compared to that comedy shitshow, and let's not forget the war in Ukraine and every other horror story from around the world, someone stealing some old books wasn't even local news. No one cared. And here the robbers showed a certain level of smarts. Had they taken everything that was available to them, this would've been a much bigger story.'

'But then, it wouldn't have been a story about stolen books,' said Buchan. 'The books themselves would've got lost amongst everything else.'

'True. We think they made that calculation. They were

betting that if it was just about the books, the overall value wasn't too great, and the police wouldn't allocate much time to it.' A pause, another small shrug, and then, 'And they were right. We just don't have the manpower.'

She made a gesture that was meant to indicate the number of empty desks in the open-plan outside the office door.

'You make any kind of inroads?'

'Some, sure. We think the whole thing was masterminded by a gang working out of Gdańsk. Headed up by a character by the name of Jan Baltazar. Yeah, I don't know, he probably made that up after watching some movie or other.'

'Or reading the Bible.'

Savage laughed.

'Right. Anyway, to be fair to him, this guy is straight out a movie. To be honest, bloody glad he's not one of ours on a regular basis. Get this. No one knows what he looks like.'

Buchan couldn't keep the flash of dismay, or perhaps contempt, from his face. A cardboard cut-out, action movie villain. Just what the day needed.

'We've been in touch with Polish counterparts, everything being done through Europol, of course. However, like I said, we didn't really have the time to allocate to it. I've tried, I've had a few arguments with,' and she jerked a thumb up to the next floor, 'but ultimately, the theft of antique books isn't high on anyone's radar.'

'So, this gang flew in, or drove in, ostensibly on business or on holiday or whatever, carried out the robbery, and headed off back home?'

'We're not sure how many actually came in. It was a Polish-orchestrated operation, but we think they had a Scottish partner. So, whether those books are back in Poland now... well, frankly, we have no idea.'

'Who's the Scottish partner?'

'You might know them. Just a regular Glasgow southside lot. Head guy's called Davie Bancroft.'

Buchan's face may not have been very expressive, but his body language gave away his interest, his shoulders straightening, sitting forward a little in the seat.

'You know Davie, then,' said Savage, nodding.

For the first time since he'd spoken to Liddell that morning, Buchan felt the excitement of a new case.

'Tell me where Claire Avercamp comes in,' he said.

11

Buchan drove the Facel out of the car park of police HQ in Dalmarnock, and began the short drive along the south bank of the river, back to the SCU building by the old Glasgow Bridge.

The car in the rear-view mirror was there, just as he'd thought it might be. He'd noticed it on the short drive from Avercamp's house to Dalmarnock, and there was something then that made him think he'd already seen it that morning. Now, as he drove along the long, straight boulevard, he saw it again.

It was sitting three cars behind, and too far back for him to get a clear view of the marque and the registration plate.

He bided his time until he came to a blind corner, then swung the Facel round, and parked just out of sight, around the corner. His tail was about to follow him round before realising how quickly Buchan had stopped.

Buchan reached for his phone, as the cars in between drove straight on, and then the black Ford Fiesta came round, and he caught a look of consternation on the driver's face, and then the car sped past, Buchan managing to get a picture of the rear of the car, before it was lost in traffic, heading away from the city centre.

Buchan cursed himself for not getting the camera up in time to get the driver face-on, then he checked his mirrors, waited, then did a wide U-turn and stopped at the lights, waiting to head back out onto the main road.

'Amateur hour,' he muttered.

12

'Wow, you really know your stuff about this Claire Avercamp woman,' said Kane. 'Didn't realise you kept up-to-date with all the celebrity goss.'

She was laughing. Buchan leaned forward on the table in the ops room, tapping the plastic lid of his coffee cup.

'I've done my reading,' he said, unnecessarily.

'You've been busy.'

She was still smiling. As was Houston.

It hadn't taken long, but Buchan had decided to escalate. He hadn't been able to get hold of Liddell, but it didn't matter. He was being followed, and the story also turned out to intersect with the other main business of the day, the interview with Davie Bancroft. There was more than enough reason to bring in the team.

'So, in the last three months Avercamp has interviewed DI Savage four times. Once on the record, the rest of the time... Looks like Savage was kind of using her. She was quite happy to have someone to do the legwork, as she didn't have the resource to do it herself. As cover for the police, part of the cooperative quid pro quo was that Avercamp would claim Savage was getting pissed off at her sticking her nose in.'

'Not a good look for us to be seen to have journalists do the work for us.'

'Nope. I guess Savage was thinking that when the movie gets made, she was going to want to look good, but...'

'Can't blame her,' said Houston.

'So, did she have anything interesting to bring to the party on Claire Avercamp?'

Buchan took a drink of coffee, then set the cup back down on the table.

'Claire liked the theory they came after something in particular, that they were searching for a specific book, or something within a specific book. However, the inspector thought she was searching for a narrative, trying to create something that wasn't there. To her, it's a story about book trafficking. That's all. There's enough money there for that to be worthwhile. She thought Avercamp was keen on specificity as it would make for a more enthralling narrative. Rather than being about money, it was about, I don't know, an unknown Chopin score or a lost Canterbury tale, or another Voynich, something like that.'

'I don't know Voynich,' said Houston.

'It's not relevant,' said Buchan, not wanting to get side-tracked. 'So as far as Savage was concerned, Claire had nothing, but perhaps Claire did, and she wasn't sharing.'

'And you said you called Stuey?'

Stuey was his contact at Apple.

'I called Stuey. He was excited to hear from me.'

Kane laughed.

'I don't know how he'll handle it his end, but he said he'll get on it today. If he can give me anything, we'll have it by mid-afternoon. We just need to make sure the paperwork's in order so he has cover.'

'You want me to…?' said Houston, and Buchan nodded and said, 'Thanks, Ian.'

'Did you tell him what you were looking for?' asked Kane.

'Didn't make it that easy for him,' said Buchan. 'Hopefully what we're looking for will be quite unexciting. It'll jump out at us, but not him. I didn't want him to know how much power he had in this thing.'

'Doesn't everyone at Apple know they're the ones with the power?' said Houston, ruefully.

'And the other interesting thing about Claire was that she had an insider. A mole. Someone she called Starbuck.'

Houston and Kane looked sceptically across the table.

'Because they met in a Starbucks?' asked Kane. 'Like, when they were exchanging information? Like Woodward meeting Deep Throat in a basement garage?'

'Like who meeting who?' said Houston. There was a look on his face that said he didn't like being the one who never got the references.

'This guy called himself the voice of reason,' said Buchan. 'Apparently this relates to the character Starbuck in *Moby Dick*.'

'Which is where the coffee name came from, right?'

'I'm meddling with forces I don't understand,' said Buchan. 'Have never been in a Starbucks, have never read *Moby Dick*, and neither of those things matter. What does matter is that

Claire has a mole, and the trouble is, we have no idea whether this was in the Polish end of the story, or with Davie Bancroft's mob. Or, for that matter, in the police service.'

'Davie's lot seems most likely,' said Kane. 'Just from a location perspective.'

The door opened, and Cherry entered quickly. A nod around the table, then he took his seat.

'Anything?' asked Buchan.

'Car's registered to Samuel Hawthorne,' said Cherry.

'Sammy,' said Buchan, nodding.

'Yep, one of Bancroft's goons.'

'It wasn't him driving, though,' said Buchan. 'Interesting.'

'You think you could do an e-fit of the driver?' asked Houston.

'Not a chance,' said Buchan, head shaking. 'I know it wasn't Sammy though.'

His phone buzzed, he took it from his pocket, saw Roth's name, and quickly put the phone away.

'Any contact yet with Malky Seymour?'

Seymour was Davie Bancroft's number two. If Bancroft was out of commission, Seymour would currently be running things. If Bancroft was hiding, but still in control, Seymour would know where he was. Not that it would be information he would share, but it was a case of Buchan having to use his wits.

'Just a phone call,' said Kane. 'You want me to get round there?'

'I'll go,' said Buchan, getting to his feet as he said it. 'What'd he say anyway?'

'Started off with his usual, I've no idea who you're talking about, carrying on through the occasional, sure we've met, but I barely know him, to finally answering the question with a familiar straight bat. Said Bancroft must have got side-tracked somewhere, and that he'd be along any minute.'

'K, thanks,' said Buchan, and then he was at the door, and turning as he was leaving.

'I'll send Savage's report on the Eurocentral theft to all three of you. If you could split it, Sam, please? Read up, get everything you think we might need, and in particular how it relates to Davie Bancroft.'

'Will get a one-page drawn up,' said Kane.

Buchan nodded, included the others in it, and then turned away and was walking quickly down the corridor.

—

13

Neither Malky Seymour nor Davie Bancroft would openly recognise Seymour as being Bancroft's number two. In fact, by their own reckoning, they barely even knew each other.

Nevertheless, that denial was made with the awareness that the police knew it was a blatant lie, but since truth didn't seem to matter to anyone anymore, regardless of their walk of life, it certainly wasn't going to matter to the leadership in a criminal gang.

Buchan's interview with Seymour would also be conducted in the shadow of the possibility it was Seymour who'd made Bancroft disappear. Everything, Buchan had observed to Kane, was on the table.

He parked outside the large former council house in the southside. The home had previously been adjoining semi-detached properties. Seymour had bought them both, and combined them. The house was painted a pastel pink, as though it was on the seafront at Tobermory. The neighbours had not joined them, the rest of the houses in the street a more familiar white or grey, neither a yellow nor pastel blue in sight.

Aware of just how conspicuous the Facel was in this setting, Buchan walked up the garden path, rang the bell and stood back.

One beat to the next. He turned and looked across the road. Not so much as a curtain twitched.

Seymour himself opened the door, having obviously seen Buchan coming. No surprise on his face, and he stood with his legs parted, his arms folded over a large stomach.

'What?' he said.

'Thought we might have a chat about Davie Bancroft,' said Buchan.

'I don't know him,' said Seymour, expressionless.

'He's missing.'

'Don't know him.'

'Interesting, given that we've got photographs of the two of you talking to each other on at least seventeen occasions in the past five years.'

'What does that tell us?' said Seymour.

'It tells us that you two know each other.'

'It tells us that you lot are guilty of harassment. And it tells us that you can all fuck off, starting with you, right now.'

He left it a moment to see if there was going to be an instant reaction, and when there wasn't, he started closing the door.

'And you don't know why anyone would be driving Sammy Hawthorne's car around town, then?'

Seymour stared grimly back across the entrance. Chin lowered, face downturned, eyes narrowed. Everything about him spoke of contempt. All part of the game, thought Buchan.

'You'd better come in,' he said.

*

They stood at the kitchen window. Buchan often wondered about the kitchens people seemed to have nowadays, so many of their interviews conducted in opulent settings, with islands and peninsulas and flagstone floors and Agas and double doors leading out to a kitchen garden. Seymour's kitchen, however, was the original from one of the two semi-detached houses. Small and cramped, with a square table thrust in the corner.

The back garden had been mostly paved over. In the centre, a mock Renaissance statue spouting water. In the far corner, a kid's trampoline.

'For the grandkids,' said Seymour, indicating the trampoline with his mug. 'No idea why Lizzie married that fucking spanner, but the kids are nice. Maggie's a lovely wee thing. She laughs a lot. I like that. I like her laugh. Not sure about Tyler, though. Think he might be a bit funny, you know.' Another pause. 'Gay,' he added. 'Or one of they other things. It's a fucking minefield these days for the likes of us.'

Buchan was watching the water pouring steadily from the mouth of Venus.

'Tell me about Davie,' he said, to move things along.

He took a drink of tea. It was perfect. Nothing fancy.

These are my people.

'What about him? He goes to Ibrox and he's still listening to Oasis. What else d'you want to know?'

'What's happened to him?'

'What does that mean?'

Buchan took a drink, still looking out over the garden. At the borders it was an array of colour. He didn't know any of the flowers. He presumed they had someone come in. On one side there was a table and six chairs, and a few feet away, a barbeque, the lid closed.

'You know what serendipity means?' asked Buchan.

Seymour took a loud drink of tea, then said, 'Too long a word for me.'

'I was called into my boss's office this morning,' said Buchan. 'Got a job for you, she said. There's a woman missing. A movie director, Claire Avercamp. Go and investigate. When she says this I'm not very impressed. Seems like a bit of a dead end. I'm not up myself or anything, but it seems the kind of thing a local constable should be doing, not the senior inspector at SCU. And it's particularly bad, because I'm going to be busy today. I'm going to be interviewing Davie Bancroft.

'As it happens, Davie doesn't show up. Meanwhile, I start investigating the life of this missing woman. Seems she herself is investigating a crime. Antique book theft. I speak to the police officer who's been investigating the antique book theft. She mentions a gang based in Gdańsk, and their Scottish counterparts. Or rather, their Scottish... I don't know, what's the word? Counterparts doesn't seem right. Bitches? I think that covers it.' Seymour scowled. 'I ask her who that is, and she says, it's Davie Bancroft and his lot. Well, that's interesting, I think. I've got two different cases, and it turns out they're connected. You know what you call that?'

'A cunt?'

'Serendipity, if you like. Everything coming together. Very convenient for the police officer who thinks he's been pulled in too many directions, when it turns out there's just the one direction. Tell me about the Baltazar mob in Gdańsk.'

'I don't know them,' said Seymour, after a few moments.

'You think they might have had something to do with Davie vanishing off the face of the earth, or was that you?'

'It wasn't...'

Seymour stopped himself. He sucked air, sucked his teeth, head twitched.

'You know, boss,' he said, 'you're not the first person to say that. I've had about fifteen calls this morning. I have no fucking idea why Davie didn't turn up at your place. No idea.' A loud slurp of tea, then, 'No fucking idea.'

'You don't think it might be connected to the Baltazar mob?'

Another drink of tea. Silence.

Dammit, thought Buchan. Well, at least there's that. Confirmation in the silence. This is one hundred per cent connected to the Poles.

'You know Claire Avercamp?'

'Don't know the name,' said Seymour.

'She's been in the news.'

'Lots of people are in the news.'

The interview was stalling. When that happened, Buchan usually blamed himself. It was a skill to keep a reluctant interviewee talking, and more and more Buchan felt it was one he'd lost.

'I'm not saying we need to work together, Malky,' said Buchan. 'Eventually I'm going to win, and you're getting nicked. But if you're worried about Davie, you need to help us. We can get something done.'

Seymour laughed.

Silence.

In the silence, the sound of the fountain made its way into the kitchen, through the small open window to their left.

'I'm not sure you can,' said Seymour after a while.

14

Buchan pressed call, put the phone on speaker, started the car, and began the drive back into town.

Kane answered after two rings.

'What's up?' asked Buchan, by way of introduction.

'Boss,' said Kane. 'This Baltazar mob are pretty hard core. People trafficking from Ukraine and Moldova and Belarus. Prostitution, drugs, cigarettes, alcohol. There's talk of them having extensive political connections.'

'With PiS?'

Kane hesitated, then said, 'I'm not sure who they are. They're a political party?'

'Ruling party, yes.'

'I don't know. I'll dig. You know about Polish politics?'

'At a level of the BBC,' said Buchan. 'So, alongside all the standard major gang tropes, they do a line in antique book smuggling?'

A short silence, and he pictured Kane nodding to herself.

'This is interesting, because the basic answer is no, which is weird given that that's how we've come to them.'

Buchan accelerated out onto the main road, on the way back into town. A busy late morning, not much chance to pick up speed.

There was no rush.

'Go on,' he said.

'Well, that's just it,' said Kane, 'there's nothing. They're clearly major euro-crime players, but there's nothing to suggest they deal in any of this kind of thing. They smuggle booze, cigarettes, drugs and women, period. They don't do art, they don't do antiques, they don't do old-ass books.'

'But we know they're involved in this?'

'The Polish police are certain. Not sure Savage ever completely got to the bottom of why, but... I guess she took their word for it, which is fair enough, right? We barely have enough time to investigate criminals, never mind checking up on the authorities.'

Buchan slowed as he approached a red light. Dropped a gear, brake, another gear, coasted up behind a white VW. *Brakes feel soft*, he thought, and one part of his brain tried to recall how long it had been since the pads had been changed.

'You think they're partners in this, the Poles and Davie Bancroft, or d'you think Davie's working for them as a kind of local contractor?'

'I've got to say the latter,' said Kane. 'This is like... it's like the difference between the Clyde and some river in central Europe we've never heard of. Our lives are around the Clyde, and because of ship-building and whatever, we think of it in pretty major terms. Then you're on holiday somewhere in Europe, and you come across some massive-ass river in the middle of nowhere, that makes the Clyde look like a backwater stream. I've never heard of the Baltazars, but next to them, Davie and his gang are the Famous Five. Like our guys are playing at crime. These people have a turnover at least a hundred times that of Davie. They kill, they maim, they traffic, they kidnap, they control lives in a way that Davie... well, I'm not even going to say he dreams of this kind of thing. If Davie turned against them, then we're in an Albion Rovers versus Real Madrid situation.'

'Not out of the question he escapes with a nil-nil draw, but more than likely he loses thirty-nine-nil on aggregate.'

'Exactly.'

The lights changed, and he was off, accelerating with the traffic.

'What did Seymour have to say for himself?'

'Unsurprisingly cagey,' said Buchan. 'Nevertheless, he said Davie had been getting bolshie with the Poles. He claimed not to know what about, but he was lying. However, that's where we are. There was a disagreement between them, and when gangs fall out... Davie's on home turf, at least.'

'Liverpool beat Rangers seven-one at Ibrox last year,' tossed in Kane.

'I need to speak to an antique books expert,' said Buchan. 'Can you find me someone? Would prefer if I can pay them a visit, so if there's anyone in town.'

'Boss.'

Lights had changed up ahead, the chain of red brake lights snaking along the road towards him. He waited a few moments, then braked.

Nothing.

He automatically pumped it, pressing it to the floor.

'Fuck,' he spat.

Braced himself, pulled the hand brake. Nothing.

'Boss?'

'Fuck,' shot once more from Buchan's lips.

He pumped the brakes another couple of times, but it was automatic, a gut reaction, and utterly useless. The white VW ahead was coming rapidly back to meet him.

'Boss!'

He swerved dramatically, last second, over the low kerb in the centre of the four lanes, and into the outside lane of the oncoming traffic. Dropped to second gear, the engine growling angrily at him, the car juddering. Three cars approaching. A sharp outburst of horns. Quickly a cacophony. Foot still uselessly working the brake, now frantically looking ahead for somewhere he could go, somewhere he'd cause the least amount of damage.

A BMW clipped a Vauxhall as it changed lane to avoid him. Angry faces, shouting. Thirty-three miles an hour and falling. Slow, most other times, now it felt like he was doing a hundred as the lights approached. He fumbled into the glove compartment, lowered the window, slammed the blue light on top. Siren blaring. Cars skidded out of the way. Another small crash. He reached the lights, racing through. A white car at an angle, another white car clipping its rear end. More cars coming towards him, horns blaring. He moved left, the Facel bumping over the low kerb in the middle, then onto the right lane. Cars scattering on both carriageways.

Up ahead, his opportunity. A stationary bus, signed Not In Service. Aimed the car a yard to the side, and then as he came up alongside, he swerved into the side of the bus. The Facel crunched at the impact, it scraped along the side, and then caught on the front wheel arch, and span across the dual carriageway. Clipped the middle kerb, threatened to overturn, held its ground, spun again, hit the kerb again, hopped it this time, then smacked into a central lamppost side on. Buchan thrown against the door, head banging against the window. The window broke. The car settled with another bump off the kerb.

Buchan settled in his seat, staring groggily ahead. A moment, and his head began to clear. He touched the side of his face. Blood.

15

The tow truck was lining up in front of the Facel. Buchan standing with his arms folded, watching. Kane beside him. Blood on his jacket and shirt. The ambulance was still at the side of the road, but the paramedics' work was done. There had been no other reported injuries, and the wound in the side of Buchan's face had been cleaned up. Two rough stitches done on the spot, the wound dressed. They'd said he should go to A&E, he'd asked that they sort him out where he stood. There was no time to sit in a hospital waiting room.

The mechanic approached Buchan, rubbing his hands in a rag. Buchan had summoned Derek from the garage in Rutherglen, the man who always serviced his car. Derek dragged a thumb across his neck.

'Someone messed with the brakes, right enough,' he said.

'Dammit,' said Buchan.

He felt guilty about the havoc he'd wreaked along the road, although it could have ended up a lot worse. At least it hadn't been his own fault, a result of negligent car maintenance.

'Wouldn't the boss have felt the brakes, I don't know, they'd have been soft as soon as he started, right?' said Kane. 'That thing you get in the movies, where brakes suddenly fail in the middle of a journey, it's not really going to play out like that?'

Derek turned and looked at the car, then turned back to Buchan.

'The fluid's leaked, but it didn't look like someone cut the lines. It looks like they were blown.'

'The fu…,' said Kane, though she stopped herself going through with the expletive.

'Remotely?' asked Buchan.

'If it had been before you started driving, you'd have noticed the first time you pressed the pedal. This must've been sometime after you drove off. That's my guess.'

'I noticed they were soft at the lights prior to them completely failing.'

'They'd have been blown just before that, and then a minute later,' and he made a small gesture indicating the crash. 'I'll take it back to the garage, but you might want your, what d'you call it people, your CSI types, to go over it before I do anything. But it seems to me what you have here is the perfect combination of modern technology – the remotely detonated nano-explosion – with your antique car here, which doesn't have the capability to recognise a brake issue as and when it happens. A modern car would've been flashing a hundred different warning lights at you as soon as the brake fluid started hosing.'

'We're good, inspector?' asked one of the paramedics, approaching from across the road.

The road was closed back to the set of lights that Buchan had crashed through, six officers on the scene. Once they got the car moved, there would be a clean-up, the bus was in the process of being collected, and they'd be able to get the road re-opened.

'Yep,' said Buchan. 'Thanks for your help.'

The paramedic raised a closed fist.

'How many fingers am I holding up?' she asked, Buchan answered with a weak smile, and she turned away.

'All right, thanks, Derek. Get the old girl back to your place, and I'll get Sgt Meyers to send someone round.'

'Boss,' said Derek. He nodded at Kane, and then turned away, back to the Facel.

Buchan and Kane watched the scene for a few moments. The aftermath. Not too much damage, life beginning to return to normal. No casualties.

'That could've been a lot worse,' he said. 'The bus saved the day.'

'We can't let that detract from where we are now, boss,' said Kane. 'This is one hell of an escalation.'

Buchan nodded. It was, and suddenly everything they'd been doing was going to have to be ramped up.

'This looks a little more like the work of the Baltazar mob, rather than our Davie,' said Kane.

'Yeah, but let's not jump to conclusions.'

He looked down at his shirt and jacket, brushing himself as though that might get rid of the blood.

'Can I get the car you came in? I'll drop you back at HQ, then dive home and change. Shouldn't be long, then we can get into how we ramp this up when I get back.'

'Boss,' said Kane, nodding.

—

38

16

Buchan let himself into the apartment. Noticed the two pieces of mail on the small table in the hallway, thinking Roth would have put them there on her way out. Checked the time again. She would've been gone a while. Into the open-plan.

Roth was in the seat by the window, curled up, the MacBook open in her lap. She turned and looked at him a little warily, and then she was up, placing the laptop where she'd been sitting.

'Shit, boss, you all right?'

'Why are you here, Agnes?'

They stood in the middle of the room. Silent for a moment. She looked at the blood on his shirt, the small compress on the side of his face.

'Are you all right?' she said again.

'Car accident,' said Buchan. 'No one got hurt. I got a cut, but it's not a big deal.' He indicated the blood. 'This makes it look much worse than it is. Why are you here?'

Roth stared blankly for a moment, the young woman momentarily lost in the face of authority, and then she found herself.

'I haven't seen Dr Kennedy in a couple of weeks.'

Buchan wasn't sure what to say. In all his years leading a team, the team itself had always run smoothly. He'd never had any personnel issues to deal with. Managing people was not his strong point. Treating the people as a resource, and managing that resource, he could do. But that was work. The personal side he managed by ensuring the team worked well, everyone knew their place, and everyone felt valued.

'We need to talk,' he said.

'I know.'

'Are you seeing your mum for lunch?'

Another silence, then a head shake.

'Agnes, really?'

She held his look for a few moments, and then indicated her computer.

'I've got some of that stuff you were looking for.'

Another silence arrived. One second to the next. Buchan needed Kane for these kinds of moments, but Kane didn't even know Roth was staying with him. If and when Kane found out, she was going to be annoyed. This moment was a turning point, and he didn't know what to do with it. And nor did he have the time.

'I need to get cleaned up,' he said, and he turned away, walking through to the bedroom.

*

'Daniel Maplethorpe's name was all over a small investment firm in Edinburgh, Wynn-Harvey Global. He ran security. But dig a little deeper, and there's more. The job at Wynn-Harvey was actually just part of the portfolio of a massive private security business called Poznań Secure. And it took a little more digging, but the chief director of Poznań Secure, is Daniel Maplethorpe. I feel that perhaps the Wynn-Harvey thing was early days in his security business empire, and the information with his name on it has kind of hung around the Internet. Now he's a much bigger fish in the international security sphere.'

'You got the Wynn-Harvey detail in the public Internet space, but had to use our systems for the rest?'

'That's correct.'

'And this Poznań Secure, that's Poznań as in Poznań, Poland?'

'I presume. Is that significant, you think?'

Buchan, his hands thrust in his pockets, turned away from Roth, who was back in her spot, and looked out of the window. The Clyde glinted back at him in the late morning sun.

'You have a list of their clients?' he asked, without turning.

'I have a list of names, none of which really mean anything. You want me to dig a little further?'

Buchan nodded, and then turned.

'Would you come into the office to do it?'

She stared blankly back at him. She still looks lost, he thought. And I am out of my depth.

'OK,' he said to her silence. 'Yes, please. But… I'll need to organise the team when I get back, and it might be that one of them takes it on. You can do it for now, and I'll… Maybe I should get you signed back into work, and you can work from

—

40

home for a while. I can speak to the boss.'

The look on Roth's face, the nothing look, had not changed. Eventually she nodded.

'Maybe,' she said.

He didn't stand for long, but he didn't have time to stand there at all. Yet he'd come home, blundering into a conversation he could have had on so many different occasions over the past three months, at a moment when he was ill-prepared.

'I'm going to have to tell the boss you're here,' he said eventually.

'It won't look good.'

'No.'

'I should leave,' she said. 'Move back to my own place. If I go this afternoon, then we can, you know, I can just be at home, and we can say I've been at home all along, and you can say that you called to see how I was doing, and that I said I'd do some background work for you.'

Another silent stare. Buchan sighed, shook his head, started to move away.

'Do you want to go home?' he asked.

She didn't have a reply.

'Don't go home, not if you're not ready,' he said. 'I'll deal with the boss, and anyone else who wants to...' and he finished the sentence with a dismissive gesture. 'Did you get a chance to look at Harriet Blake's career?'

'Sure,' said Roth. She indicated the MacBook, but didn't need to look at it. 'I wrote it up. I'll send it over now, with some stuff on Maplethorpe. Nothing leaping off the page. Fairly regulation career in film, by the looks of things. Did a degree in business, then got a job in a film financing company, worked her way up, then made the switch and started putting films together. Nothing major. Couple of Scottish BAFTA nominations, but that's about that. Has obviously done some work with Avercamp.'

'OK, thanks.'

He puffed out his cheeks, turned away from the window, looked at the door as though he needed to establish his exit route.

'No idea when I'll get in this evening, but when I do, we need to talk.'

Roth nodded.

'And, you know, try to be ready to talk, Agnes. Try to... I

don't know, have some sort of plan, some sort of way forward.'

Roth smiled weakly.

'I'm sorry, boss.'

'Don't be. We just need to make sure you get better.'

She nodded. They both thought he sounded uncomfortably like he was reading lines for a TV show, and he turned away quickly, jacket on at the door, and then he was out onto the landing, and jogging quickly down the stairs.

17

'You're not dead then,' said Malky Seymour on the phone.

'Good spot,' said Buchan, drily.

'Well, it wasn't me. I mean, it wasn't one of our people.'

'Didn't think it was,' said Buchan. 'The brake pipes were damaged by remote-controlled, nano-explosion...'

'No fucking way, man,' said Seymour. 'That is quality.'

'Certainly what I thought,' said Buchan. 'So the devices could've been fitted at any point, didn't have to be while the car was outside your place. Nevertheless, we'd like to check the car's environs everywhere it's been left parked this morning. Can your people look at the CCTV outside your house?'

Seymour barked down the phone.

'Sure.'

'I'm serious, Malky. I'm not threatening you with anything, but if someone tampered with my car, it could well be the same person who's tampered with Davie. There's something major going on here, and if you don't want to fall prey to it, you're probably going to have to help us out.'

There was silence down the phone while he thought it through. Buchan knew he had him.

*

'Poznań Secure?' said Liddell.

'Yes.'

'So, this is circling back to Poland, which is where the gang who perpetrated the thefts came from.'

Buchan nodded.

Kane was in the room, but this conversation was between Liddell and Buchan, and they stared warily at each other, while Liddell thought it through. Buchan, knowing what was coming, was in no rush.

'These private security people...,' said Liddell, and she let the sentence go, head shaking.

'They often have connections we're not going to be aware

43

of,' said Buchan.

'Exactly.' A pause, and then, 'I don't like it. Sorry, inspector, I don't mean to stick my nose in, but don't do anything on Maplethorpe for the moment. Let me look into it. I'll make some enquiries.'

'If you're sure. I don't mind.'

'Leave it with me.'

'K.'

'You got this stuff off our Prism Network?' she asked.

Buchan nodded again.

'OK, I'll take a look. Make a couple of calls. Clearly we need to unravel this thing as quickly as possible.'

'You did that when you went home, boss?' said Kane, curiously. 'You hardly had time.'

Well, that didn't take long, thought Buchan. Not that he was going to be surprised by Kane's perspicacity.

'I asked Agnes to do it,' he said.

Silence. They both regarded him warily.

'She's not signed back on yet,' said Liddell.

'No.'

'You called her? You've been in touch with her?'

Of the two, Kane's look was the more suspicious.

'About ten days after her kidnap,' he said, launching into the short speech which he'd meant to make to one or both Liddell and Kane at some point over the previous few months, 'she came to see me. We all thought she'd been recovering at home the previous ten days. It turned out she hadn't spent any nights in her apartment. She'd tried a few times, but always ended up leaving and heading out into town. Most nights she booked into a hotel. One night she ended up getting the bus out to the airport, and sitting out there until eight the following morning.'

'Jesus,' said Liddell.

'I was about to head to Switzerland on holiday for two weeks. She asked if she could stay at my place.'

He left it at that for a moment, before dropping the full truth of it. The hesitation told the rest of the story.

'And she's still there?' said Liddell.

'Yes.'

'Inspector, seriously? She's a junior officer.'

He had nothing to say, now that it was out there. He'd said what had to be said, now he wanted to drop it and get on with the job.

'Tell me she's in the spare room,' said Liddell.

'She's in the spare room,' said Buchan.

'And how's she doing?'

'Worse than I thought. I just discovered now, when I went home, that she's not seen her doctor in the last fortnight.'

'She's been lying to you,' said Kane. 'And us, given we all thought she was at home, or staying with her mum.'

'Yes,' said Buchan.

Liddell glanced at her phone, closed her eyes momentarily, shook her head.

'I've had a couple of messages to call Dr Kennedy. Hadn't got around to it yet. Dammit.'

Buchan looked between the two of them, then decided the spell had to be broken.

'I know. I know everything you're going to say. It doesn't mean you don't get to say it, but it's not a conversation for now. Chief, if you don't mind, if you're going to take on the Poznań Secure line, then please, make some calls. The sergeant and I, meanwhile, have about fifty bases to cover.'

Liddell leant forward, her hands clasped, the end of an unlit cigarette sticking out of one, her chin resting against them.

'You're right, inspector, I will get to say all the things you know I'm going to say. But yes, for now, you can go. Keep me updated, and I'll let you know if my enquiries on Maplethorpe come up with anything.'

*

'Did you find me an antique books dealer I can talk to?' asked Buchan.

Kane nodded.

Walking down the stairs at a clip.

She stopped him at the bottom of the stairs before they went back through to the office.

'You're not lying?' she said.

'How d'you mean?'

'Agnes is in the spare room?'

'Agnes is in the spare room.'

'Do you find yourself visiting the spare room on occasion?'

Buchan held her gaze. The question irritated him. He took a moment, not wanting to answer in anger.

'No. I'm like her dad, or something. And that, sadly, extends to the fact that I can't really talk to her. We just exist in the same space. Occasionally we eat together. That's about the size of it. I hope it's allowing her a gentle recovery, but... I'm not sure it is. I've not been sure for a while.'

Kane was annoyed at him, regardless of whether she found the explanation convincing.

'You're not in love with her?' she said.

Buchan felt another stab of aggravation. But then, hadn't he started asking himself the same question? Hadn't he asked himself the same question when he'd looked in the mirror that morning? Hadn't he started to enjoy having Roth around, regardless of how distant the two of them could seem when they were in the same room? Wasn't that one of the reasons he felt so guilty about her living in his house?

'Because Agnes has feelings for you,' said Kane. 'She has had for a while, and you opening the house up to her...'

'No one's in love with anyone,' said Buchan, as Kane let the sentence drift off.

He didn't want to examine his own annoyance.

'Come on,' he said, 'I'll be available for all your opprobrium at a time in the near future. We need to crack on.'

He pushed open the door to the open-plan, held it briefly for her, and then walked quickly to his desk.

18

Buchan walked into the small, independent book store just off the Gallowgate. Now that he was here, he recognised it, was aware that he'd long known about it. Nevertheless, it was the kind of small shop that he would never have given any thought to, so far off his radar that it hadn't even occurred to him to come here when they'd first started looking for contacts in the business.

The smell of the shop was wonderful. A rich, smoky warmth, that spoke of the library in some well-heeled Highland hotel. He thought of weekends away with Janey, back in the early days, when they'd allowed themselves the luxury of those kinds of breaks. It had always been the time that had been the luxury, not the expense, and gradually Buchan had stopped giving up his time.

'Inspector Buchan?' said the woman behind the counter. She was frowning, and it took a moment for him to realise it was because of the bandage and bruising on his face.

She'd been sitting down, but now walked around the side of the counter as he approached.

He took out his ID.

'This is the before photograph,' he said.

'You're all right?'

'Hell of a day so far,' he said. 'Mrs Bannerman?'

'Call me Carol,' she said, smiling. 'How can I be of help?'

The shop had a simple design, a small space filled with second-hand books. Shelves down both walls, and covering one side of the front of the shop, beside the door and the window. A double shelf, to head height, down the middle of the shop. Plenty of space in between, so that perhaps another central shelf, another row could have been added, but that would have been a desperate squeeze.

At the top of the shop, in front of the counter, a locked glass case with six volumes on display, two of them opened at pages of illustrations.

Buchan glanced at the case, and walked over to look inside.

He supposed he recognised he was looking at old books, and that those books, the quality of them, must represent something, but he wasn't a reader, and he was never going to feel a connection with them.

'Maybe if there was a first edition *Ellington at Newport*,' he said quietly to himself.

'Sorry?'

She was smiling curiously.

'Tell me about these,' he said, indicating the books. 'These are your rarest items?'

'For now,' she said. 'There's a selection amongst the six. The most expensive is the small one in the corner here. Early edition, *Alice in Wonderland*, but not, sadly, a first edition. It might have Lewis Caroll's signature, however.'

'Might have?'

'There's a signature. The dealer couldn't get it authenticated. I've done some investigation, and I agree. So if it was first edition with a verified signature, you're looking at several hundred thousand pounds in value. This is a third edition from 1866, and potentially just signed by any old hobgoblin off the street, and I've got it for sale here at four and a half thousand.'

'What'd you pay for it?'

'Two and a half.'

Another world, he thought. Seemed insane to him. What did you do with the book once you got it? At least art you put on a wall, music you put on a record player. What was the use of the old book once you'd read it, if you ever even could?

'Have you spoken recently to a filmmaker named Claire Avercamp?'

'Yes, of course. Terrible what's happened. You're investigating her disappearance?'

'Yes. When was the last time you spoke to her?'

'A month, maybe. We'd spoken a couple of times. She'd said she was putting a film together about the Eurocentral theft last year. I thought that would've been a pretty cool movie. Still will be, if it happens.'

Buchan turned to face her. In the small shop, this close, books all around, the wonderful atmosphere of the place which he somehow couldn't dissociate from romance, he felt strangely uncomfortable.

'Can we go and sit and talk somewhere?' he asked.

'Sure, there's a café just along the road. I don't mind closing for twenty minutes.'

*

'There are buyers in the UK, there are buyers in the US. And, in this business at least, there's actually more money in the UK. I mean, obviously it's in London rather than Glasgow or Edinburgh, but there's plenty of it floating around for such things as the pointless luxury of the old book, even if it's so old you're afraid to pick it up in case it falls apart. So, sometimes books pass through Scotland because the auctioneer's head office is here, sometimes bidders are sought, sometimes it's a paperwork issue. All sorts of reasons.'

'And the books that were stolen last October, they were an exceptional batch, or that kind of thing is passing through here all the time?'

She took a drink of coffee, Buchan followed. He hadn't wanted another coffee, but he'd been feeling uncomfortable, and the coffee, as so often was the case, was an easy crutch.

'I'm not sure it was exceptional, but it was probably the highest value batch that's ever passed through Scotland.'

'That sounds like it might have been exceptional.'

She smiled.

'Right. Let's just say, it wasn't that much higher than normal. A little higher, likely the highest ever, but I think exceptional makes it sound like it was...,' and she lifted her hand above her head to finish the sentence.

'And how easy would it be to get rid of them afterwards?'

'To sell them on?'

'Yes.'

'It's going to have to be black market, so it depends on your connections. Claire said she was working on there being some sort of European gang involved. I feel that makes more sense. You take these things to Eastern Europe, Italy maybe, somewhere like that, they're going to be a lot easier to fence than trying to do it in Scotland, or London even.'

'Have you heard tell of any of them coming to the market in the last year?'

She smiled again. Buchan had always liked women who smiled easily.

'I stay well away from that market,' she said. 'The black

one. Everything above board.'

'So, you think this was a regular heist, or were they looking for something specific?' asked Buchan, and he smiled weakly as he said it, aware that the question was a reach.

'I don't really know, sorry.'

'Did Claire?'

'She could be a little cagey. I know she was working on the basis it was some high-end, you know, top of the range, rare book. She was wondering if it was possibly something that wasn't included in the manifest. I wondered if that was wishful thinking on her part. Something to make her movie more exciting.'

'What kind of thing would that be?'

'You know, there's all sorts. Early Bibles, of course, early printed volumes, original editions of iconic works, you know, the Magna Carta, Declaration of Independence, that kind of thing. Not that anything like that's going to be passing through here from Poland. On that route, you're likely looking at an original, you know, Beethoven or Mozart, especially if it's signed. Or an original scientific textbook, like Galileo, Newton, Copernicus, one of those guys.'

'I heard about original Copernicus manuscripts going for about a fifth of a Tom Brady sports card?' said Buchan, and Bannerman laughed.

'Well, I heard that too, but really... I'm not sure it's true, and if it is, it's about people paying stupid amounts for the sports card. There are a couple of original Copernicus works which have gone for well over a million.'

Buchan's phone rang, and he made a small apology and took it from his pocket.

Malky Seymour.

'Mr Seymour,' he said.

'Got one of my people to check,' said Seymour. 'This thing, these cool mini-bombs, didn't get fitted at my place.'

Buchan thought to say, *unless it was done on your instruction*, but then, the request for Seymour to look at the CCTV had been made in good faith. Buchan could have doubts if he chose to, but if he wanted any help from Seymour in this, he had to keep them to himself for now.

'OK, thanks. Any word from Davie?'

'No.'

'Any ideas?'

A pause, and then, 'No.'

'When was the last time anyone had contact with him?'

'I presume when he saw Janet this morning. None of our lot have spoken to him today.'

Buchan looked across the table at Carol Bannerman, looking through her, thinking about Seymour.

'What does the name Starbuck mean to you?' he asked.

A short silence, then, '*Moby Dick*.'

'Really?'

'We've all read *Moby Dick*,' said Seymour. 'Terrific novel. I love a study in obsession.'

His delivery was dry enough that Buchan had no idea whether he was telling the truth. Something about it made it feel like he was mocking Buchan for his own lack of interest in reading, but that was just projection on Buchan's part. How could Seymour know Buchan hadn't recreationally read an entire book in over thirty years?

'Keep in touch,' said Buchan.

Seymour laughed grimly and ended the call. Buchan placed the phone back in his pocket, looked at Bannerman, the consternation still on his face as though it was aimed at her, and then he shook it off and lifted his coffee cup.

'Starbuck?' said Bannerman.

'Did Claire ever mention the name?'

'The coffee shop or the first mate on the Pequod?'

'The first mate on the Pequod?

'*Moby Dick*.'

Keep up, he muttered to himself.

'I don't know,' said Buchan. 'Just a name, not the coffee shop.'

Bannerman shook her head.

'Sorry, don't think I've heard it used as a name, other than for coffee.'

'No one's been in asking for a copy of *Moby Dick*?'

Bannerman smiled and shook her head.

19

'Danny, can you start checking all channels, everything public and private you can see, social media, personal e-mail we have access to, for any reference to Starbuck?'

'Seriously?'

They were in the ops room, the small team. Buchan with the sergeants, Kane and Houston, plus DC Cherry and Ellie Dawkins.

'Exclude Star*bucks*, just do Starbuck, that might narrow it down. We need to find some other mention of the name. I don't want to say this guy, this woman, whoever it is, is a key player. Could be nothing. But if they exist…'

'I'm on it,' said Cherry.

He'd written *Starbuck!* on the notepad in front of him.

'K. So, Seymour says his people checked the CCTV outside of his house, and…'

'We're trusting him on this?' asked Kane.

'Nope. But let's say he's telling the truth for now. It has a pretty big asterisk on it, but we'll run with it. So, the boss asks me to investigate this thing at eight this morning. I've got the list of where my car's been since then. We've got here, obviously, in our carpark, then at Harriet Blake's place in Shawlands, outside Claire Avercamp's apartment, then to Dalmarnock HQ, back here, then Malky's, then boom.'

'Busy morning,' said Houston.

'So, Ellie, I'll give you the addresses for Blake and Avercamp's, and can you check if there's any footage in the vicinity. Given the nature of the devices, far as we know at the moment, before we hear anything from Ruth, these things could've been fitted at any time. Yesterday, last week, a year ago, whenever. Maybe it's nothing to do with Claire Avercamp or Davie Bancroft, but if it's not, then we're in coincidence territory, so let's say for now, that it is. Which means…' He hesitated, then finally said what he'd been thinking since his last phone call with Seymour. 'Look, I don't want to get into any kind of dramatic *Where Eagles Dare* kind of, I don't know, fifth columnist, saboteur absurdity, but I'd like you to check the footage for our car park and Dalmarnock's.'

Houston made an *interesting* face, which Kane then voiced.

'Interesting choice,' she said.

'Let's just cover the bases.'

'On it, boss,' said Dawkins.

Buchan hurriedly scribbled some numbers on a notepad, tore off the top sheet, then passed it over.

'The rough times I was at each of the places.'

'Boss.'

'Sam, I'd like you on this Baltazar mob. Can we do a list of any of their operatives known to have travelled to the UK, and their movements here as much as we can get them?'

'Boss.'

'Ian, likewise, with Bancroft and his crew. We've obviously got plenty on them already, but we need to look at it from an angle we haven't previously considered. Relations with Poland, and the Baltazars in particular. Any mention of Poznań Security, or any of their off-shoots. Any mention of Starbuck. That's the kind of thing we could easily have missed before, as we likely would just have thought it meant the café.'

'Boss,' said Houston.

'All right, folks, up and at 'em.'

He stood, he looked at the clock.

'Don't forget to grab some lunch,' he added.

*

Kane waited for him as the others left the small, windowless situation room.

'Sam, we cool?'

'Just wanted to apologise, sir,' said Kane.

'Why?'

They stopped in the corridor, but it wouldn't be for long. Buchan had a sense of urgency he would try to take through the rest of the day.

'I was too judgemental. Sorry. I know you mean well. I'm just... you know, I'm worried about Agnes, and...'

He was shaking his head.

'It's OK. It's a shitty situation, and I'll admit I'm out of my depth. This has been good. It was good I went home and found her still there today. Whoever blew my brakes did us a favour.'

He smiled weakly.

'So, how is she, by the way? I was kind of hoping she'd, I don't know, gone off somewhere to recuperate. You know, like a sanatorium in the Alps or something.'

'Sure, because of all of us, Agnes belongs in the nineteenth century.'

Kane laughed.

'What does she do all day? Does she leave your flat. I mean…'

'Not as much as she led me to believe, but yes. When I was leaving earlier I checked with Carter on the door. He says she goes out every day, so she's not been lying about that, at least. She's spent a lot of time in Kelvingrove. She likes the lunchtime organ recital. And a couple of times a week she does Tai Chi in the park.' He shrugged.

'How's the pink hair doing?'

Buchan took a moment, addressing the fact that he was discussing a young woman's hair, which didn't fit with his feelings of determination to crack on with the case. He was also uncomfortable, because he realised he liked talking about her, and it wasn't something he wanted to like.

'After a few weeks, when the roots were really showing, she shaved the pink off. Bit of a buzzcut. Been letting her hair grow out since then.'

'Wow. Are we going to recognise her?'

Buchan stared at the floor. He thought of Roth sitting in the chair by the window, with her black-rimmed spectacles, her knees up at her chin, a million miles from the woman who'd been the life of their office three months previously.

He stopped himself smiling.

'Not sure that you will,' he said.

He kind of shrugged. A small accompanying movement of his facial features to bring the conversation to an end.

'We should move,' he said.

'One more thing.' She winced uncomfortably as she said it, and Buchan indicated for her to continue. 'You should tell Danny. He's been worried about her.'

Buchan nodded.

'Leave it with me,' he said.

20

Liddell was on edge. Buchan had called, she'd said to meet her in the canteen. The unlit cigarette was set down at the side of her plate, as though it was a utensil. She was eating a sandwich, a wholemeal roll, lettuce and pieces of ham sticking out from all sides. Taking no enjoyment in it, the food just something that was happening to her mouth at that moment. She also had a small bottle of sparkling elderflower, though she was yet to pour it into the moulded plastic cup.

Buchan was eating a tuna salad. He hadn't wanted anything.

'I don't like this one bit,' said Liddell.

Buchan was eating lettuce, his face deadpan. He gave Liddell the space to talk in between mouthfuls.

'I was feeling troubled at first. It bothered me that I'd brought you on board, asked you to look into this Avercamp business, and then you could've been killed. But, of course, it turns out to be tied to Davie Bancroft, there may well be something pretty major playing out, and it's right we're in the middle of it. Should've been involved sooner, in fact.'

He made a small gesture with his fork. No one was blaming anyone for that.

'What did you do about Maplethorpe?' he asked.

She took another bite of the sandwich, chewed for a moment, and then this time she cracked open the cap of the elderflower, poured the entire bottle into the cup, and took a drink.

'I asked around. Didn't learn too much in the first instance. I think perhaps you can get one of the team to get digging. Then I called him.'

'There's a tactic,' said Buchan, smiling.

'I hope you don't mind me just blundering in like that.'

'How'd it go?' he asked, not answering the question.

'I asked him about Avercamp. He immediately got cagey, but you know, not in the way we usually see. Not in a streets of Glasgow way. But like…,' and she took another bite of sandwich, angry eating, her face etched with bitterness, 'like some government minister caught with his face in the trough, and he weasels his way out of it. Nothing to see here. I'm a Tory and I can do what I like, and it's none of your damned business.'

She apologised as she said it, as though Buchan was going to complain about the Conservatives being traduced.

'He denied having any contact with her?'

'Neither confirmed nor denied.'

'Did you mention the Baltazars?'

'Yes. That was interesting. He played a nice hand there. Didn't deny all knowledge, as some might have done. *I've heard of them, of course*, he said. Of course. But, as far as he was aware, Poznań Secure have never had specific dealings with them.'

'So, they don't do much business in Poland?'

'He wouldn't say.'

'Where does the company name Poznań come from then?'

'He said that was where he and his wife had their honeymoon. He's had a soft spot for it ever since. When he started the company, the UK was still in the EU, and at the time Poland was an advantageous place to set up. This, he says, does not mean that he actually conducts much of the business there.'

She stared across the top of her sandwich.

'What d'you want me to do with this?' he asked, before finally taking a mouthful of salad.

Liddell took another bite of sandwich, and now she laid it back on the plate. She finished chewing, she took a drink, and this time she shook her head.

'You know, the thing I hate most about modern life is that everyone's so damned prissy.' She made a gesture with the glass of elderflower. 'What was wrong with a glass of chardonnay at lunch? Really, what harm did that do anyone? But look at it. Look at the preposterous glass case at the counter. Three hundred bottles of Coke Zero. Sure, because that doesn't do anyone any harm.'

Buchan smiled, enjoying, as ever, the burst of exasperation from the chief.

'Sorry,' said Liddell. 'I'll focus. Do what you will, inspector. I'm done with it. Aside from speaking to him, I got nowhere with anyone else. I should learn to keep my old head out of this kind of thing, and leave the detective work to the detectives.'

'OK, thanks,' said Buchan.

'I should let you get back to work,' said Liddell. 'I was going to talk to you about Agnes, but I guess Agnes isn't going anywhere. We can have the conversation tomorrow.'

Buchan nodded, took another mouthful of salad, regretted it again, then lifted the plate and the bottle, placed the plate on the shelves of discarded trays, and left the canteen, bottle of water at his lips.

*

He stopped off at Cherry's desk. Quick look around the office, no one else within earshot. It wasn't a secret anymore anyway, so it hardly mattered.

'I know you've got the Starbuck thing, but you can take half an hour to nip round to my apartment. You know where it is, right?'

'Sure,' he said, asking the question with a furrowed brow.

'Agnes has been staying with me for a while. Recovering. You should go and speak to her.'

'I thought she was at her mum's?'

'Sam and the boss know,' said Buchan. 'No one else, just leave it at that for the moment.'

'OK,' said Cherry. He looked uncertain. Buchan nodded and left the room, leaving him with his uncertainty.

21

Buchan found Malky Seymour on the Clydeway driving range, between Uddingston and Blantyre. A pleasant day for it. The sound of the M74 in the background, the crematorium just across the river.

Seymour became aware of Buchan's presence standing to the side and behind, turned and held him with a stare for a few moments, raised an eyebrow and nothing more at the marks on Buchan's face, then looked at the man swinging a club in the next bay along.

'Would be a shame if the inspector took an inadvertent two-iron to the forehead, right?' said Seymour. He said it completely deadpan, the other man staring blankly at him wondering whether it had actually been an instruction, then Seymour burst out laughing, and the man joined him.

'I need to have another word,' said Buchan.

'Sure you do,' said Seymour.

He lined up, stretched his neck in an affected manner, then let rip a two-iron long and straight. He followed the flight of the ball, took a moment, then lined up another, went through his pre-shot routine, and played an identical shot. Again he followed the path of the ball, and then he turned to Buchan.

'It's the same every day at this place,' he said. 'Shot after shot, just like that metronomic, boring bastard Faldo in his prime. Then I take it out on the course, and phht... I hit the ball like the club's made of limp cocks.' Then, 'What d'you want?'

'I need to know if any of the Baltazar gang are in town at the moment,' said Buchan.

Seymour tipped the club upside down, and then leant forward, putting his weight on the club head.

'I thought I told you I'd never heard of them?'

'You did.'

'Well, there we are. I've never heard of them.'

'You give me two types of answers, Malky. You lie, and I decide to let it go; or, you lie, and I stand here until you tell me the truth. Guess which one this is.'

Seymour barked out a laugh.

'I don't always lie,' he said.

'I need names.'

Buchan received the well-practised look of consideration. They all used it, the likes of Malky Seymour. Letting the officer know that he was at least worthy of consideration. Not that he was sure yet whether he'd pass anything on, but he was thinking about it. The police officer, in this case Buchan, should be grateful.

Seymour turned the club around, lining his hands up on the grip. Tapped the club head a couple of times on the artificial turf. The other man had appeared on the edge of the tee, holding a nine-iron. A short club, wedged for an effective, and brutal attack. Buchan felt no threat. This wasn't about backing Seymour into a corner, where he would be forced to fight, regardless of the circumstances. That day would likely come, but not yet.

The consideration was still taking place. Buchan hadn't been here long, but he was already feeling the time pressure. He wasn't entirely sure where it was coming from, this wasn't some deadline-related drama, where everything had to be wrapped up by midnight or someone would be dead, the thing would be lost, whatever ancient manuscript everyone was after would be gone. Or, if it was, he didn't actually know it yet. Nevertheless, the sense of urgency was coming from somewhere.

'Let me think out loud for you,' said Buchan. 'You have information that I need, of course you do. This is what our game is. You know things you don't want me to find out. You have dealings with the Baltazar mob. However you frame it to yourselves, you know you're the junior partners. They're a massive, pan-European operation, you control a bit of the south side of Glasgow. They would be tough people to rat out to the police. And if they discover you ratted them out, then who knows where that goes. And yet... Davie's gone. You have no idea where. But there's something at play here. I don't know what it is. But the only thing in play that's big enough to lead to Davie vanishing involves the Baltazars. So you're standing there thinking, if we need to come up against the Baltazars, have we got the manpower, or would we be better leaving that to the po–'

'I thought you weren't supposed to talk much?' snapped Seymour.

Buchan didn't reply. They were getting there, coming to it

eventually.

'If they find out this came from us, inspector,' he said, then he tapped the club head on the turf another couple of times, 'if they find out this came from us, we are at war. You and me, we're at war. That will get ugly very quickly.'

Buchan held his gaze. Didn't respond. He sometimes thought it might be better if the police and this kind of gang existed in a state of war, although he only thought that because he imagined, probably wrongly, that the police would triumph, and things would look better for everyone on the other side. As if the void would not be filled by the next thug off the conveyor belt.

'They have a house. A nothing kind of a place, city end of Baillieston. Don't think they've had it long.'

'You've had it watched today?'

'Of course. Nothing doing. Not sure if there's even anyone there at the moment.'

'Why are you watching it, then?'

Seymour scowled.

'Lenny'll give you the address.'

Buchan looked at Lenny, then turned back to Seymour.

'Thank you.'

'And I'm not telling my guy out there that you're coming. His job is just to keep an eye on the place, but if you end up getting into any kind of shit with him, that's on you. This goes no further than me, you and Lenny. And Lenny's an idiot, and'll forget all about it by the time you've left.'

Buchan nodded a thank you. A moment, then Seymour turned away, and began lining up another shot.

'One more thing,' said Buchan.

Seymour grunted, but didn't turn.

'Have you given any thought to who Starbuck might be?'

Seymour didn't move. Buchan couldn't see his face. Eventually he turned, his eyes sweeping past Buchan, he exchanged a look with Lenny, a significant look Buchan couldn't read, before turning back.

'I'm afraid I can't help you with that, inspector.'

'I think that might be one of those lies again, Mr Seymour.'

'Goodbye.'

Seymour turned away, took a moment, lined up a shot, and this time shanked it horribly short and to the right.

'Fuck,' he spat at the early afternoon.

22

Buchan sat in his car on Baillieston main street. Taking a moment, wondering if Seymour's man would be obvious, but from a low vantage point on a busy road, cars parked most of the way along both sides, it was always going to be difficult to spot someone else.

A regulation high street in central Scotland. One and two-storey buildings, the shop fronts a depressing fusion of bookies, barbershops, hairdressers, charity shops, a small grocers, a tanning salon, a newsagent, a phone shop, in amongst several other boarded-up shop fronts, including a long-departed Chinese carry out. The address Seymour had given was a first-floor flat above the former premises of the Orient Express.

Time to move. He checked his phone to make sure he hadn't missed any messages, and then got out of the anonymous white Golf, locked the door and walked quickly along the road.

Before speaking to Seymour he'd put a quick call through to Roth. Her own phone, as she never answered his land line. Not that anyone ever called that land line. Buchan just happened to belong to the last generation who would have a land line as a matter of course.

'Boss,' she'd said.

'You getting anywhere?'

'I think I might be the wrong person to be looking at this. It's a quagmire of dodgy businesses and shell companies and overseas investment portfolios. There's a lot of digital and online security stuff. There's stuff about Swiss banks, Cayman Island banks. It's all pretty weird, and I feel I'm kind of bogged down in it. You know Eddie, down in Finance? Constable Barnes?'

'Of course.'

'You should get him to take a look.'

'OK, thanks, I will do. But... maybe you could stay on it too. Focus on their Scottish and Polish operations if they have any.'

'Right.'

'Anything with the name Baltazar anywhere near it. And I really doubt there'll be anything that involves our man Davie Bancroft, but if there are any connections with his lot, that'd be worth noting. And I mean, maybe Davie targeted something that turned out to be being protected by Poznań. That's the kind of peculiar connection we're looking for.'

'Boss.'

'And the name Starbuck, if that pops up anywhere.'

'Just Starbuck? Like the Moby Dick guy?'

'Exactly.'

'K, boss, I'm on it.'

Typical Roth, he'd thought. No questions, just an acceptance of the instructions and a willingness to crack on with it.

'One more thing.'

'Yep?'

'I told Danny where you were. He'll be around to see you shortly.'

Silence.

He'd left it a moment.

'You OK with that?'

'Sure. It'll be nice.'

'Don't go out.'

He'd imagined her smiling sadly at the other end of the phone.

'I won't,' she'd said.

Arriving at the locked door to the close on Baillieston main street, he quickly worked the lock with the small pick, didn't bother with the furtive glance over his shoulder as depicted in fiction every time someone surreptitiously unlocks a door, and then he was along the short, featureless, concrete corridor, up the stairs and outside the door of flat 1B.

He stood still for a moment, taking the time to listen to what was happening inside. There was a TV playing loudly in the apartment across the narrow hallway, the sound interfering with anything Buchan might have been able to catch from inside the Baltazar place.

From nowhere, the hairs started standing on the back of his neck. He glanced back at the door across the hall, looked at the peephole, wondering if someone was staring out at him. Dragged his look away, turning back to the Baltazar door.

He'd been going to knock, but something had changed his

mind. Hairs on the back of his neck? Was that all? A gut feeling?

There was no time to examine where it had come from. If this really was the safe house of a Polish crime gang, he had no qualms about breaking in. And if he was being set up to do something foolish by Malky Seymour, then he'd just have to take the fallout when it came.

Again he worked the Yale lock, as ever it taking no more than a few seconds, and then he very gently opened the door, in case it was going to meet the sudden resistance of a chain. When it was clear that wasn't an issue, he swung the door open and stepped into the apartment.

The door opened straight into a small kitchen/diner. Beige flooring, beige walls, beige cabinets. A couple of mugs, a plate, a beer glass beside the sink. The smell of stale onions. The window behind the sink was closed, and Buchan had to stop himself instinctively opening it to let in some air.

Two doors off, one leading to a short corridor, the other into the sitting room.

Buchan hesitated in the middle of the kitchen, taking the temperature of the house. Trying to sense if there was anyone here, although he felt the quiet of it already. He didn't know where the tension was coming from, that thing that was playing with his spine, but he was also getting the feeling that the place was empty.

He glanced back at the dirty plate. Leftover baked beans, not entirely dried in. Hadn't been there too long.

Get on with it, he chided himself.

He walked quickly into the sitting room. One step through the door, and he stopped abruptly.

The man was sitting upright in the armchair, his eyes closed. It would have looked a peculiarly formal position in which to fall asleep, except he obviously wasn't sleeping.

The bloody bullet wound in the middle of his forehead told its own story.

23

The block was closed off. Officers, including DC Dawkins, were going door to door around the neighbouring apartments and shops. CCTV footage was being checked in the hope that the perpetrator might show up somewhere, however fleetingly, albeit the police had to admit they didn't know what or who they were looking for.

The woman across the hallway had answered the door to Buchan, who'd rung her bell even before the rest of the team had arrived at the apartment building. The bell had sounded loud inside. Before she'd even come to the door, Buchan had known she was going to be deaf.

The conversation had not gone well. After a couple of questions, the woman had signed a question back to him. He assumed it was a question. She could have been telling him to leave her alone, although at least there had been nothing obviously rude in it.

They were waiting for a constable from Dalmarnock to come to interview her.

The victim had not been left in possession of any ID. However, in his wallet, a few Polish złoty, a Slavic look about his face. That was all they had to go on. Of course, he could have been Polish, and he could still have been in Glasgow all his life, working for the Bancrofts or anyone else. Equally, planting a bit of Polish money in someone's wallet would have been a very easy, if obvious, piece of mis-direction.

'Dead no more than two hours,' said Donoghue, the pathologist. 'Nothing more than what we see here. A single bullet shot to the head. And as you've already noted for yourselves, he was shot where he sits, the bullet passing through his head, the back of the chair, and lodging in the wall.'

'We don't see much gun crime around here,' said Kane, her tone almost absent-minded.

'I don't suppose you do, sergeant,' said Donoghue. 'Brings a whole other level to the party. So often we see killers take precautions before killing their victims. Doing *something* to make sure they can't fight back. When you have a gun, you have a gun. You tell someone to sit on their backside, and they usually do. In this case, it sadly didn't do him an awful lot of good. It did make him a very easy target for his killer.'

'No more than two hours ago?'

'Late morning at the earliest.'

Donoghue looked between Buchan and Kane, and then began to wrap it up.

'I've got everything I need. I'll take another look when we get him back to the lab, but I'm not sure on this occasion there'll be much worth reporting. A gun's a gun for a' that,' as the Bard said.'

She smiled, she seemed, thought Buchan, to be unusually chipper at the use of a firearm, and then she turned away and left them to the room. Just Buchan and Kane, another local officer at the door, three SOCO's, and the victim's body in the place where it had been left.

There was nothing obvious to indicate that anyone else had been in the flat. The baked beans had been a meal for one. One glass had been used, one set of cutlery. There was a double bed, but it appeared only one person had been sleeping in it. One toothbrush in the bathroom, one set of clothes. There were also no obvious signs of someone clearing up after themselves, removing all trace. If that had been done, it had been carried out by a consummate professional, Kane had observed. Whoever had committed the murder had more than likely arrived at the house at some point during the morning, and been allowed in.

'Are we taking the złoty and the whatever at face value?' asked Kane. 'He looks Polish, we've found him in a house that, according to Malky Seymour at least, is a Baltazar house, so ergo, he was one of their gang?'

'We have to be sceptical, but I like it. Feels right. Obviously we're not taking it for granted, but we'll work on this basis for the moment.'

'Yes,' said Kane.

'Now, I'm inclined to leave this with the locals,' said Buchan. Kane was nodding. 'Get back to the station, get the ops room cranked up. The boss said right at the off if I needed to ramp it up, to speak to her. Well, the damn thing keeps ramping itself up. First thing this morning there was nothing, and now we've got fifty different angles, and we've no idea from which direction the shit's actually flowing.'

—

'We should leave Ellie here, she can let us know if anything comes up from speaking to the local shops.'

'Yep,' said Buchan. 'I'm going to head back and get started. Can you wrap your end up here, and make sure Ellie's on top of everything?'

'Boss.'

And Buchan was out of the small, depressing sitting room, and through the small, depressing kitchen, and down the stairs, his feet clipping noisily as he went.

24

Still early afternoon, Buchan and his crew back in the ops room. Buchan had made a start on filling up the whiteboards. Kane and Houston were there, Liddell too, seeming to want to make herself more of a part of it, perhaps feeling some responsibility for the whole thing going so wildly awry from what she'd originally imagined it might. 'Even if you hadn't asked me to look into Avercamp,' Buchan had said, 'we'd certainly be doing it by now.' Cherry had arrived, giving Buchan a bit of a sideways glance. Whatever thoughts he had on Roth staying at Buchan's apartment had yet to play out. Dawkins remained at the crime scene.

'Before we really get into this mire, we shouldn't get away from the basic question that started this all off,' said Buchan. 'What's happened to Claire Avercamp? We've become distracted with talk of Starbuck, the missing books, Bancroft's mob, the Baltazar mob, this Maplethorpe guy, and now this, what looks like a fairly straightforward gangland hit. The whole thing seems to be travelling at five hundred miles an hour. It feels like it should already be the middle of next week, yet we're still here, early afternoon, Tuesday. So, let's start at the beginning. Anyone with anything on Avercamp?'

He looked around the room.

'I've got something that's ultimately pretty minor, but it's fitting the narrative,' said Houston, and Buchan indicated for him to continue. 'She was seen having a drink with Davie Bancroft a few weeks ago. You know, the guys on the fourth floor, they're just running basic surveillance on him. As we know, prior to today, they didn't have an awful lot to report, they weren't much help with our protection racket case built around the Gallowgate newsagent's. Lunching with Avercamp seemed a little odd to them, but it was hardly a showstopper. That wasn't the kind of thing they were looking for.'

'And no one thought to pick it back up when she went missing?'

Houston kind of shrugged, acknowledging it was something

that would've slipped under the radar. It happened, especially when the police remained as understaffed as they were.

Buchan drew a line from Avercamp to Bancroft, studied the board for a moment, and then turned back.

'That means she knew they knew something about the books,' said Buchan.

'Maybe she got it from Savage,' said Kane, and Buchan nodded.

'Quite possibly.'

'Or maybe Starbuck,' said Houston.

There was something about the name Starbuck that amused him.

'Before we get to Starbuck, anything else on Avercamp? She hasn't popped up on any other radar?'

Head shakes around the room.

'K, we'll park her for now, but we can't forget about her. She's obviously at the heart of this. So, Starbuck, anyone? Danny, how are you getting on?'

'Sorry, I got distracted, sir, but I've been on it the last hour or so. And... I've got nothing. There's literally nothing. Feel like I might be wasting my time. It could be that this name, this Starbuck, was a codename between Avercamp and her contact. That's it.'

'In which case, there's no point in looking any further.'

Cherry nodded.

'K, park it for now. Hopefully I should be hearing from my Apple guy fairly soon. If we get a data dump, you can delve into that. That might give us a steer.'

He looked around the others.

'Anyone?'

Head shakes and blank faces in reply.

'OK, that maybe points to what Danny's saying.'

Buchan's phone started ringing, he took it out of his pocket, laid it on the table. A call from Sgt Meyers, leader of the SOCO team that had been at the flat in Baillieston. Buchan answered the phone.

'Ruth,' he said. 'You're on speaker.'

'Got something significant,' said Meyers. 'The victim was shot by a Glock-17, and we know from the round left embedded in the wall, the weapon used was the same one that was used to kill Rab Jones and Sally Kilbride last autumn.'

Buchan stared at Liddell, who had straightened in her seat.

'You're a hundred per cent?' he asked.

'More than that,' said Meyers, with grim certainty.

'That's great, Ruth, thanks. You'll send a detailed report over?'

'Stuart's just working it up now. Won't be long.'

They ended the call, Buchan nodding as he did so.

The murders of Jones and Kilbride had crossed their desks nine months previously. A gang hit, widely recognised as being carried out by Davie Bancroft's crew against a rival gang on the south side. The Lansdowne family. The police had feared an escalation, but it hadn't happened. No one knew why. And despite being sure of why the murders had been committed, they'd never been able to pin it on specific members of Bancroft's gang. The deaths had become just another couple of gang murders that went unsolved. The kind of thing that ate away at Buchan, that made him feel inadequate, made him feel the futility of what they were all doing some days.

'Malky's going to be sick of me,' said Buchan.

'You going to bring him in?' asked Liddell.

'Yep,' said Buchan. 'It's time. Every damn thing seems to lead back to him.'

'You want me to lead it?' said Kane.

The door opened, Dawkins entered. She looked around the room, as if counting off the names of everyone who was there.

'Sir,' she said.

'What's up? Anything else from the crime scene?'

Dawkins shook her head.

'Ellie?' said Buchan.

She looked around the faces again, was obviously feeling awkward.

'I've got something. It's pretty sensitive. I'm not sure… maybe you just want to look at it yourself first. But then… sorry, that feels like, I don't mean to imply I'm suspicious of anyone.'

She shook her head, then added, 'Sorry, I should've thought this through.'

'What've you got, Ellie?' asked Buchan. 'There's no one here that should be kept out the loop.'

'OK,' she said. She looked at Liddell, Liddell seemed to say something in the look she gave her, as though imparting authority, and Dawkins added, 'This can't leave the room.'

She took her phone from her pocket, and placed it on the table. Everyone leant in a little, to see what she was going to show them.

'I got access to the CCTV footage for this morning when your car was parked at various places, sir. When I was out at the crime location, things had settled down, everyone was pretty much doing what they were supposed to be doing, so I took the time to skim through some more of it.' A pause, and then, 'I found what we were looking for.'

She opened her phone, the clip was ready to play, and then she ran a black and white film of the Facel Vega in a car park. The location was not clear, little in sight other than several unmarked cars. A slight figure with a hoodie pulled up, wearing a black face covering of the type that had become so common over the previous three years. Everything about the figure and movement suggested it was a woman, although it was not entirely clear. She took a moment, a quick look around, and then she bent down out of sight at the far side of the car. The clip ran on, but now there was nothing to see, as the woman did her work.

'She's small,' said Buchan, grimly. 'She's going to have been able to reach further beneath the car without having to take the time to jack it up.'

'Whoever gave her the brief, had given it that much thought,' said Dawkins, nodding.

After a minute or so, the woman straightened up, and now walked quickly away from the car without taking any further look around. A few seconds, and she was out of sight.

Liddell looked at Dawkins, then at Buchan. She could see that Buchan's face had changed. The look in his eyes she recognised when they were filled with cold fury.

'Where was this?' asked Liddell.

Buchan stared across the desk, then looked at Dawkins.

Dawkins swallowed. She wasn't playing the moment, but she might not have done anything differently if she had been. Eventually she found the words.

'The HQ in Dalmarnock, ma'am.'

25

Six of them in the room, three simultaneous conversations. Buchan was trying to listen to Kane, but he couldn't properly pay attention. Through it, he heard Dawkins say she'd checked the footage of the camera aimed at the perimeter fence, and as far as she could make out, no one had broken in.

Finally Buchan snapped, bringing his hand swiftly down on the table. Having done so, he made a small gesture to Kane in apology at having cut her off.

Silence. Liddell gave him an eyebrow, but she hadn't minded him taking charge of the tumult.

'Sam and I will bring in Malky Seymour. Ian, I need you and Danny and Ellie to continue the work on the two gangs we're dealing with here. If we can get anything else on Seymour before we bring him in for questioning, that'd be perfect. If I get anything from Apple in the meantime, I'll forward it on to you. Boss…' He looked at Liddell, and she nodded, knowing what he'd been going to say.

'Leave it with me,' she said. 'I'll take it to Reynolds in Dalmarnock. He probably won't want to see me, but I think this little clip is something of a door opener. Can you forward it to me, please, constable?'

Dawkins nodded.

'And everyone,' said Liddell, 'we don't know what this is yet. Constable Dawkins was quite right to be cagey showing us all. Hopefully this is going to turn out to be a case of someone climbing the fence, or finding some other way to make their way into the facility, in order to attack the inspector's car. However, there's always the possibility of… well, we all know. And we know the likes of Bancroft's gang is going to have people on the inside. Try as we might, we're never ridding the force of that kind of corruption. For now, this goes no further.'

A look around the room, nods all round.

'OK,' said Buchan, 'let's get to it. Sam, five minutes and we'll head. Can you identify Seymour's whereabouts, please?'

'Boss,' said Kane, and she led the team from the room.

Buchan and Liddell watched them go, and then Buchan closed the door on the corridor, turning back to face the boss.

'What d'you think?' he said.

Liddell shook her head.

'I'm not sure going over there's going to accomplish much this afternoon, but I'm damned well going to try. Reynolds won't like me turning up and losing my rag at him, but that part will be unavoidable. But... it's a big building, there are a lot of people working there. There are bad actors in every organisation, and we are sadly no different.'

Buchan nodded, couldn't think of anything else to say, and then made for the door again. Stopped with his fingers on the door handle.

'Maybe you should take someone with you to sit in the car while you go inside,' he said.

'That, inspector, is a grim suggestion, but you know what...'

She nodded in agreement, then walked to the door and led him out.

26

'I'm seeing your problem here,' said Seymour.

Buchan and Kane on one side of the table, Seymour and his lawyer on the other.

It hadn't taken long. They'd called ahead, and although they'd been reasonably quick about it, by the time they'd arrived, Seymour was already consulting with his lawyer at the kitchen table. And now the four of them had moved scene, to a different table, in an interview room at SCU, three bland walls, and a room-length mirror in the fourth.

'What we have here is a classic case of police over-reach. Or let's call it a logical fallacy. You start with this fact with which no one's arguing. The gun that was used to kill Jonesy and that lassie Kilbride was the same gun that was used to kill this Polish lad today. I can see you in court now, with your diagrams and your *science*. Very impressive. The jury are on the edge of their seats. So who, asks the prosecution counsel, killed Jonesy? You look at the jury, stiff upper lipped and straight backed, and boldly say... I'm not sure. We *think* it was one of Bancroft's mob. Can't be certain. But probably. Well, let's say possibly. And, of course, that gun could have changed hands, and God knows what else went on with it, but let's say it *was* one of Bancroft's mob who used it on Jonesy and Kilbride, chances are it's one of Bancroft's mob who used it to do the Polish lad.'

He paused, he looked deadpan across the table. If Buchan had bothered looking at the lawyer, he would have been able to detect something of a smirk around the edges of her mouth.

'And then the prosecution counsel might ask how you came to find the Polish lad's corpse in the first place, and you wouldn't be able to say, because you'd promised to keep it a secret. But the thing is, you'd know. Deep inside, you'd know. And you'd think to yourself, if it was one of Davie's gang who committed the murder, why did Malky Seymour tell me where to find the corpse? What would be the point in that? And you'd stand there staring at the jury, dumbstruck. Or maybe you'd

---

mumble some shitty answer, but you wouldn't be feeling it. And the jury would see your lack of conviction, and they would know this one undeniable fact: you have no case. Whatever it is that's led you to bring Malky Seymour to court on these ridiculous charges, it's a falsehood. A pipedream. Who is this inspector we see before us, who drags us away from our daily lives? We thought this might be fun. Interesting. And this is who we get for the prosecution. A flibbertigibbet, a will-o'-the wisp, a clown.'

'What?' said Buchan.

Seymour laughed. He looked at his lawyer, and smiled. She looked coolly across the table.

'It seems Mr Seymour likes show tunes,' said Kane.

'Everybody likes show tunes,' said Seymour, still smiling, and then, with a snap of the fingers, the smile vanished.

'Inspector,' he said, 'we're all professionals here, we've all got work to do, we're all busy. I've had my break today on the driving range, and I had been intending to get out on the course this evening. But it turns out it's a busy day and I've no time for it. Which means I've no time for this. So, can we cut to it, please, or shall I instruct Ms Butterfield here to start proceedings against the police right now for wrongful arrest?'

Buchan held his look across the table. Felt Kane lean forward beside him. A signal that she was about to speak, giving him the second or two to stop her, but he let her continue.

'We can prove to a jury that your team committed the crime. That the gun belongs to someone at your outfit. That there is a clear connection that runs from the weapon to Davie Bancroft and his people. Then we have the curious case that you, and not some unidentifiable member of your team, literally told us where to find the body. X marks the spot. It's a small apartment, we have scenes of crime all over it, samples currently being taken from every damn surface and fibre, every inch of the corpse and his clothing. And we're lining up the resources, and about to pull the trigger, to bust your entire mob. Every last one of you. By the end of the afternoon, we'll have samples from each of you, and unless the perpetrator jumped in a warm bath of acid, there'll be some trace of weapons discharge on him or his clothes. There always is. So, maybe you can add all that up and it comes to nothing, but that's for you to decide. Or else, we can work together on this. You don't want some European uber-gang muscling in on your patch, any more than we want them here.'

Seymour let the silence linger, then finally, with a shrug in the tone, said, 'Was there a question in there anywhere? I mean, if there was, I missed it.'

Kane held his look, deadpan.

Nothing.

'When was the last time you spoke to Davie?' asked Buchan.

Seymour now shifted his look to Buchan, as though the process had been a slow, mechanical movement, a turning of the crankshaft.

'Last night.'

'What did you talk about?'

'Rangers.'

'Did you discuss the Baltazar gang?'

'Not last night'

'When was the last time?'

Seymour held his gaze, considering his words. Butterfield lifted her hand, the familiar *you don't have to say anything* gesture. Seymour shook his head, directed at her, even though he was continuing to look at Buchan.

'You might want to speak to William Lansdowne,' said Seymour.

'Lansdowne?'

'Sure. That's what we always say around these parts, isn't it? All the dodgy roads lead to Lansdowne.'

He laughed humourlessly.

'I don't think this one does,' said Buchan.

'We said, and this you cannot deny, that the murders of Jonesy and Kilbride were an internal power struggle. You lot thought there'd be an escalation afterwards, and there wasn't. And that was because that lot were too busy fighting each other. Plus, they had no reason, other than the usual, to come after us in any case.'

Buchan's phone buzzed, and he took it from his pocket to have a quick look. A one-line message with an attachment. **We're all square**.

Buchan placed the phone back in his pocket.

'Message from the King?' said Seymour, accompanied by another grim laugh.

'Tell us about Claire Avercamp.'

'Nothing to tell.'

'There's been no contact between you and Claire Avercamp?'

'I thought I told you earlier I'd never heard of her.'

'We know that Claire met up with Davie a few weeks ago,' said Buchan, and Seymour laughed.

'When you say met up...?' said Seymour, laughing, and he gestured crudely.

'We just received all Claire's personal correspondence,' continued Buchan, humourlessly. 'All the work she's been doing on the stolen books project, all the contact she's had with the Baltazars, the police, Europol, experts in the field. We'll know soon enough if she's had any contact with William Lansdowne.' They stared harshly at each other over the few feet of the desk. 'And we'll know how much contact she had with the Bancroft gang.'

'Again one of you two with the soliloquy and no question,' said Seymour. 'It's like you're getting your lines written by Shakespeare or something.'

Buchan abruptly pushed his seat back, getting to his feet.

'We'll be back,' he said, then Kane rose to join him, and they walked to the door.

'Is my client free to go?' asked Butterfield, quietly to their backs.

'If he was, we wouldn't be coming back, would we?' snapped Buchan.

They left, closing the door abruptly behind them.

27

Lansdowne was old school. Or, at any rate, what he liked to think of as old school. He'd been making money the same way, off the same things, since the seventies. High street shakedowns, small-time drug deals, women. His sons had wanted to move with the times, but that wasn't William Lansdowne. *You stay here, the rules are the rules*, he said. The game hadn't changed, and it wasn't going to now. He occasionally wondered if they'd ever try to usurp him, but he knew neither of them was strong enough. Both now in their forties, both too beholden to his legacy. One day, he thought, he'd die. Comes to everyone. Might be at the hand of some rival gang, but it wouldn't be from within. Everyone was too craven. Then the elder son would finally assume what he considered to be his rightful position, and he'd be lucky if he lasted a month. You needed to command respect, and his sons barely commanded acknowledgement of their existence.

Big house, up the hill at Cathkin, a view from the patio at the rear, down over the city. Not the best view on earth, but expansive. Would look good at night, thought Buchan, and on the rare occasions it snowed.

Buchan hadn't bothered taking the seat offered to him. Lansdowne was sitting at a wooden table, leaning forward, straight on to the view. In front of him was a small chess set, on which he was charting the moves of a game he was playing on his phone. Buchan thought of Roth for the first time in an hour.

He had passed the download from Stuey at Apple straight on to Kane, asking her to first of all make sure it was as extensive as they'd been hoping, and presuming it was, to then break it down and pass it amongst the team. Kane had pre-empted him by asking if she should include Roth, and Buchan said that she should. He'd also asked that she check the most recent activity on any of Avercamp's accounts and devices to see whether she was active somewhere. As he'd arrived at the Lansdowne house, he'd received her text to say there was nothing to report. Last activity, ten days previously, the day before her disappearance had been made known. Other than that worrying news, there was a lot to download.

'What happened to your face?' asked Lansdowne.

'Life,' said Buchan. It sounded cheap.

'Ha,' said Lansdowne, dully. 'So, why are you here, Buchan?'

He was seventy-five, and was sitting outside in a white, collarless shirt, sleeves rolled up, fat belly tight against the material. *Time to move up a size*, thought Buchan. By his right hand there was a glass of neat whisky, and a lit cigarette propped in a large, glass, unmarked ashtray.

Buchan turned away and looked out over the view. You could see the pollution today. Whatever it was about the warm, early May day, the air not circulating quickly enough, not enough of a breeze coming from the west, whatever it was, the light smog was sitting over the city and the land between them and the Campsie Fells in the distance.

'Tell me about the Baltazar gang,' said Buchan, turning to look at him.

Lansdowne smiled, his index finger placed on top of the black queen, poised to move. As if whoever was playing him could see he had his hand on the piece and would complain if he removed it.

'Hard bunch of fuckers from Poland, the way I hear it,' said Lansdowne. 'What you asking about them for?'

'We think one of their crew got hit in Baillieston this afternoon.'

Lansdowne turned quickly, eyeing Buchan to try to get a sense of whether he was making that up. He looked a little uncomfortable, his finger still on the black queen, his arm pressing against his bulging stomach, and then he finally removed his finger from the piece.

'Did they, now?'

'Gunshot wound to the head.'

'Well, there's a story,' said Lansdowne. 'You make any arrests?'

Buchan shook his head.

'Really? I heard you'd taken Malky into custody. I was wondering what that was about. That was odd, and now up comes old, plodding Buchan telling tales of Polish mobsters being hit, in fucking Baillieston of all places. That's not a coincidence, that's a shitstorm.'

'We're not arresting Malky for the murder.'

'No? Too bad. What'd he have to say about it?'

'That one of your lot probably did it.'

Lansdowne burst out laughing, a loud belly laugh, full-throated, though it died quickly. He laughed like he'd been smoking sixty cigarettes a day since his teens. He lifted the one from the ashtray and took a long draw. The laugh had gone, but he still had a smile on his face.

'Does that sound like my m.o., detective inspector? Because I don't think it does. That stupid boy of mine would probably love me to get involved with some bunch of goons from the continent, not realising we'd be overrun in a week. They would kill us. You have to know your place. You know that, or at least, I thought you did. Yet, here you are, turning up on my day off, asking stupid questions.'

'You heard Davie Bancroft's disappeared?'

Again the throaty laugh. It could be amusing, the laugh in itself, under other circumstances.

'Thought it sounded a bit strange, you know?' said Lansdowne. 'But now we have your tales of Euro-gang members getting killed, and it's clear as the light of day. There's a turf war down there,' and he made a vague gesture in the direction of the city, 'and it's nothing to do with us. More than likely, Davie's brought it on himself. Must've invited that lot in, and now he's gone. Stupid bastard. Sad tale all round.' A pause, and then, 'Makes the lot of us in Glasgow look bad. Small. Diminished.'

'Had you heard tell of the Baltazar gang in town?'

Lansdowne took a last draw of the cigarette and then extinguished it in the ashtray, leaving a thin trail of smoke to clutch to existence for a few seconds. Then he lifted his glass and took a drink, eyeing Buchan as he did so.

'Damn it, Bill,' said Buchan, hating the chumminess of it. This wasn't him, cosying up to the opposition, making friends, playing one off against the other. Yet the sense of urgency he'd felt since this morning had not left him. There was no reason why everything should be coming to a head just as Buchan and the team had been brought into what had already obviously been a long game, but that was how it was playing out.

'Damn it, Bill?' said Lansdowne. 'We friends all of a sudden?'

'Help me out here. There's a chance here for you. Let's not

mess around and pretend I'm on your side, *in any way*, but you have to consider your position. You spend your life in perpetual conflict with Davie's lot. Something's happened to Davie. Something's happened to one of the Baltazar mob. This could get ugly very quickly, and at the end of it, it's liable to fall out to your advantage. So why don't you just help me out here, and –'

'Why?' said Lansdowne with a barked laugh, cutting him off. 'If those daft bastards are going to wipe each other out, who benefits?' He stared at the sky, he shrugged, he smiled. 'You're going to have to give me better logic than that, chief inspector.'

'Really? I'm guessing you know who the Baltazars are. Davie's gone already, and soon enough, the likelihood is his team are going to get crushed. There is no *wiping each other out*. There's only going to be one winner. And sure, they're Polish, and the bulk of their ops are in Poland. But they're also in the Baltic states, they have some action in Germany and Hungary, some in various states in former Yugoslavia. They're expanding. And if you think they're going to come in here, crush the opposition in a new territory, then say, well that was a nice holiday, we'll leave everyone else alone now ...' He left the gap for a few moments, then added the unnecessary, 'You're wrong. Today Davie, tomorrow you. That's how this is going to play out. And that leaves us facing this European mega-gang, rather than you lot.'

The whisky was still in Lansdowne's hands, and he put it to his lips and drained the glass. Tapped the glass against his closed lips for a moment, drained the dregs, then set it down on the table, letting out a long, throaty sigh.

'You know that old gag, the problem with you is that all your brains are in your heid? That's you, Buchan. I fucking hate it when you come round here. Maybe once you could turn up with a tin of biscuits and have a cup of tea.' He continued to look out over the view, tapping the glass against the table. 'But you never bring biscuits. You bring shitburgers.'

'The audience is weeping for you, Bill. Tell me what you've heard.'

Another tap of the glass on the table, then he turned and took a glance over his shoulder. Perhaps a look back in the direction of the bottle, somewhere inside, contemplating another. Or perhaps checking to see if there was anyone around who might be listening.

Another loud sigh. Buchan kept the eye roll to himself at

the tortured pain of the reluctant witness.

'There was talk all along about the book raid out at Eurocentral. We were never that arsed with it. Just something that happened. Heard that Davie and his mob might've had something to do with it. Because the books had come from Poland, folk were thinking there was a Polish gang involved 'n all. Didn't hear a name for a while. Didn't take much interest, to be honest. But you know how it is. There was a bit of a buzz around. I mean, there's always a buzz about something, but this one refused to go anywhere. Refused to die down.' He sniffed, scratched his nose, lifted the glass and drained the non-existent dregs. 'Word was that they were looking for something in particular.'

'What?'

Lansdowne laughed.

'Don't know. Don't care. Just thought it was pretty fucking funny, by the way, that's all. They did this massive raid, got what by all accounts is a big-ass payload, and still didn't find what they were looking for. I mean, did you see that shit? There was a literal fucking Da Vinci, like signed drawing or something in there, man. That's like quarter of a million straight off the bat. But it wasn't enough. Must've been something, you know...'

All that nonsense about how disinterested he was, thought Buchan. He could see it now, as Lansdowne talked. The light in the eyes, unable to keep the smile from his face.

'Aye, it comes to it, inspector. This is, I don't know, Indiana Jones territory or something. There's something out there,' and he turned and swept his hand over the city, 'there's something. It was getting moved from Poland to the US, via here. Don't know why. Don't ask me. It was supposed to be in the Eurocentral shipment, and either it was, and someone's nicked it again, or it wasn't there in the first place. And the funny thing is that a lot of the people in the game don't even know what it is they're looking for.' He barked a laugh.

'What about you?' asked Buchan.

'You're a funny cunt sometimes, Buchan. I don't know any better than anyone else, and I'm not looking anyway.' He looked over the sweep of the city, and made another gesture to include it all. 'I'm just sitting here watching the wheels go round.'

He laughed again, possibly because he'd quoted John Lennon, and possibly because he just amused himself with everything he said.

28

They were all in the ops room when he got back, all sitting looking at laptops. Kane, Houston, Cherry, Dawkins. Liddell was there too, one of the crowd, a laptop open in front of her, nothing to distinguish her as the senior officer in the room.

Silence as Buchan entered. A few acknowledgements, then Cherry, Dawkins and Houston immediately looked back at their screens.

'Close the door, inspector,' said Liddell. Buchan closed the door, though he wasn't intending to stay. The urgency remained with him, and he was about to go and find Maplethorpe. He'd been meaning to speak to him since the name had first been mentioned. Beyond that, beyond putting himself in front of the man, he hadn't really thought anything through. There was also the matter of Malky Seymour, and what else they could get out of him, but he needed something more to take into the interview room, or else it would be a repeat of what had happened earlier. Soon enough they were going to have to release him.

'Without wishing to sound too dramatic, inspector,' said Liddell, 'there's a very big game afoot.'

'What have we got?'

'There's a lot to cover. Take a seat.'

Buchan gave the crowd a bit of eyebrow, then pulled a chair out and sat at the table, the only one not covered by a laptop. Liddell automatically closed the lid of hers, Kane resumed whatever task she'd been doing when Buchan entered.

'Whoever planted the explosive device on your car, they one hundred per cent came from within Dalmarnock HQ. We have footage of them leaving the building, and returning to the building. I'd say it's definitely a woman. There are currently four hundred and seventeen women working in that building, of whom three hundred and sixty-three were in the office. We obviously shouldn't assume anything, but under normal circumstances, this would not be the work of a commanding officer. This is the work of a foot soldier. However, at the other end of the scale, indicating that somewhere there is a commanding officer in play, you will find Malky Seymour is no longer in custody.'

Buchan's face hardened. This was becoming a day when nothing surprised him.

'Tell me.'

'Internal politics, someone pulling someone else's strings. I showed Reynolds the footage. Presented him with the fact that someone from within his building tried to kill one of my officers. He took it the way you'd expect. He's a defensive son-of-a-bitch. Cagey. I'm not taking that as complicity, by the way, just that he didn't like a subordinate officer bringing him something this ugly, when he had no idea what was to be done about it. He questioned my use of the word kill. He preferred *derail*. That was his take. Whoever this is, he said, they were able to plant a remote-controlled device beneath the Facel. It could easily have been a bomb, big enough to kill. They chose not to do that. He said that as you were driving around the city, you were never likely to find your brakes giving out at seventy miles an hour. Or, unless you went up the top end of town, to find yourself on a steep hill.'

'Jesus,' muttered Kane, eyes still on her laptop, ears obviously on Liddell.

'What about Seymour?' asked Buchan.

He didn't want to linger on Reynold's defensiveness. It was an inevitability. Discovering one of your own crew was trying to sabotage a fellow officer, regardless of whether it was a design to kill, maim, or just interfere with the investigation, was always going to lead to wariness, until such times he was made fully aware of what was going on, and was in a position to do something about it.

'He tossed it in at the end. I'm just about to leave, and you understand I was extremely pissed off and he was not helping in that regard, and he says, oh, by the way, *we've had to release Malky Seymour*. I pointed out it wasn't his call, he said it hadn't been. You don't have enough to hold him, he said. With Davie Bancroft missing, this is a delicate time. Can't afford to put a foot wrong. There will be people thinking it's the police that have made Bancroft disappear.'

'Who the fuck is thinking that?' snapped Buchan, then he shook his head and quickly held up his hand.

'Inspector,' said Liddell, 'those were exactly the words I used to the superintendent, which did not play well.'

They held the shared look of annoyance across the desk, then Liddell made a gesture to dismiss the news.

'This is where we are. And, sad to say, it puts us in a position where I'm not sure we can trust anyone other than who's here in the room.' She shook her head as soon as she said it. 'I am confident we're good with the people in this building, although of course we can't know. I should say that I'd like to keep this as much as possible here so we're not exposing too many people to whatever the hell is going on out there.'

'Keep it tight,' said Buchan, nodding.

'Yes. Although it does leave the matter of Constable Roth.'

A couple of them glanced at Buchan, eyes then quickly averted.

'I asked Sam to include her,' said Buchan. 'She's already been looking into some things for me, and –'

'That wasn't what I meant,' said Liddell, and Buchan intimated for her to continue. 'As you say, inspector, we need to keep things tight. I'd like Agnes in here for now. Let's see how the day plays out. There's just a feeling that, I don't know, something major's going to happen. Sure, it could be next week or next month, or never, or it could be tomorrow and it's in Edinburgh, we don't know. But these people have already targeted your car. Maybe your apartment is vulnerable. She should be here, at the very least until you're done for the day and go home.'

Buchan was nodding along by the time she'd finished.

'I'll go and get her,' he said. 'We can worry about the return-to-work paperwork later.'

'Thank you.'

'We getting anywhere?' he asked, tossing the question around the room.

A couple of raised heads again, this time everyone deferring to Kane, who'd obviously been collating the information gathered from Avercamp's iCloud files.

'The most useful stuff here is in her notes for the movie. That's what the folder's called. Notes For The Movie. Here she's got a list of contacts, information gathered from each of them, the story so far, a movie treatment, a working script itself, albeit I think that's the most speculative thing. Some of that is clearly wishful thinking, searching for drama that's not necessarily backed up elsewhere. Perhaps what she hoped she was going to be able to say.

'So, she definitely has an insider called Starbuck, but we don't know where or who this is. It's possible he or she might be one of us. There's certainly plenty of discussion on the police investigation. Some insight, the inner working and thinking of the police service. But if it was the police, they had no control over what Avercamp then did with that information.'

'They could've been feeding her false info,' said Cherry. 'Playing her.' A pause, then he kind of smiled. 'Using her as a pawn.'

'Do we think this is DI Savage?' asked Buchan.

'Not necessarily. She wasn't working the case alone. It's a small team, but it doesn't really end there. It could easily have been anyone over there who just logged into a computer and read the latest notes on the case. And, like Danny said, it could've been someone pretending to be the police, having an educated stab at what we might be doing. Maybe Avercamp thought it was the police.'

'Had she worked out what everyone was looking for?'

'She thought she had, but didn't yet have confirmation. Given the origin, and the fact that the Baltazar mob are so keen to get their hands on it, she's pinned it down to a Chopin manuscript. An original draft of his second symphony. So, in Chopin's own hand. A similar piece, the composer's first symphony, went for seven hundred and fifty thousand a few years ago. Apparently, well according to Avercamp, Chopin Two, as she calls it, is his *Bohemian Rhapsody* or *Hey Jude* or whatever. She thought it would likely go for upwards of two million.'

'Savage mentioned a Chopin manuscript, but she was dismissive enough that I don't think she was giving it any credibility. Did Claire have any proof? It wasn't listed in amongst the pieces that had gone missing, was it?'

'No and no. It's all supposition. And maybe she's batting at the level of a conspiracy theorist, but she manages to sound convincing, I'll give her that.'

'Albeit, these are her own notes, so she's only trying to convince herself?' said Buchan.

'Yes, looks like she hadn't sent them anywhere else. But the manuscript, this Chopin, hasn't been seen since the war. Generally it's presumed to have been either destroyed, or to be currently sitting amongst the private piano music collection of some ex-Nazi family in a South American jungle.' She made a small gesture to wave away the trivially generic Nazi joke. 'She's managed to find some talk of it, just in general in antique music circles. She's finagled an argument that says there was a particularly rare piece amongst the shipment travelling from Warsaw to New York, that was never announced. Top secret. It was going to be the big reveal when they got to the States, the intention being that the news of it would drive the price up even more. And, of course, it all comes back to Chopin, the great Polish musical hero. The maestro. You can imagine some Polish mobster wanting this piece of his country's history. He might not be able to tell everyone he's got it, but he'll know. *People* will know.'

Liddell was nodding as Kane spoke.

'Like the sergeant said,' she said, 'it sounds convincing, but it's not necessarily based on anything solid. We'll keep looking. Plenty more where all this came from. You got a plan for what's next?'

'I need to speak to this Maplethorpe character,' said Buchan. 'Been meaning to do it for the last couple of hours.'

'Of course,' said Liddell. 'But, first Constable Roth, if you wouldn't mind.'

Buchan nodded and was gone.

29

Buchan let himself into the apartment. He hadn't called ahead, and as he'd walked up the stairs, he'd begun to wonder if Roth would be there, and in an instant had created a scenario where she was gone, and not answering her phone.

When he entered, she was sitting at the kitchen table, the laptop open, cup of tea beside her, the remnants of a piece of toast on a plate, the smell of it invitingly in the air.

'Boss,' she said.

'How're you getting on?'

'Nothing doing, really. I've just got Claire's private e-mail account here.'

'She kept her work completely separate?'

'Seems like it. She was very compartmentalised. So, to be honest, the sarge hasn't given me much to do. There's nothing consequential. Turns out she wasn't as on the wagon as was generally believed, but she seems, or at least she thought, she was handling it. Occasional managed benders, is how she describes it to one of her friends, which sounds not unlike Elon Musk's space craft and its rapid unscheduled disassembly.'

'She wasn't talking privately to anyone about work?'

'There's nothing. She mentions quite often she's got something on, that she's working, she has plans et cetera. Very positive, but if anyone pushes her on it, she goes all super secretive, but... I'd say most people believed her. It's really just a random scattering of friends, a couple of whom I assume are family. You can always tell the different tone. I'm chasing some of these people down at the moment, making a list of those it'll be worthwhile contacting to see if they might have any idea. But, as I guess was already noted, there's nothing outgoing from her accounts in the past ten days.'

Buchan nodded his thanks, and then looked at the window, and then, as he always did in this room, found himself drawn to it, and he walked over, and stood looking down at the river. Beside him on the table, the chess set had been reset. Edelman was curled up on Roth's usual chair, fast asleep.

When he turned back, she was watching him, her chin resting in her hand. She showed no sign of awkwardness at being caught looking at him.

'You taking a break?' she asked. 'Or are you done for the day?' She checked the time.

'The boss wants me to bring you in,' said Buchan.

She stared back, no emotion on her face. Nothing to say.

'Are you all right with that?' asked Buchan.

'I don't think so,' said Roth, and when Buchan started talking again he got no further than, 'There's been a –,' when she cut him off with, 'I'm sorry. This just feels like... you know, I understand you had to tell the chief, and I can understand that you felt you had to tell sarge. I just thought, this is going to escalate, and now...' She made an exploding gesture.

'You spoke to Danny?'

'Sure.'

Buchan asked the question with silence, and she sort of shrugged.

'It was fine. It was nice to see him. I like Danny.' A pause, the worry on her face. 'I feel like you're pushing me.'

'Don't say that,' said Buchan. That clawing feeling of being out of his depth. Janey would know what to say in this situation. Real life. A trauma survivor. Maybe not just Janey. Lots of people. He wasn't one of them.

'It's pretty fast,' she said, 'that's all,' and she made a small gesture to her computer. 'Obviously the sarge doesn't want to give me much, and you know, I can't blame her. I should stand down, leave you guys to get on with it.'

'Whoever tampered with my car did so while it was parked at the HQ in Dalmarnock.'

'What? But not someone from the actual... not, you know...'

'Yes, someone from the building. Hood up, unidentifiable, left the building, sabotaged the Facel, went back into the building.'

'Jesus.'

'We had Malky Seymour in custody. It was tenuous, I admit, but we needed to put pressure on him. Someone, we don't know who, ordered his release. He's gone. Chances of finding him again today, pretty near zero, I would've thought. There's a fight coming between Davie's mob and this gang from Poland. It's already started. One dead, as far as we know, but it could

—

88

already be more, we just haven't found the bodies yet.'

'Kicking off,' said Roth, her tone neutral.

'Yes. And we are, sadly, in a don't know who we can trust situation. Not a good place to be. We'd like you in the office, so we can keep the small team working on this together.'

'As I said, I'll stop working on it.'

'There's a lot going on that suggests someone within the force is playing for the opposition, and we have no idea who that is, and what they know. But they've already targeted my car, so how can we know they won't target my apartment?'

In the silence of the large, open-plan room, her swallow sounded loud. She self-consciously lifted the tea and took a drink.

'I know it's going to be hard, but everyone in the office knows. They know you're coming, they know how difficult it's going to be for you. None of them will pretend to be pleased to see you.'

He said it deadpan, then couldn't stop the slight, sad smile.

She tried to join him in it. She looked pale and sad, a faded version of herself. *She's right*, thought Buchan, *it's too fast*. He didn't think they had any other option.

*

There had been smiles and nods as she walked through the office. Most people had had the moment of surprise, at not recognising her straight off, as she no longer had what had been her most distinguishable feature. Indeed, if it weren't for the fact they'd been warned Buchan would be returning with her to the office that afternoon, it was possible some of them wouldn't even have recognised her. Curious, for someone usually so striking.

The ops room door was closed, as it had been most of the day. Buchan entered, Roth following behind. Kane, Houston, Cherry and Dawkins looked up. Dawkins and Kane immediately stood. Liddell was no longer in the room.

'Oh my God, Agnes,' said Dawkins. 'So good to see you. You look amazing!'

Dawkins gave her a hug, then stood back, trying to downplay her reaction, looking at Buchan.

'Sorry, sorry, we were told. Sorry!'

'It's OK,' said Roth. 'It's nice to be back.'

She smiled weakly at Dawkins, then looked around the table. The others were watching her supportively. Roth was not one to be the centre of attention for long, however.

'Right, boss,' she said to Kane, 'where are we?'

She pulled a seat out at the table. When she turned to look at Buchan it was to see the door closing on his departure.

—

30

'Mr Maplethorpe is busy right now. He can see you first thing tomorrow morning, if that's suitable.'

'He's in the office?' asked Buchan.

'Yes, but as I said, he's busy.'

'You can get him on the phone?'

'I'm not sure. As I said, he's busy.'

'Get him on the phone, and tell him I'm here, and will see him now. If he doesn't want to see me now, then I can hang around in the lobby until twenty of my colleagues have arrived. I could obviously arrest him myself, but you know what us heavy-handed coppers are like. Nothing we enjoy more than a show of force.'

The man on reception straightened his shoulders, which was a feat, thought Buchan, given how ramrod straight he'd made himself as soon as Buchan had announced his presence and why he was here.

'This will not wash.'

'You need to call Mr Maplethorpe, and find out what washes,' he said. Left it a moment, then added, 'Now.'

The man on reception left enough of gap that he imagined he had regained some of the control he'd never actually had, then he lifted the phone.

'We have a Detective Chief Inspector Buchan here to see Mr Maplethorpe.'

A pause, the look in the eyes that said where the story was going, then he hung up.

'Go straight up,' he said quickly. 'Mr Maplethorpe is on the ninth floor. The elevator is to your left.'

'Thank you,' said Buchan. He started to walk off, stopping himself after a couple of paces. 'And thanks for the promotion. Would be great if you could let my pay section know.'

*

'I'm not sure I appreciate the visit, Inspector Buchan,' said

Maplethorpe.

'Appreciation is not something we usually care about.'

'How may I help you?'

They were in a large office in the centre of town. The top floor of a new, glass building, views over the older sandstone of the magnificent nineteenth and early twentieth century buildings that dominated the city centre. The university to the west, the Kingston Bridge a few blocks south and to their left.

'Claire Avercamp's disappearance had not been on my team's radar before today. My boss asked me to take it on. We find out Claire was running an investigation into the theft of antique books, which had arrived at Eurocentral from Poland, last October. Something else that had not been on my team's radar. Suddenly events start moving at a hundred miles an hour. There's a storm coming. There's a gang in Glasgow we've been keeping tabs on, a case we were going to be working on today, who are involved in the book theft in some way. The head of that gang goes missing.' He snapped his fingers. 'There's another lot, the Baltazar group from Gdańsk, involved. One of their crew turns up with a bullet in the brain.' Snapped his fingers again. 'Someone sabotages my car, someone pulls some strings to get a suspect released from custody. Like I say, everything moving at a hundred miles an hour. When that happens, we start looking around for peculiarities, or things that seem a little too neat. And we have Claire Avercamp speaking to you, we have the Polish crime gang, we have books travelling from Poland to Scotland, and we have you, owner of a Polish-registered security company.'

Maplethorpe was sitting behind his desk. Expensive suit, expensive white shirt, expensive dark green tie. Expensive haircut, expensive teeth. No time for the likes of Buchan. Indeed, thought Buchan, he was surprised he'd had the time for Claire Avercamp. The arts of any description, did not seem like this man's usual territory.

'Coincidence, inspector? Life, if you take the time to look around you, is full of them.'

'Not in this line of work,' said Buchan. 'Things fall into line for a reason, and I'd like to know the reason you were speaking to Claire Avercamp.'

Maplethorpe casually rubbed the palm of his right hand, affectedly scratching an itch. Something to do while he pretended to debate with himself over whether to cooperate with the police.

'Were you investigating the theft of the books at Eurocentral last October?' asked Buchan.

'Why would we investigate anything? We're in security, not private investigations. We protect things.'

'Did you have anything to do with the security on the haulage of the Eurocentral books from Poland to the US?' asked Buchan, and Maplethorpe emitted a low, barked laugh.

'I can assure you that if we had, they would never have been stolen.'

The smug over-confidence and absolute certainty of the rich, thought Buchan.

'You've never had dealings with the Baltazar group?' he asked.

'As I said to your boss when she rather rudely interrupted my meeting a while ago, they are the *kind* of operation with whom we have to deal. But that's it. As for specificity, I have nothing to tell you. I do not recall any particular instance of having to deal with them directly. I think you might find that we move in rather different circles. The kind of crimes we protect our clients from, are not the kind of gangland thuggery this crowd are involved in.'

You could talk to these people and it would seem like you were getting nothing in return. And yet, here he was, and the lies were piling up. And once you had proof of the lies, it made it so much easier to come back. *Keep talking*, thought Buchan.

'You know the name Jan Baltazar?' he asked.

'Part of this Baltazar group, presumably?'

Buchan nodded.

'No.'

'You know Davie Bancroft and William Lansdowne?'

'Sound Scottish,' said Maplethorpe.

'Yes.'

'Don't know them.'

'Two of the main gang leaders on the south side of the city,' said Buchan.

'Not really our territory. We have this office here, but that's entirely because of my wife's family. I don't spend much time in Scotland. Our business is global with a capital G, inspector. Small-town crime of the likes which may well be your bread and butter means nothing to us.'

Buchan's phone buzzed in his pocket. He held

Maplethorpe's look while he removed the phone, then he read the text message, slipped the phone back into his pocket, and lifted his eyes once again across the desk.

'When was the last time you had contact with Claire Avercamp?' he asked.

Maplethorpe stared blankly back at him. He's calculating now, thought Buchan. He doesn't know what I know. Did I just receive something that made me ask that question? Although, I've already asked a couple of questions that are clearly clutching, so perhaps this is just more of the same.

'Claire Avercamp wrote to you two months ago,' said Buchan.

'Did she? I don't recall. Lots of people write to me, inspector. I more often than not do not reply, particularly with personal requests for information. More than likely, the name would have meant nothing to me.'

'You replied.'

'Did I?'

He looked vague, and shrugged.

'You're obviously trying to implicate me in something here, inspector, but I can assure you I have no idea where you're trying to go with this, and what you think you're going to achieve.'

'You discussed the theft of the books. You discussed the involvement of the Baltazar gang. She asked if you had any connection to them, and a channel through which she'd be able to meet Jan Baltazar. You replied to say leave it with me.'

'I did?' He laughed. 'That's exactly the kind of thing that happens. I do not recall.'

'It would be reasonable to assume from your reply that you know Jan Baltazar.'

'Assume what you like, inspector, though perhaps you might want to work on the basis of fact, rather than assumption.'

'The implications of what she wrote are that you were, in some way, already involved in the Eurocentral case.'

'Implications belong in the same bin as assumptions.'

Buchan was annoyed by him, his annoyance made worse by the growing sense they all felt at SCU that something was happening, something bad and dark and dangerous, and that time was running out to stop it. This man was in security, and nominally on the same side as the police. People were always going to be cagey with business information, particularly in a fluid situation such as this one, but everything about this man said he was in fact working against Buchan.

'Someone's been murdered,' said Buchan. 'There's the possibility others will follow. If you really are on the side of someone's security in this,' and he could see Maplethorpe actively having to stop the eye roll, 'then the best way to achieve that is to work with the police. We have access to systems and information you do not. We have –'

'I'm not involved in it,' said Maplethorpe. 'My company is not involved in it.'

'Did you meet Claire Avercamp?'

For all his own annoyance, Buchan could still sense the anger that was being silently directed back at him from across the desk.

'Since you persist, Ms Avercamp funded her cocaine habit by selling sex,' said Maplethorpe. 'I was not her only client. I'm sure, being one of the city's leading detectives, you'll be able to identify others.'

'I don't believe you.'

'Believe what you like, Inspector Buchan. I'm rarely in Glasgow, but when I'm here, I like to pay for sex. I usually find it's worth it.'

Buchan stared harshly across the desk. This was what he hated. The lies. The chutzpah to be presented with facts by the police, and say they mean nothing. The balls of it. And sometimes you'd see it from the likes of Bancroft and Lansdowne, and there would be a sly smile, a nod and a wink, everyone knowing that everyone else was playing a game. But this sort, Maplethorpe, it was a conviction borne of education and family life that told him he was always right. He didn't have to justify anything. He didn't need reasons.

Buchan abruptly turned and walked from the office. As he closed the door behind him, he caught the movement of Maplethorpe's hand as he lifted the phone.

31

Buchan returned to his car to find it hooked up to the back of a tow truck. A woman driving the truck, working the tow chain, a man standing on the pavement making sure everything was properly aligned.

'What are you doing?' said Buchan.

The man gave him a glance, head to toe, then shrugged.

'My job. Someone's got to do it.'

'It's not illegally parked there,' said Buchan.

'Got a call from the feds that it should be brought in.'

Buchan read the name on the side of the truck. McMurray Pick-Up.

'You got a call from someone to bring this car in?'

The man gave Buchan a bit more of a look.

'This your car?'

Buchan showed him his ID, nodding.

A look at the card, eyes drifting back up to Buchan. He smiled.

'You've been in the wars, eh? You gone rogue, or what?'

'Who asked you to pick it up?'

'That's not how this works, chief. We get e-mails –'

'You just said you got a call.'

'It's a call-out, man, come on. It's an e-mail. No name, no reason, just a generic thing from traffic at Police Scotland saying, go to street X, pick up car Y, bring it back to the pound.' A gap, then he shrugged. 'End of.'

'OK, good to know,' said Buchan. 'But I'm an officer, this is my car, so can you desist, please?'

'Nope.'

Buchan held the gaze from a couple of feet. Already knew he was in an argument he was going to lose.

'I'm showing you my ID,' he ventured.

'Sorry, chief. Orders is orders. If I start making calls on what e-mails I should listen to and the ones I can ignore,' and he dragged a thumb across his throat. 'It's not going to be my contract for very much longer, is it?'

Buchan had nothing to say. He turned away and began the walk back to the river, and the SCU HQ on the other side. After half a block he suddenly wondered if someone would have worked out his straightest route home and this was about setting some other trap for him. He stopped, he stood and considered for several moments whether he was being unnecessarily dramatic, and then he turned away along a different route, and crossed the river two bridges along from the one he would normally have taken.

32

'Oh my damned God,' said Liddell, when Buchan told her about the car.

It was trivial, but at the same time, something about its triviality made it worse. Whoever was working against them from inside, was throwing everything at them. Nothing was too small to try. They had yet to discover whether there was anything too big, or whether this thing was going to get worse before the day was done.

'You think we'll be able to trace this back if we get on to traffic?' she asked.

'If whoever did it was careless,' said Buchan. 'Obviously we need to check, but I doubt we should hold out much hope.'

'Yes,' said Liddell. She was tapping the end of the cigarette on the desk. 'Leave it with me,' she added.

Buchan waited.

'What's next?' she asked.

'I want to locate Seymour. We can't bring him in again, but I want eyes on him. Find some of his people, try to get a feel for what they're up to. The team are still all over Avercamp's files, still trying to pin down Starbuck. Agnes is working on establishing a connection between Poznań Secure and either Bancroft or Baltazar, however nebulous. There must be something.'

Buchan's phone buzzed, and he took it from his pocket. A message from Kane.

Better get back down here. Break-in at the Bannerman bookshop.

He held his phone out so that Liddell could see the message. Her eyes lingered over it for a while, but she wasn't trying to recall the part the Bannerman bookshop had so far played in the day's events. She'd read the report, she remembered it. She was just trying to think it through.

'Better get over there,' she said, 'but don't spend too much time on it. Let the locals deal with the wrap-up if there's nothing too significant.'

Buchan nodded, turning away. He hadn't needed the instruction. He felt Liddell's impotence, stuck behind her desk, wanting to grab this thing by the neck. She would be back down in the ops room soon enough.

Buchan entered the office no more than a minute and a half after receiving Kane's text. The room was buzzing with phone calls, and although everyone was sitting at a desk, there was an energy about the place that was usually only to be found in an imminent crisis.

He stood beside Kane's desk, said, 'What's up?' when she ended her call.

'Got another bookstore break-in call thirty seconds after the Bannerman. Someplace else that sells antiques. We've identified nine places that sell antique books in and around the city. We're just...,' and as she indicated the room and the staff working the phones, Cherry said, 'Yep, Forrester Antiques have just been hit.'

He dialled another number.

'Leatherbound in Clarkston,' said Dawkins. 'Same.'

'What are we talking about here in terms of being hit?' said Buchan. He made a gun with his thumb and forefinger. Could feel the urgency surging inside him, ready to move.

'Doesn't appear to be the m.o. No deaths currently reported.'

'Ops room,' said Buchan, indicating for Kane to follow him. 'We need a list of all the shops, we need to make sure the locals are on it, but I want one of us to go to every affected shop. Agnes can coordinate. We'll get the boss in on it too, she looks like she wants to get her hands dirty.'

Kane clapped her hands as they headed to the door.

'Ops room, people, let's move!'

33

They'd done a thorough job, not a book left on a shelf, as if the room had been laid waste by a thousand poltergeists.

There were two other officers there, one of whom was taking photographs of the shop on her phone, the other talking to Carol Bannerman at the counter. Bannerman was leaning forward, her face expressionless. Like she'd shut down as a mechanism to get through the rest of the day. Maybe she'd taken something.

They turned towards Buchan as he entered. Now there was a slight shift in her look towards disdain.

'Can you leave, please?' said the officer with the phone, and Buchan held forward his ID, saying, 'DI Buchan,' as he did so.

'Sir.'

'Keep taking the photos. Constable...?' he said to the one talking to Bannerman, and she said, 'Jess Robson,' and Buchan said, 'Jess, can you work the street, see if there's anyone with a story to tell?' and she nodded, acknowledged Bannerman, and then turned away, picked her way through the detritus, and left the shop.

While the other constable continued her work, Buchan and Bannerman stared at each other over the remnants of the raid. He'd been in the shop for less than a minute, and her face had already darkened considerably. If she was looking for someone to blame, she'd found him.

Buchan carefully stepped through the mess, his eyes picking out occasional titles along the way. *A Farewell To Arms. Deacon's British Flora and Fauna. Of Mice And Men. A Study In Obdurate Determinism (1878-91). A Study In Scarlet. Battles of The British Army 1710-1895.*

'Are you all right?' he asked, arriving at the counter, bending to move a couple of books to give himself some floorspace. He wondered where Robson had put her feet.

'Just tickety-boo,' she said. Voice deadpan. The expression sounded strange from her. She seemed annoyed at herself for using it in the first place.

'They didn't hurt you?'

She stared grimly across the counter.

'You don't need to be mad at me,' he said.

'You think?'

'Yes. You're presuming this happened because I came to see you earlier –'

She cut him off with a sharp, bitter laugh.

'Certain amount of cause and effect going on here, yes,' she said.

'There wasn't,' said Buchan. 'You know Forrester books? Bellocq and Bristol? Leatherbound?'

Her brow furrowed, she nodded.

'They all got hit at the same time. You getting hit was nothing to do with me turning up. We chose you at random, as I was looking for someone with a little inside knowledge. Whoever did this, chose *everyone*.'

'Shit. Are they… Did anyone get hurt?'

'I don't know yet. You all got hit at the same time. A very coordinated attack. And while some presumably took longer to go through than others, it would appear that all the shops were locked down for the same length of time, so that the calls to the police came in together.'

'Even Sturdy & Son? I know they at least have an emergency alarm button under the front desk.'

'Didn't get the chance to use it, as far as I'm aware. My sergeant's heading there now. We're in a very active situation, so we don't have all the details. Tell me what happened.'

She looked more worried now than when he'd come in, no comfort in being part of a collective.

'Nearly the end of the day, there were no customers when they arrived,' she said. A pause, she looked away from him, over the scene of devastation. 'I thought they'd picked their moment, but if this was coordinated with other shops, presumably that didn't make any difference. God…'

'We can't worry about others just now. Tell me what happened.'

'I'd really like to call Lance at Sturdy if that's OK.'

'There are officers there already. If there were any major injuries, anything beyond what we have here, I'd've been notified. Just run me through it, please, you can make your call in a few minutes.'

'Sure,' she said, impatience creeping into her voice.

'So, there were no customers,' said Buchan, ushering her back into the explanation.

'Three men. Face coverings, bobble hats. It was obvious, straight from the off, what was coming. I was here, behind the counter, but I never got that alarm fitted. I lifted my phone, but they were like,' and she rapidly snapped her fingers three times, 'boom, all over it. Guy with a gun, straight off the bat. Meanwhile, the other two are at the front of the shop, *Closed* sign pulled over, door locked, blinds lowered. Lights on, and they started searching.'

'They tell you what they were looking for?'

'Nope.'

'This third guy, the one with his gun on you?'

'That was his job. Keep me where I was, make sure I didn't do anything to interfere with the search. I had to stand here, except when they came to search behind the counter, then they ushered me out to stand where you are.'

'Did they talk at all?'

'Nothing.'

'The guy with the gun just spoke with the gun?'

She made a few gestures to indicate him moving her around with the weapon, then she said, 'Yes.'

'Did they speak to each other?'

'Not at all.'

'Did you say anything?'

'I asked what they were looking for. The guy put the gun to his lips.' She mimicked putting a gun to her lips.

'Did you feel any threat?'

She looked at Buchan for a moment, expressionless, then curious, then a rueful laugh, and then scornful confusion.

'Did I feel any threat from the guy pointing the gun at me? I don't know. Let me think about that.'

'Most people pointing a gun have no intention of using it,' said Buchan, his voice level. 'It's a tool, something to get a job done. In the moment, what was your gut telling you? I would not expect you to have taken a chance if you thought the guy wasn't actually going to do anything, I'm just looking for...' He let it go, he shook his head. 'Your gut reaction, that's it. Did you think, as it progressed, they would kill you anyway?'

She sighed, looking away from him. Every time her eyes revisited the scene of the book-splaying, she seemed to suffer anew, a shadow crossing her face.

'All right,' she said. 'I was scared at first, but soon enough... I think it was when I spoke to him and he did the gun thing. You know, put it to his lips. There was a look in his eyes. Just something that said, don't do anything stupid, and we'll be gone shortly. By the end... I felt like a spectator, rather than a victim or a hostage or anything. Maybe I was being naïve or stupid, albeit it turned out I was right, but I thought they'd find what they were looking for, or not, then they'd go.'

'How did it end?'

The officer taking the photos approached carefully through the mess.

'I'm done here for the moment, sir,' she said to Buchan. 'I'll join Jess, yeah?'

'Please,' said Buchan, then he nodded at Bannerman to continue.

'My guy, the gun guy, he was the time keeper. Kept looking at his watch, though every time he did it, he held his wrist up beside the gun hand.' Again, she mimicked the movement. 'I guess so he wasn't looking away from me, as if I was going to pull some sort of *Atomic Blonde* bullshit.' As ever, Buchan didn't get the cultural reference. 'They looked like they'd gone over everything, then started again. Then at one point he snapped his fingers three times, then twice, I guess a minute later, then he did it once and I finally cottoned he was counting down. Began to feel a little nervous then. Anyway, he snapped his fingers once, again, and that was the signal to leave. The other two guys just walked out, my guy followed, gun inside his jacket as soon as he turned away.'

'And they never took anything?'

'Not that I saw. I mean, I was distracted by my guy a couple of times, but they were definitely looking for something in particular, and I don't think they found it.'

'You have a storeroom back there?'

'Part store room, part office.'

'And they looked there too?'

'Yes.'

'And they didn't want you to hear them talking?'

'That's how it seemed.'

'Height, build, any features standing out about them, any hair sticking from beneath the hats?'

'Nothing exceptional. They weren't all wearing black or

anything. Jeans, long-sleeved whatever. Jumper, sweatshirt, whatever you'd call them. No hair showing. Average builds.'

'All men, though?'

'Far as I could tell.'

'No chance of making an ID?'

She laughed.

'You can fill your boots on my CCTV, inspector.'

34

'That's twenty-seven people involved in simultaneous raids,' said Buchan. Back in the ops room for the reassembling. The reports had all come in for Roth to amalgamate, although not all the team had yet returned.

The raids had all followed the same pattern as the one on Bannerman's bookshop. Two people out of the nine shops had attempted what Bannerman had described as an *Atomic Blonde* manoeuvre. One shop owner, one customer. They'd both been summarily shot in the kneecap. There had been no discussion. No verbal threat. None of the twenty-seven had spoken.

'Do we suppose no one spoke,' said Roth, 'because they didn't want to give away that they were Polish, or could it have been Davie Bancroft's mob, or even William Lansdowne's, and they wanted us to believe they had something to hide in their speech?'

She was by the whiteboards, phone sticking out of her back pocket, blue marker in hand, updating the boards as the information arrived. It seemed that none of the nine teams of three had found what they were looking for.

'I'd tend towards the former,' said Buchan, 'but you're right, there's a war happening here, and they're both going to want us on their side. This could easily be part of that.'

Roth pointed to another note on the board, three lines drawn together.

'This is the most worrying point,' she said.

The door opened, Liddell entered. She had a look about her that Buchan hadn't seen before. The thrill of the chase. Interestingly she wasn't holding a cigarette.

'Where are we?' she asked.

'I was just saying,' said Roth, 'this is the most worrying thing from our perspective. They knew beforehand which shops were connected to the alarm system. Someone had given them that inside knowledge. Those three establishments were approached a little differently, allowing the attackers to cut off any chance of anyone pressing the emergency call button.'

Liddell was nodding. 'I thought as much,' she said, indicating the board. 'Vintage Books was one of mine, and I wondered if it would've been the same at the others.'

'Have you spoken to Reynolds again?' asked Buchan.

'I skipped him this time,' said Liddell. 'Called the chief. He was in Edinburgh, visiting the shiny new transport HQ with the First Minister.'

'You must be employee of the month.'

'Took a while getting him to the phone, took a while once he was there persuading him of the seriousness of this, but I got there. He's sending a team.'

'Reynolds should be calling any minute.'

Liddell smiled grimly.

'He called already. I didn't take it. And, I should say, if he calls anyone else, put him on to me. I may still not take it, but I don't want anyone having to put up with any of his shit. We're probably best avoiding him until the team get through from Edinburgh. Shouldn't take them too long. Thereafter, he'll have them to deal with, and we won't have to worry about them.'

She took a step closer to the board, taking in all the information. Seeing her standing next to Roth like this, he realised that Roth too was looking the most energetic and engaged he'd seen her in three months, and he kicked himself for not having done something to get her into the office earlier.

Houston and Cherry were already in the room. The door opened, Kane entered, acknowledged them all, took a quick look at the board.

'Jesus,' she said. 'So they'd been tipped off about the alarms. I knew it. Are we doing someth –'

'It's in hand,' said Liddell. 'It's been escalated.'

'You had one of the kneecappings?' asked Buchan.

'Yes. Young woman, a customer. She's been watching too many movies. I managed to have a quick word. She said she was a black belt karate. She has moves, that was what she said. *I have moves*. She didn't get anywhere near making her moves, though. Took one step towards the guy with the gun, and he floored her. Single gunshot, silencer attachment, and she was down. She cried out, she was making a lot of noise, he put the gun to his lips and indicated the other knee. She resorted to sobbing quietly at that point. I spoke to her mother, who'd arrived by the time the ambulance was ready to leave. Turns out she's never done any karate training in her life. She's watched the *Karate Kid* like a hundred times, spent several months practising taking her jacket on and off, and decided she was a black belt.' She paused, raised an eyebrow, then quoted the mother quoting her daughter. *'If some guy can stick on a dress and some lippy and call himself a woman, I can say I'm a black belt and everyone can lump it.'* She shared a shrug with the room. 'Not that it mattered. I don't think there's a martial art that's stopping you taking a bullet in the knee.'

Buchan asked if there was anything else exceptional about the raid, anything that hadn't already been communicated to Roth, with a pair of raised eyebrows, then he turned back to the boards, everyone else following his lead.

'So, we have no idea what they were looking for, right?'

Agreement from around the room.

'Do we think they themselves didn't know what they were looking for, and it was a know it when they find it scenario?'

'Seems unlikely,' said Kane. 'More likely they knew exactly what it was. Sounds like they were laser-focussed. They'd scoped each location, they knew how long it would take. They timed the length of each raid to suit the longest predicted search. This was very professional.'

'Yes,' said Buchan, nodding. 'Do we think Davie's mob has got the capacity to carry this out?' No one immediately answered, and he continued, 'I will say I'm very sceptical. The efficiency and ease with which this was executed firmly points to the Baltazar gang. Of course, we don't know them well, we don't know how likely they are to botch things, we...'

'They're not,' said Roth, interrupting. 'Sorry, boss...'

'No, go on.'

'Everything I've read about them so far says this is who they are. They've been running something like twenty-five years now, and they're a precision gang. They're good, very professional, very organised. When they come to a new territory, they swallow up, they subsume. They're literally the Borg. If they use this to get into Glasgow, we could be in trouble. I know I postulated earlier that maybe this was Davie's mob trying to implicate someone else, but everything about the raid says it was the Baltazar gang.'

'We don't suppose the Bancrofts are capable of impersonating efficiency?' said Liddell.

'If they could impersonate it, why wouldn't they just do it? said Roth.

107

'Good point, constable. So, what's next, inspector?'

Buchan looked over the board, taking a moment, getting his thoughts in order. Still, though, the sense of urgency that had been with him the entire day, was not leaving.

'We need to find out why this thing is being driven forwards the way it is,' he said. 'Out of nowhere, we suddenly have all the pieces moving, all sorts of things in play. There's been a drama building that we didn't know anything about, and it appears to be culminating today. Something's driving it. I'm going to see DI Savage again. For now, I need everyone on what they were already doing. The Bancroft gang, the Baltazars, I'm prepared to throw in William Lansdowne's lot for now, because there's no doubt there's a chance this all falls to his advantage. We need to hunt the Baltazars down, try to establish if they have anywhere else in town. I mean, they must have. If they're capable of sending out twenty-seven people, then they have an HQ.'

'Claire Avercamp?' said Houston, who'd had little to contribute so far.

'I feel like she's a bystander at the moment,' said Buchan. 'Potentially collateral damage. But nothing that's happened today, after we got called in to this thing, has actually related to her personally. We can't get away from the possibility of her being some sort of catalyst, but she's not the one orchestrating anything.' He snapped his fingers, thinking of something else. 'And we need to know who's running this Baltazar operation. Any ideas?'

'You mean the head of the gang in Poland, or the…'

'In the UK. Presumably this Jan Baltazar character doesn't make field trips. Even if he did, he's likely to have generals running ops. We need their IC in Scotland. And boss,' said Buchan to Liddell, 'I think we need you in with our people through from Edinburgh. If we don't, there'll be a bunch of meetings behind closed doors in Dalmarnock, and we'll get snippets here and there, *if we're lucky*. We need someone in the room.'

'Of course.'

'Sam, you OK, to coordinate here? I'll speak to Savage,' said Buchan, 'and I'll call it in when I'm done. Boss, you want to come with me over there.'

Liddell nodded, and got out of her seat, still with a rare energy about her, and they were gone.

35

Eleven minutes in the car, mostly sitting in traffic.

'You think Reynolds is in on it?' asked Buchan, halfway through. Unusually, he was uncomfortable with the silence, borne of the need to get on. The need to not be sitting at traffic lights.

'I have no idea,' said Liddell. 'There's no more reason it should be Reynolds than anyone else. Reynolds... well, he's an idiot, he's far higher up the chain of command than anyone like him ever ought to be, but that doesn't mean he's open to blackmail, or is just a plain bad actor in our force. And we should remember that much of the information that appears to have been put into the hands of the Baltazars or the Bancrofts, whoever this is, could have been provided by virtually anyone in Dalmarnock. They all have access to this. The only thing giving it the stench of being from someone higher up, is the release of Seymour. But then, perhaps that was just Malky using one of his contacts, or his lawyer using a contact, and his release was nothing to do with the rest of this garbage that's been taking place today. When I'm here I'm going to push for a full and immediate investigation into anyone who's been accessing records who shouldn't have been.' A pause, and then, 'God knows how long it'll take.' Another pause, and then she took Buchan by surprise with, 'Agnes is blossoming before our eyes now that she's back. You should have brought her in sooner.'

'I wasn't keeping her for myself,' said Buchan, defensively, an unusual churlishness in his tone, and then he held his hand aloft.

'I know. But she's flourishing on it. We need to get her signed back on, although Dr Kennedy might have something to say about it.'

The traffic was moving. Silence returned to the car. Eventually Buchan said, 'You're right, though. This has been good for her.'

36

'You're not willing to take any responsibility for this, inspector?'

Buchan was standing at the window in Savage's office, Savage turned in her seat, looking down on the river. This was where Buchan had found her, cup of coffee in hand. Despite being by the window, he'd barely glanced at the water.

'We need to work together,' he said. It was bland, stopping well short of the rebuke he wanted to make.

'Seems to me you've just been bludgeoning everyone in front of you, and look where it's getting us. One man dead, two people kneecapped, nine bookshops raided, you nearly get killed while destroying a bus, your face looks like that...,' Buchan had completely forgotten the bandage on his cheekbone, the bruising around his eyes, 'bloody lucky no one else got hurt, and no nearer finding Claire Avercamp, which, according to you, was your initial brief. Would you like me to work with you to mitigate the damage you've been inflicting?'

'Jesus, Rose,' said Buchan, 'can we park it? We're being played. We're all being played. My chief knows Avercamp's father. He asked for her help, that's it. The guy is not involved in this drama *at all*. He checks out.' He took a moment, said what he was hesitating to say. 'I checked him out independently of the boss. He runs a tiny gin company, but largely spends his life playing golf and going on two-month cruises with his wife.

'Thereafter, one thing has blended seamlessly into the next, this is a cavalcade of shit, and we're all being made to look hapless and helpless. And you can be glib, but the guy who got the bullet in the head, the shops that were busted, obviously had nothing to do with us.'

Savage didn't look particularly impressed with the speech, but made a go-ahead gesture.

'You know a guy called Maplethorpe?' he asked.

'I don't know him, no.' Her tone had not softened much.

'You know the name, though?'

She took a deep breath in through her nose. Loud,

contemplative. He waited.

'Claire asked me about him,' she said. 'I'd never heard of him, nor of this Poznań Secure he supposedly runs. She thought there was some relationship between his firm and the Baltazars, but then when I turned the tables on her, so it was me asking the questions, she didn't like that. Downplayed his involvement, and changed the subject, like there was nothing to see here.'

'You didn't chase it?' he asked, and he could see the defences go up as the words left his mouth.

'I chased him all over, actually,' she said, hiding behind superficiality. 'Weirdly, I had literally nothing else on my desk, so I could afford all this amazing time to go hunting some random guy whose name had just been mentioned in passing. *This* is police work, I thought, as I sat in first class on my British Airways flight to Warsaw. There were some people in the office questioning why I had to fly via Singapore, but I said, that was absolutely the cheapest ticket.'

'Are you done?'

'I don't know, I'm quite enjoying it.'

'Why today?' said Buchan, trying not to rise to her disdain. 'What's bringing it to a head today, after all this time?'

'I genuinely don't know,' said Savage.

'Can we work it out?'

'What does that mean?'

'They raided nine bookshops, they trashed them, they didn't steal anything. It would seem Claire Avercamp was right, they're looking for something specific.'

'I suppose I have to give you that. Although, have you given any thought to the possibility this is nothing whatsoever to do with the break-in at Eurocentral, or to do with Claire Avercamp?'

'Frankly, no,' said Buchan. 'This thing is escalating off the charts, and part of that escalation, as we've already established, is them trying to kill me. Or, at least, as Reynolds says, delay me. My boss got us involved off the back of a chance request, and someone else doesn't want us to be. It's impossible to imagine that all these things are unconnected. In her notes, Avercamp thought they were after an original, signed manuscript of Chopin's second symphony.'

'Yes, she thought that was it.'

'And?'

'I don't know, inspector. It wasn't on the manifest, there's never been any mention of it come across my desk. I think she was clutching, because it seemed like the kind of thing a Pole might be interested in.'

'Poles are going to be interested in all sorts of things,' said Buchan. 'She must have heard tell of it from somewhere in the first instance.'

'She had.'

Buchan asked the question with raised hands.

'This infernal informant of hers. Starbuck.'

'You don't know who that is?' said Buchan.

'I have no idea. And I never knew enough about what they were telling her, to know whether they were playing her. But that was where she got this cockamamie bullshit story about the Chopin.'

'Why cockamamie bullshit?' asked Buchan. 'It must be exactly the kind of thing that went missing after the war.'

'Sure, but a lot of the stuff that went missing was because the Allies bombed the shit out of Germany. There was a war on, that was the point. A lot of European history went up in smoke. I made a couple of enquiries, because Avercamp had her sweet theory about, you know, there being some secret item not included as part of the manifest, and she sucked me in briefly. I asked around, and I was pretty much laughed at. If I was to summarise the answers to all my questions, it would be, once you've found the lost Chopin, you can move on to the Ark of the Covenant, then Atlantis and Shangri-La. It's a myth, inspector. It's the literal Holy Grail.'

'There were plenty of artefacts survived the war,' said Buchan. 'Maybe it was one of them.'

'It was known to have been in the possession of Ludwig Schütz, a well-known composer of the Reich. He died in Dresden, along with his family. There was nothing left of his house.'

'Nevertheless,' said Buchan, 'today's search makes it look like she was right about the single item. Maybe it was another Chopin, and… I don't know, she got the number wrong. It was Chopin One, or Three, or Five Hundred.'

'Maybe all sorts of things, inspector.'

'But ultimately it doesn't matter, because what really matters is that it's *something*. There's a something, somewhere, and these people are searching for it, or fighting over it, and it's today. What the hell is it about today?'

112

She lifted her hands.

'We're six months removed from the raid,' said Buchan, not wanting to lapse into silence. 'In all this time, there's been no sign of any of the titles coming to market?'

'Complete radio silence, which is kind of weird in itself,' she said. 'I've had regular updates from Europol, and there's been nothing. Largely nothing.'

He regarded her warily for a moment.

'Something's gone missing from the stash,' said Buchan, 'Davie Bancroft might well have been the one who took it, and that's started the war that's been playing out all day.'

Savage folded her arms, but he didn't get the feeling she was being defensive.

'It would seem that way,' she said.

'So what does *largely* nothing mean?'

'Look, I know I'm being facetious 'n all, inspector, but I've spent the day on it since you stopped by earlier. We had Davie working with the Baltazars. The only sign that any of the books had been moved was two guys getting picked up in Warsaw a couple of months after the event. They were stopped at customs with three antique books of little value or significance. Turned out they were from the Eurocentral raid. The books themselves got sent on to New York a couple of weeks ago. No one seems terribly excited about them. Whatever this is today, it's not about those books.'

'Why didn't we know about these two guys before?'

Savage answered with a look that said today was the first time she'd actually spent any extended time on the case, and she'd missed it. Without her to tell Claire Avercamp, Avercamp quite possibly had also been unaware.

'What happened to them?' asked Buchan.

'Released without charge, as far as we know,' and she made a gesture to indicate that they'd flown. 'That aside, and with the exception of Claire Avercamp making noises, this thing had been completely dead. Now, all of a sudden... My guess is that the Baltazars finally came looking for their share, or perhaps the whole thing, however the deal went down initially, and discovered something was missing. Davie Bancroft is either,' and she ran her thumb across her throat, 'or else, he got himself the fuck out of Dodge, leaving his team to take the fall. Although, far as we know, his team are unscathed, right?'

Buchan nodded. He looked at his watch. He'd left the

others attempting to locate as many of the Bancroft gang as they could. So far he hadn't heard back.

'Maybe,' he added to the nod.

'What does that mean?'

'It's been a couple of hours, and things are moving. I've got my people tracking them down, all Bancroft's usual suspects, and I've got nothing back yet.' He paused, he added, 'Just got one of those creeping, uncomfortable feelings.'

She regarded him warily, said, 'Let me make a call.'

Buchan nodded, stood his ground, glanced at the river. She was staring at him.

'You want me to leave the room?' said Buchan, after a moment.

'It's delicate, inspector, that's all.'

'You have someone on the inside? You have a mole in Bancroft's gang?'

The answer seemed to be in the silence.

Dammit, thought Buchan. It was the inevitability of the creation of the SCU. It wasn't like there weren't other officers, in local stations and other departments, dealing with the crap that resulted from people like Bancroft, whose operations crossed so many different city boundaries, covering so many different aspects of crime.

Buchan would have killed for an insider.

He turned away, left the office, closing the door behind him.

Standing outside in the open-plan he wondered, not for the first time, how it was the DIs in Dalmarnock got their own office, something that always made him smile grimly. He knew he himself needed the open-plan, the chatter and the buzz of being around his team.

His phone vibrated. A call from Kane.

'Sam,' he said, phone to his ear, voice low.

There was a dull thud from the door to Savage's office, and he looked at it curiously.

'We just got a call from Harriet Blake,' said Kane, an urgency in her tone. 'You know, Averc –'

'Avercamp's producer, yes,' said Buchan.

'Claire called her. Sounded desperate. Said she was in some apartment somewhere. No idea where. She ended the call after about twenty seconds, so didn't get to say much.'

Buchan checked the time. Another twisting of the stomach.

What was it that was driving the day on like this?

'I'll go round and speak to her now,' said Buchan. 'Almost done with Savage.'

'Anything new?'

'Too early to say. I'll call on the way to Blake's house and we can catch up.'

They hung up. Buchan remembered the quiet thud against Savage's door, then opened it curiously. She was at her desk, no longer on the phone. She ushered him in. Buchan noted the small stress ball lying on the floor by the door.

He lifted the ball and placed it on her desk, thinking, as he did so, that maybe he could get one of these for Liddell.

'Sorry,' she said, indicating the ball.

'I wouldn't want you to have to get up,' said Buchan.

'How d'you know I can?'

He looked at her, he looked at the seat to see if she was in a wheelchair, or if there was any evidence to suggest it that he might have missed.

'I'm havering,' she said, waving it away. 'Anyway, can't get my guy. I mean, it's not unusual. He's pretty careful, and if he's with any of his crew at the moment, he ain't answering.'

'Given everything that's been happening today, wouldn't you expect him to have given you a shout?'

She answered once again in silence, eventually tacking a small nod on to the end of it.

'Dammit,' muttered Buchan. 'I need to get on. We can stay in touch?'

'Of course.'

He was going to ask what she was doing, but then decided the better of it. He would leave her to do her own thing, coming at it from whatever angle she saw fit without his interference, and he could hope it might produce something positive. Of course, given the time, there was always the possibility she was just about to knock off for the day.

He made an *I'll call* gesture, turned away and was gone.

37

'Boss,' said Kane, on the phone again as Buchan sat in the VW on the way to see Harriet Blake.

'How's it looking?'

'Been speaking to Eddie in finance. You know, DC Bar –'

'What's he got?'

'Poznań Secure get murkier by the minute. They are one hundred per cent balancing on the edge of the law. Huge business, never pay tax. Profits safely secured all over the place. They have connections everywhere. They do government work, they do private business, they have some very unsavoury acquaintances. They whore themselves out to anyone and everyone, often enough to competing interests. And those government connections are enough to make sure that when they trip over onto the wrong side of the law, there's someone there to make sure nothing gets done about it.'

'There isn't a situation on earth that the involvement of politicians can't make a hundred times worse,' muttered Buchan.

'And our friend Maplethorpe was at Davos this year…'

'Terrific. On holiday, or attending the World Economic Forum?' asked Buchan glibly, and Kane laughed.

'You guessed it. This man is a player. The serious kind, the most dangerous kind. No one knows who he is, there's nothing about him on the Internet, he exists in the margins. But he has money and he has contacts, and with those…'

'Come power,' said Buchan. 'And power without visibility means absolutely zero responsibility.'

'Yep.'

'Dammit,' muttered Buchan. 'Anything else going on? Any more detail on this lost Chopin manuscript Avercamp thought everyone was looking for? Savage thought she was wrong, by the way.'

'Oh, nope, nothing. But… it's just weird. These people are passing up a lot of stuff. Maybe there was nothing hugely valuable in any of the shops they raided today, but if they'd taken the time to sweep books into bags, across all nine shops, that's hundreds of thousands of pounds worth. Probably millions. And they pass it all up for a Chopin?'

'You're projecting,' said Buchan. 'You don't care about Chopin, doesn't mean they don't.'

He liked the idea of the Chopin, the objections of others making him like the sound of it even more.

'I don't think the argument's about the Chopin or not, though. It's about them passing up money. Crime syndicates are no different from any other business. They're interested in money, that's it. So this seems kind of weird. And if this Baltazar lot are as omnipotent in pan-European crime as they appear to be, you'd think they'd be able to fence some stolen books.'

'Yep, I get that.'

He thought of adding something about not having enough information yet to make an accurate judgement, and typically decided not to bother.

'Any luck finding any of the Bancroft bunch?' he asked instead.

'Nothing,' said Kane. A pause, then she added, 'Getting a strong, uneasy feeling about that, I have to say.'

'Aye,' said Buchan. Then, 'Nearly at Blake's house. I'll call later.'

They hung up. Buchan changed down the gears. Usually when he drove a car other than the Facel he missed it, but not today.

*

'What the hell happened to you?' said Harriet Blake. There was an uneasiness about her.

Buchan had to think about it.

'It's been a long day,' he said.

'You'd better come in.' She held the door open, wincing as he walked by.

'I have gin,' she added.

*

They were in the sitting room. A room of books. Bookshelves on every wall. A small television. No art, as there was no space for it. Books on the floor, and books on the two small tables,

117

alongside three unwashed mugs, a plate with toast crumbs.

'You've read all of these?' he couldn't stop himself asking, even though Blake was obviously agitated.

'Almost all,' she said. Distracted. She indicated the table. 'Got a couple there at the weekend, that's the to-be-read pile.'

He glanced around. *Kubrick on Film. Andrei Tarkovsky: A Life on the Cross. Lawrence d'Arabie de David Lean: Les Fiches Cinéma d'Universalis.* He stopped looking.

'Tell me,' he said.

'Phone rang. Unknown number. I wouldn't usually answer it…'

'Landline or mobile?'

'Mobile. Wouldn't usually answer, but I got a feeling. I don't know. Picked it up, there was nothing for a moment. I said hello again, then Claire comes on. She's whispering. Not whispering, but, you know, that horrible combination, juxtaposition, of desperate restraint.'

She paused. She stared at the carpet. Buchan didn't bother with the obvious question.

'Hari? That's what she said. Hari. She always called me Hari. No one else ever calls me that. I suppose I've been waiting for the phone to ring. Jesus, Claire, where are you, I said, then she said Hari again. Then she said, I don't know where I am, but it's all kicking off. Fuck me. And I said, are you a prisoner, and she said yes, like really insistently, yes, but there's something happening.'

'She said there was something happening?'

'Yes. And then, I could hear, there was like shouting in the background, a door slamming. The phone went dead.'

'OK,' said Buchan. 'That's everything? She didn't know where she was. It's all kicking off. Yes, she's a prisoner, and there's something happening. Shouting, door slam, call ended.'

She stared at Buchan, her face a blank canvas of concentration, and then, 'Yes.'

'The shouting?'

'What about it?'

'What did they shout?'

The same look on her face, and then a small head shake.

'I don't know. It was just like a bark.'

'Could it have been a dog?'

Consternation, and then, 'No, no, not that kind of bark. Just a, I don't know, just a shout. Hoy, or something, but not hoy.'

'Had Claire ever done any acting?'

'What?'

'Was she an actress? Had she ever appeared in any of her films?'

'Seriously?'

Buchan answered the scepticism with a familiar look.

'Wait, are you asking if she was pretending to be terrified and in the gravest, I don't know, peril?'

'Yes,' said Buchan, bluntly.

Further consternation, and then the look switched to giving the question serious consideration, coming out the other side with a head shake.

'No, that wasn't her. No, is the answer to the question. She never appeared in her own films, she never trained as an actress. We talked about this. She trained as a journalist, that was it. I never knew her to act.'

'She sounded convincing?'

'Yes!'

'Think about the barked shout again. Can you hear it?'

'Can I hear it?'

'If you think about it, can you replay it in your head?'

More staring.

'Yes. But there's nothing specific.'

'Any other sounds. Cars going past, a television, a plane overhead, anything?'

'No.'

'When you were relaying what she said, you never mentioned that she actually sounded terrified, then you said it in response to me asking if she might have been acting. Did she really sound terrified?'

The face again. Coming off the high of fear and stress, made to think through the call more forensically.

'No,' she said eventually. 'I don't think... maybe terrified isn't the word. There was something in her voice. I thought... maybe this sounds wrong, maybe it is completely wrong, but there was something in her voice, like an excitement. The thrill of it. I'm scared for her, and she's obviously in danger, but I wonder if the filmmaker in her, the filmmaker in Claire, is thinking, now *this* is a movie. This is the kind of narrative twist we need.'

'Is that what you think she was thinking, or is that what you're thinking now?'

'Oh, please…'

*

'Danny, need you to get on to tech, get a call tracked.'

'K,' said Cherry, and Buchan could hear him moving a notepad, pictured him lifting the pen. 'You got the number and the time?'

38

Buchan walked back into the open-plan. Heads down at every desk, a couple of people on phones. He noted Roth wasn't there.

'Agnes is in the ops room?' was the first thing he said to Kane.

'She preferred to stay in there,' said Kane. 'I thought it was OK. She's still the focal point for information collection.'

'K. I'll go and have a word. Danny, we getting anywhere on the call location?'

'Still waiting,' he said.

It hadn't been twenty minutes yet.

'Any other headway?' he asked Kane.

She shook her head by way of answer, though it was more in exasperation. 'There's so much, so many different pieces in play, or players on the move, however you want to put it.'

'Aye.'

Buchan remembered he hadn't had anything to eat or drink all afternoon. Glanced over his shoulder at the coffee machine, looked back at Kane.

'I'm good,' said Kane.

'Agnes had anything?'

'Not sure.'

Buchan nodded, turned away. Set the coffee machine going, two mugs.

Kane watched his back for a moment, had that uneasy feeling again, then turned back to her computer.

*

'Oh, thanks, I could kill for that,' said Roth.

Buchan left the ops room door open, and stood at the far side of the desk, looking at the whiteboards. Coffee to his lips. Took a moment to enjoy the first taste.

'How are you doing?' he asked.

'I'm OK.'

'Happy to be back?'

The question felt flippant.

'I'm doing OK,' she said. 'Head down.' A pause, and then, 'Kind of missing home.'

Then she looked at him uneasily, aware of how that had just slipped out. They both knew she didn't mean her own apartment.

'Sorry.'

'That's OK. You can take Edelman with you when you go,' he added glibly, no less uncomfortable than usual. She smiled, she looked back at the screen.

'We need certainties, Agnes,' he said. 'There's too much speculation, too many things we don't know.'

'You want to know what the certainties are?'

'Yes.'

And then, still feeling discomfited, and thinking better of just having this conversation with Roth, he stepped back quickly into the open-plan and indicated for Kane to join them. The three of them in the room, he closed the door, and he and Kane took their places at the table.

'We need certainties, we need a solid take on what we're doing next,' said Buchan. He checked his watch. Another hour and a half of daylight yet, for all that mattered. There was cloud coming from the west.

'You don't want the team in?' asked Kane.

'There's too much needing done. We can't all be just talking.' He indicated the board. 'What are the certainties?'

'Claire Avercamp has been missing for nine days,' said Roth, looking at her screen, as though she'd written up the list while Buchan had stepped briefly into the open-plan. 'She's just managed to make a call to Harriet Blake. She's alive. And this points to something that the certainties keep returning to, which is, whatever this story's about, it's all coming together today.

'The story itself revolves around a stash of stolen antique books. It's no certainty, but everything we now learn points to this being about one particular book, which means,' and she paused and looked between Buchan and Kane, 'we might be in a kind of Maltese Falcon situation. There's something that a lot of people are after, and we don't know what. There's potential it's a Chopin manuscript, but that detail is far from definite.

'The Baltazar gang and the Bancroft gang have been working together, but we don't know how that arrangement's holding up. I would suggest, if I can stray briefly from the remit, that the reason everything seems to be coalescing today, is that the two gangs have fallen out and we're getting caught up in the middle of it.

'It would appear there's someone in the police service, likely based in Dalmarnock, working for one or other of the sides. Possibly both. But the definite is that this person, whoever it is, is looking to get in our way.

'What else? Bancroft has gone missing, and now, they've all gone missing. The entire Bancroft collective.' She snapped her fingers. 'A presumed Baltazar gang member dead, shot by a gun that was used to take out two of the Lansdowne mob last year. Which, of course, introduces the Lansdownes to the fray.'

She puffed out her cheeks, shook her head.

'It's a shitshow, and we're no nearer sorting any of it out?' she said, again taking them both in with a look.

'That's about the size of it,' said Kane. 'The trouble being, even when Agnes was making a solid effort to list the things we're sure of, she was still drifting unavoidably into speculation.'

'Do we have anyone on to immigration trying to get names of people who've come in from Poland in the last few days?' asked Buchan.

'Ian's on it,' said Kane, then she added, 'UK Borders,' with a shrug. No one was getting their hopes up.

A knock at the door, Houston entered, as though on cue.

'Boss,' he said. 'Been trying to get info on Bancroft safe houses in the city. I was speaking to an old contact of mine. Guy who used to be one of their crew. Got out, went to live in Kilmarnock, hadn't had anything to do with them in a couple of years. He didn't want to talk, told me he had nothing. I thought it was done. Anyway, he went away, decided to start calling a few folk, to let them know that SCU are sniffing around. And he couldn't get hold of anyone. *Anyone.* He hears word that something major's playing out in the city, but no one really seems to know what. He said he'd thought about coming up here, but it was his wife who'd dragged him off to Kilmarnock in the first place, happily married on the basis he was through with the Bancrofts. She wouldn't let him come. Long story short, he gave me a couple of addresses.'

He brandished a piece of paper.

Buchan got straight to his feet, said, 'Sam, you're with me, Ian, get Ellie, we'll take them simultaneously.'

He looked at the piece of paper, read the addresses, thought through the routes they'd take.

'You take Pollock, we'll take Parkhead?'

'Boss,' said Houston, and with that they were gone, out the situation room, closing the door behind them.

Roth stared at the door, and felt the strange tingle of fear that had been her companion for the past three months.

'Jesus, Agnes, come on,' she muttered to herself, 'there's work to do.'

39

The apartment was stark and grim.

A functional kitchen. A kettle, a hob that looked like it was never used, a small table, two chairs. Only partially floored, bare boards beneath the table. The sitting room had an old sofa rescued from recycling. Two small tables set up in front of it. Dirty net curtains across the windows. A side table on which sat a black router, green lights blinking.

There was one other room. A bedroom without a bed. A sleeping bag dumped in a corner, a lamp on the floor next to it.

The bathroom was small and cramped and hadn't been cleaned in years.

The sitting room was where drugs were repackaged for onward sale. Larger bags of hash and cocaine divided up. There were quantities of both strewn across the floor. One of the small tables was at such an angle as to suggest it had been roughly pushed aside, or perhaps toppled over and hurriedly righted.

Kane bent down, lifted some of the hash, aimlessly put it to her nose.

'You think this happened today?' asked Buchan.

'Normally I'd be cagier, and say that it happened sometime in the past few days, relatively recently at least, but given what we're in the middle of, this has today written all over it, doesn't it?'

Buchan nodded. Stared at the floor and the strewn drugs for a little longer, then walked back through to the bedroom to take a closer look.

He pulled on a pair of nitrile gloves and knelt down beside the sleeping bag. The zipper was mostly open, and he pulled it down to the bottom and opened out the bag. It was tired and old and stained. He lifted it, put it to his nose, dropped it again. Turned it over, examined it a little further, then got to his feet.

'Smell test revealing, was it?' asked Kane.

Buchan smiled grimly, then stood looking around the room, trying to see if there were any small details they might have missed.

'Nothing. Musty. Maybe someone slept in it last night, maybe not. There's no fresh smell of sweat or anything else.'

'Grim, either way,' said Kane, and Buchan nodded.

'There's nothing else leaping out at us,' he said, walking into the bathroom, which had already shown it had little to give up. 'We should get the SOCOs round. Can you call Ruth? Given the carnage we've got today, probably best if she just sends one person. We'll be lucky if she can spare that.'

Kane nodded, took out her phone, made the call.

Buchan caught sight of himself in the mirror, a glance he couldn't avoid, then turned away with a scowl. Gloves off, phone out of his pocket. As he was about to call Houston, his phone started ringing, with the call from the sergeant.

'Ian.'

'Getting a very, very bad feeling about this, sir,' said Houston.

'How's it looking?'

'Place is a shit tip. There's been a fight. One splay of blood across the carpet. Like, I don't know, looks like the result of the kind of thing you'd get in a movie. Slow motion, major punch to the jaw, the wobbling of the skin, the misshapen face, blood flying off to the side.'

'Any teeth?'

'Bingo. Just the one.'

'And it's fresh?'

'Blood still damp. The rest of the place has been trashed. In the main room, there's a table and four dining chairs, that's it. Three of the chairs are broken, the table upturned. And by broken, I mean, smashed up. Used in the fight.'

'Similar here, though not as extreme,' said Buchan. 'Looks like there was a low-level stramash, but whatever it was, it didn't last. We've got drugs here, how about –'

'Nope, nothing like that. There's a pack of cards strewn around the place. There was a radio still playing. Classic FM. A couple of water bottles, a McDonald's paper bag, stuffed with empty drinks and burger cartons. If that's anything to go by, there were three here.'

'K. Not obvious how many we had here. Doesn't really matter,' said Buchan. 'It's beginning to look like the systematic removal of the Bancroft gang. Just a second...'

He put him on speaker, looked at Kane as she was off the phone, the pair of them now back in the sitting room.

'Got Sam on speaker,' said Buchan. 'You get hold of Ruth?'

'Yep. She's snowed under, as we know. I asked her to take someone off the bookshops if need be.'

'We need to get someone round to Ian's place,' said Buchan. 'And since they have blood, that might be a better bet. Ian, call Ruth, tell her to reprioritise. If she can do both places, great, if not, yours has precedence.'

'Boss.'

'And we need to find one of the Bancrofts. Anyone, don't care who at this stage. We'll head back to HQ, we need to contact local stations, get people going round houses. Ramp this up from whatever it is we've been doing up until now, phone calls and random visits. We need people turning up at every address, every work place we have for anyone in the Bancroft gang. And we need to bring them in.'

'Boss.'

The call was ended, and Buchan was already at the door and heading out, Kane in his wake.

40

'I need a fag, man,' said Eddie Harmon. A member of the Bancroft gang. A nothing member, low grade, dispensable. A gofer, given the jobs no one else wanted.

'You can talk for five minutes first,' said Buchan.

A small interview room in Rutherglen police station. Buchan, Kane, Harmon. No one was sitting down.

The police hadn't found Harmon. Harmon had found the police.

'I talk better after nicotine.'

'Maybe you'll talk better after you've been released and allowed to walk round the city for a couple of hours, waiting to get picked off,' said Kane sharply.

Harmon shook his head, staring at the floor, but there was nothing in it. This was not a man of conviction.

'The word went round, make yourself scarce.' He wasn't looking at them. 'None of us knew what was going on.'

'Do you ever know what's going on?' asked Buchan.

The fact that he'd never had to deal with Harmon before, pointed to his lowly status in the hierarchy.

'Harsh,' said Harmon, but when he looked up he kind of shrugged. 'Fair enough. Fine. I'm not usually in the loop. I get my jobs to do, and… it's like anything, right. The better the job you do, the more duties you get, blah-de-fucking-blah.'

'Do you have quarterly chats with your line manager, and have to go on diversity training?' asked Kane.

Harmon didn't get it. Buchan couldn't keep the wry grin from his face.

'Word went round,' said Buchan. 'Make yourself scarce, no one knew what was going on,' and he indicated for Harmon to keep talking.

'Aye, right, whatever. Look, like I said, I don't usually get the inside scoop, you know, but this time no one seemed to know what was happening. The word goes round though, get to the safe houses. Trouble is… well, like we've all been saying, no one tells me nothing. I don't know where any of them are. I says to Wee Billy and Tommy Pack Horse, one of you guys going to tell me what to do, tell me where to go.' He paused, Buchan could hear the response coming from a mile away. 'Wee Billy's a hard bastard, of course, we all know that. He says, oh, I'll tell you where to go all right, son, now fuck off. We'll be in touch.'

'What was it you did?' asked Kane.

'How d'you mean?'

'Your fellow gangsters don't trust you with the addresses of the safe houses.' A pause, and then, 'At some point in the past, you must have done something.'

A scowl, a head shake. 'Aye, fine, whatever. I went away for the weekend with one of Billy Lansdowne's daughters. I mean, honestly, I didn't know who she was, she was just some bird I was shagging. I mean, she didn't know who I was either, straight up. I wasn't getting played. No way. Anyway, we come home, have nothing else to do with each other. Thought it'd be best if I kept my mouth shut.

'Word gets around though, right? When the big man found out, he wasn't best pleased. Would probably have ended up dead up the graveyard if it hadn't been for Malky. He put in a good word or two, I avoided the chop.'

He looked between Buchan and Kane and shrugged.

'Anyway, whatever. I wasn't in the fucking loop, that's it, man.'

'You been in touch with any of your crew?' asked Buchan.

Buchan had let Harmon keep his phone for now. He wasn't being charged with anything, and if they chose to hold him it would be entirely on a goodwill basis. In any case, Harmon would know already he was better off with the police, than hiding out in the city from an unseen enemy.

Harmon took his phone from his pocket, checked it, slipped it back.

'Still nothing.'

'When was the last time you heard anything?'

'When I got the word from Wee Billy, I calls Big Janice. She usually knows the score, you know. I mean, it's not like she's any higher up the fucking ladder than me, man, but pillow talk 'n all that, right? Know what I mean? Big Janice says like, I don't know man, and I'm like that, there must be something, and she's like, aye, there is, but like, no fucker knows what. Just get the fuck out of Dodge, man, you know.'

He shrugged.

'That was it?'

'Aye. She hung up on us.'

'Did she sound scared or worried or …'

'Ach, Big Janice always sounds like everything's the most exciting shit that ever happened. If everyone else hadn't been losing their shit, it wouldn't have meant nothing.'

'What d'you think?' asked Buchan.

'About what?'

'About what's happening? Why all this today?'

'All what?'

'Someone tried to kill me,' said Buchan, and Harmon ejaculated a laugh, which turned to a stupid smirk that slowly left his face as Buchan talked. 'Nine antique bookshops got raided at precisely the same time. Big budget, lots of bodies, military-grade coordination. Two people got kneecapped, and we're lucky that was it. We've just visited two of your lot's safe houses, and both of them had been cleaned out. There was blood, there'd been fighting. What there wasn't, was any sign of life.' He took a moment, then added, 'Your people are gone. Removed from the board. Just like your boss.'

'How d'you know they hadn't won the battle, but realised they'd been busted and moved someplace else safer?'

'Why take the bodies of their attackers with them?'

'Maybe they weren't dead. Maybe a bunch of stuff.'

'Your people are gone, Eddie. You know they're gone. You came to us, remember.'

As he said it, he thought of the brakes being blown on the Facel. If someone on the police had been prepared to take the life of an officer, causing who knew how many collateral deaths in an accident, Eddie Harmon might not stand much of a chance in police custody.

'Too bad you can't stay,' said Buchan.

He felt the glance from Kane, but he knew she'd understand.

'Fuck that, man, I'm not going anywhere.'

'Unless you've got anything else to tell us, you're free to go. We don't have the manpower to keep you here today. Pretty busy, as you'd imagine.'

Buchan realised this sounded like extortion. He wouldn't throw Harmon to the wolves in return for information. He had no intention of telling him the truth, however.

Harmon looked between the two of them. They recognised

the calculation. There would undoubtedly be things he could tell them, though they might not be relevant. But was it worth the risk? What if this all blew over, tomorrow was a regular day, everyone was back in position, and meanwhile he'd spilled all sorts of stories to keep himself safe from a non-existent threat?

'Decisions, decisions,' said Buchan.

Nothing.

'We don't have time for this, Eddie. You're gone.' He started moving towards the door. 'Sergeant, can you see Eddie out the premises?' He paused, he added, 'Process it properly,' which he knew Kane would understand to mean to delay it long enough that he got someone to tail Harmon when he left.

'Wait, what the fuck? Is this one of they things where you're using us as bait? Off I go, and you'll keep an eye out waiting for us to get killed, then you'se'll move in and get my killer?'

Buchan stared at him across the couple of yards of the room.

'Now that you mention it,' he said, 'that's not a bad plan.'

He left the room, leaving the door ajar.

41

The phone calls were coming in, the sense of urgency having been communicated. The police all over the city recognised the magnitude of what was happening. Every lead was being chased down, every sighting, every bolthole checked, every known member of the gang hunted, every acquaintance interviewed.

Nothing.

They were back in the ops room. Currently five of them. Buchan, Kane, Houston, Roth and Liddell. Cherry and Dawkins were still in the field.

'The brains trust,' Liddell had said, when she'd arrived two minutes earlier and looked around the other four. She'd had little to report from the meeting with the team through from Edinburgh. 'A lot of talking, a lot of willy-waving, a lot of wishful thinking that everything will be fine in the morning.'

Buchan wasn't the only one feeling an uncomfortable, crawling fear in his gut at the horror of what was unfolding.

'Has anyone checked in on William Lansdowne?' asked Liddell.

Buchan puffed out his cheeks.

'I spoke to him...,' he said, looking at the clock, and Liddell said, 'Yes, I know, but since then?' and then she shook her head at her own question. 'No, of course not, everything going at a hundred miles an hour. Maybe you should give him another call,' and Buchan said, 'I will,' and Liddell said, 'You think it's possible he could be behind any of this?' and Buchan shrugged and looked exasperated at getting something else dumped on his plate, though his exasperation was really at himself, because he knew he'd let this go when he shouldn't have done.

'Ian,' said Buchan, 'before I do that, can you just make a couple of quick calls. Not to Lansdowne, but just check in on some of his people. Is anything happening, is anyone missing, anything untoward.'

'Boss,' said Houston, and he turned away, left the room, closing the door quickly behind him.

'There we go,' said Roth suddenly.

She'd been looking at her computer the entire time, caught up in something, barely acknowledging the others as they'd come into the room. Now she had the room's attention, and she started talking without looking at anyone to see if they were listening.

'There's a book called *Incarnate* by a Polish writer named Franz Kazimierz. Published in 1909. There were only a couple of hundred printed, and there's only one known surviving copy. Kazimierz himself appears to have been a nobody in the great sweep of history. The book is a short horror story. There's not much detail on it anywhere. It wasn't reviewed anywhere, no one was much interested in it at the time, and it's of little significance. Consequently, the book itself, this one surviving copy is, in antique book terms, pretty worthless. Asking price of around five hundred euros. No big whoop. But turns out Kazimierz was the great great grandfather of a man named Jan Baltazar. We have to presume, I think, this is our Jan Baltazar. Our man Jan wants the book. In fact, Jan insists the book *belongs* to him, and that it was taken from their family during the war. So when it comes up for auction in Poland, Jan turns up and says, it's not for sale, I'll have it back, please. The seller, and the auction house say, I don't think so. Given your connection to the book, we're prepared to not put the book on the auction block, as long as you're prepared to meet the asking price of five hundred euros.'

She paused, she glanced up at them, then quickly started speaking again.

'They end up in court. I think at this stage we can surmise it was a matter of honour for Mr Baltazar. He will have spent far more on lawyers than he would have done had he just bought the book. He loses the case. There the story ends. The next time the book crops up anywhere, it's part of the shipment travelling through Scotland on its way to New York. A book which was last publicly valued at five hundred euros, in amongst books valued at half a million. No one was looking at that list and thinking, this whole thing is clearly about *Incarnate* by Franz Kazimierz.'

'Why has no one worked this out before?' said Liddell.

'That is interesting,' said Roth. 'I'm getting this from a Europol file, and then doing a lot more digging around Polish court files, having to use Google translate I might add. So, Claire

Avercamp, without access to Europol, might possibly have never been sent down that route. DI Savage though…,' and she looked at Liddell and then Buchan, shrugging her shoulders. 'Whatever the reasons for this not being an obvious strand of the investigation, I'd say we're looking at this whole thing being about *Incarnate* by Franz Kazimierz, rather than an over-priced Chopin manuscript, or anything else.'

'Bringing something personal like this into it,' said Buchan, 'instantly makes this whole thing make more sense. I like it. When rich people, powerful people, want something, they throw anything at it to get it.'

'In particular, when someone's pissed them off along the way,' said Kane.

'Yep. A rich crook throwing the kitchen sink at a problem, partly in desire, partly in petulance, is entirely on brand.'

'So,' said Roth, 'this is nothing to do with Chopin, nothing to do with actual monetary value. It's personal.'

'Have we seen any mention of *Incarnate* prior to this?' asked Liddell.

'We didn't know to look for it,' said Buchan.

'We will now,' said Roth. 'I'll run a check on Avercamp's files, give me a sec.'

'We can do the same with everything we've got on file,' said Kane. 'You want me to get to it?'

'Agnes can do it after she's done Avercamp,' said Buchan, 'it shouldn't take long,' and he nodded and looked around the others, a quality in his silence that indicated he wasn't finished, and they waited for him.

'It's good to know,' he said, 'but ultimately, it doesn't get us anywhere unless we know how to use it.'

'Do we start bandying it around?' asked Liddell.

'Yes,' said Buchan. 'I think we flood the airwaves. With Bancroft's mob out of commission, I'm not sure who there is left to speak to, but anyone we can. Maplethorpe, Lansdowne, their people, we need to put that word in front of them, and we need to see how they react. Any mention of Maplethorpe in amongst the *Incarnate* stuff from the courts or Europol?' he asked, and Roth shook her head while she looked at her laptop screen.

Buchan breathed out heavily, part sigh, part exasperation. This was useful information, but where ultimately was it going to lead? You couldn't just phone someone up and toss a word into the conversation. Seeing their reaction was the point. And

---

134

FaceTime be damned.

'Sam,' he said, 'I think it might be your turn to visit Mr Maplethorpe. I'm sure he'll be excited to see another member of the team.'

Kane chuckled.

'I'm on it,' she said.

'I'll go and see Lansdowne again, we can cover more than one base that way.'

The door opened, Houston returning to the office.

'Nothing, sir,' said Roth, chiming in before Houston could talk.

'No mention of *Incarnate*?'

'Nowhere.'

'OK, well at least we know. Ian, you heard mention of a book entitled *Incarnate*?'

'Nope. What's that?'

'Agnes'll fill you in. Anything on the Lansdowne gang?'

'Yep. Spoke to a couple of people. Palpable sense of excitement, I'd say, but nothing to report. They know there's shit going down, but no one's talking, and whatever it is, it's not happening to *them*. At least, according to my sources, it's not happening to them.'

'OK,' said Buchan, and he was once again gripped by a need to get out and do something. 'Agnes, can you brief Ian on *Incarnate*, and then, you two know what you're doing? There's still a list.'

They nodded, Buchan glanced at Liddell who shooed him away, and then Buchan and Kane were out of the door and heading quickly along the corridor.

'Call me when you're done,' he said.

'Boss.'

42

Buchan stood at the door of the large dining room. There were ten people around the table, including a young child. A family dinner, with William Lansdowne at the head. Buchan recognised both of Lansdowne's sons, though he didn't know their partners, or either of the two other men who were present. Neither of Lansdowne's daughters were there. With no expectations in the family business, thought Buchan, they don't need to put themselves through this.

As Buchan entered, Lansdowne was in the act of carving a large chicken. Perhaps it was a turkey. Buchan had no idea if you could get turkey in the UK in the spring. Either way, the table was festooned with dishes of steaming food, a Christmas dinner without the party hats and the tree in the corner, the family dishing out the side dishes, as though filming a scene for a festive Hallmark movie.

The man who had let Buchan in, having first asked Lansdowne's permission, stood at Buchan's shoulder, waiting to usher him back out when instructed.

Lansdowne paused, carving knife and fork in hand, staring grudgingly at Buchan. Buchan, for his part, felt the whole thing was an act. Lansdowne could easily have not let him in, or he could have arranged to have Buchan shown into another room. The house was certainly big enough. This, inviting him to be a witness to the family dinner, particularly with a child present, was entirely performative.

'What?' said Lansdowne, eventually.

'Merry Christmas.'

'Funny, inspector. Big dinner, every Tuesday evening. The core of family life. Too bad you don't have one.'

'Can I have a word?'

Lansdowne, who Buchan knew had every intention of talking to him in private, took the necessary amount of time to think about this, as though it might not happen, then nodded at his eldest son, indicating for him to take the carving implements.

'Sure you don't want me in there?' said the son.

Reggie Lansdowne, thirty-three going on nineteen. The Lansdowne operation, such as it was, would not be safe in his hands when William handed over the reins. Or, more likely, finally died on the job.

Lansdowne ignored him, passing over the utensils, then he pushed his seat back, ruffled the hair of the kid as he walked past, and led Buchan down a short corridor into a small sitting room.

Door closed, the dark, heavily-furnished room lit by a lamp on the ornate oakwood desk. Lansdowne sat in a large, leather armchair, indicated for Buchan to sit in the other one, Buchan shook his head, then Lansdowne took a cigarette from a small case on the table beside him, and lit up.

'Strange,' he said. Buchan didn't encourage whatever flippancy Lansdowne was going to waste his time with. 'The good money was all on the great detective having this thing wrapped up in time for supper, and yet here you are, still pounding the streets, still relentless in your quest to interview people who have absolutely nothing whatsoever to do with what you're investigating. May I be so bold as to suggest this is why you're not getting anywhere?'

'You heard anything since we last spoke?' asked Buchan.

Lansdowne smiled, shook his head. Took a draw on the cigarette, rested his arm back on the chair, the cigarette held upright between his fingers, the smoke rising straight up.

'I fucking love you some days, Buchan. It's that combination of, I don't know, the investigative ability of Clouseau and the comedy genius of Billy Connolly.'

'You heard anything since we last spoke?' repeated Buchan.

'Naw. Nothing. All quiet on the western front. Nothing to report. City seems pretty dead this evening. Work day over, everyone's gone back to their sleepy homes to settle in for a quiet evening. We'll be having our dinner, then gather round the TV for *Bake Off: The Professionals* on catch-up. It's my favourite show. The way these people make thirty-two identical little whatevers in an hour. Fucking amazing, man. How I wish I could bake like that.' He laughed. 'That's a *Bake Off: The Professionals* gag. But then, you don't really do jokes, do you, Buchan?'

'Any of your people had any contact with Davie Bancroft's lot?' asked Buchan, ignoring the rambling conversation.

137

Another performative puff, the smile, the shrug.

'We're just going about our own business,' he said. 'We don't speak to that lot, ever, anyway, so the fact that we haven't today, doesn't really mean much.'

Buchan's phone started ringing, and he wondered whether to ignore it, then automatically took it from his pocket.

'Sam?'

'That was entertaining.'

'Go on.'

'Maplethorpe's still at his office. We're not the only ones working late. He demands to know why we're bugging him again. I get my one question out, what does *Incarnate* mean to you, and he completely lost his temper at me. I got a minute-long lecture on police harassment, delivered I have to say, at quite a clip and in a state of heightened annoyance, and then he walks to the door, opens it, and says, *now fuck off.*'

'You think he was that annoyed from the second you entered, or it was the question which brought it on?'

'Fifty-fifty,' said Kane. 'Annoyed to start with, the question doubled it.'

'You think he knew the name?'

'Definitely.'

'K, thanks. I'll call back in a few minutes.'

He hung up, phone back in his pocket.

'Tell me about *Incarnate*,' said Buchan quickly.

Lansdowne impassively held his look for a moment, then made the exact movements Buchan had known he would. Cigarette to his lips, the long draw, the smile.

'*Incarnate*?'

Buchan didn't give him anything else.

'You mean the horror movie? I don't like horror movies.'

'I mean the book *Incarnate*, by Franz Kazimierz.'

The familiar knowing smile, as though Lansdowne was completely in charge of the conversation, as though he knew everything Buchan needed to find out, then he indicated the neat bookshelves that covered three sides of the room. Buchan had barely noticed them when he'd entered. Unlike the cluttered fussiness of Harriet Blake's bookshelves, these looked entirely decorative, as though no books were ever removed from them and read.

'I like a book,' said Lansdowne. 'Consider myself a bit of a collector. I've got a first edition *Treasure Island* there, that's my prize possession. First edition *Treasure Island. Dead men don't bite...*'

'Keen though you are on old books,' said Buchan, shutting him down before he could go off on another intentionally unnecessary tangent, 'I don't suppose you've ever heard of this?'

'What was it again?'

'*Incarnate* by Franz Kazimierz.'

Lansdowne turned and looked at a bookshelf to his right, then got out of the armchair, cigarette in his mouth, and started thumbing through a row of old cloth-bound hardbacks, many of which didn't have a title on the spine. He found what he was looking for, he pulled the book out, he turned and handed it to Buchan.

Took a draw from the cigarette, smoke blown out to the side.

'Can't say I've read it, to be fair, what with it being in Polish. Completely indecipherable. I mean, have you ever looked at Polish?' He laughed. 'Tell you what though, give it a sniff, inspector. Now *that* is what a book should smell like. None of your Kindle shite.'

Buchan examined the cover, opened the book, flicked through it. The words meant nothing of course, the one-word title meant nothing, but there was the name of the author, Franz Kazimierz, and the wording on the verso stated that the book had been published in Warsaw, 1909. He then lifted it closer to his face, and breathed in while he flicked through the pages. His initial feeling was that he was likely being scammed. But then, where had this certainty come from? Half an hour ago they'd never heard of *Incarnate*. Roth had picked something up from the morass of detail they were all searching through, and now they were convinced this was the Holy Grail at the heart of the maelstrom.

'Where'd you get this?'

'I buy books, inspector,' said Lansdowne, having settled back into his chair. 'Sometimes people buy me books, sometimes Reggie picks them up for me. I'll give Reggie that, to be fair. Not the sharpest tool in the shed, guaranteed to be an absolute idiot when it comes to running the family business, but he's got an eye for these. Does a nice job of picking things up.'

'He got this for you?'

'I don't remember. Maybe he did.'

'How long have you had it?'

'Let me think.' He made the pretence of thinking, staring deadpan at Buchan as he did so. 'I'm going to say, six days, more or less.'

'You've got a letter of provenance with this, a certificate of authenticity, a whatever?'

Buchan didn't know the correct term.

'Sure, I've got that somewhere.'

'This is a first edition?'

'Last one known in existence,' said Lansdowne. 'Quite the pick-up.'

'I'll need to take this,' said Buchan.

'How about we reword that? How about we say, your lawyer can speak to my lawyer.'

'If this is the only one in existence, then it was part of the haul from Eurocentral last October. This is evidence.'

'I don't know anything about that. That is exactly the kind of thing your lawyer can take up with my lawyer. Perhaps they could speak to each other tomorrow morning. A little past close of play, today.'

The door opened, and the man who'd shown Buchan into the house entered the room, closing the door behind him. He stood, his back against it, waiting further instruction, and Buchan wondered how he'd known his presence was required.

'You can give the book to Brendan, there,' said Lansdowne. 'Then maybe you can see yourself out. My dinner'll be getting cold.'

Buchan held on to the book, making the calculation. Given all the shit that seemed to be happening with their own service, and their inability to know exactly who was and wasn't on their side, did he really want to take the book away at this stage in any case? What difference did being in possession of it for now actually mean? Other than to Jan Baltazar, who was the only one who really wanted it.

'People don't like the police, inspector,' said Lansdowne. 'It doesn't matter who I am, but they don't like *you*. So Brendan here gives you a bit of a kicking one night when you turn up at my house? Well, the public'll understand. What's the situation here exactly? We have a rogue copper, he turns up at the home of a respected local businessman, kicking the door in and creating havoc, while said businessman is trying to have a quiet meal with his family. There are children present. There's a stramash, there's shouting, children are crying, they're afraid. Big nasty copper, no fucks to give, scaring the kids. No one likes that. No one's on the side of the copper.' A pause, and then, 'No matter how badly he gets the shit kicked out of him.'

Buchan looked between the two of them, and then made the call, handing the book over to Brendan, who took it while staring grimly back.

'Now, off you fuck, inspector,' said Lansdowne. 'We can resume this at a later date. I'm free tomorrow. Hmm, maybe scratch that, and let's say, I'm free fourteen months on Monday. If you are. Of course.'

He laughed, he stubbed the cigarette out in a small bowl on the table, and then got to his feet, blowing out the last puff of smoke.

43

Buchan was in his car, the evening progressing, streetlights coming on. Roth called before Buchan had been able to get his call through to Kane.

'I managed to get hold of someone from the originating antique book dealer in Warsaw,' said Roth, and Buchan couldn't help himself interrupting with, 'Gone ten o'clock in Warsaw?' and Roth said, 'I know how to bend people to my will,' and Buchan smiled and said, 'Go on.'

'I got a little more detail on how it played out with Baltazar. Firstly, and this I'd missed, sorry, lost in translation, I guess. The thing where Baltazar insisted he get the book back, started over five years ago. Took a couple of years to go to court. When it did, it was like the smallest, most insignificant court case on earth. No one paid much attention to it, then it was thrown out in seconds. He thinks Baltazar came in with all guns blazing and the kind of high-end representation you'd normally see from a multinational oil company. It really got the judge's back up. However it played out, Baltazar lost, and it was a zero story. Nevertheless, what little attention it had received, coupled with the seller's awareness of just how much Baltazar really wanted this book, meant that the seller then offered it to Baltazar for fifteen thousand euros. Baltazar, of course, said no. Time passes, Covid gets in the way, various things get in the way, and finally it gets put on a plane to go to the US. However, by then, the chance of a lucrative sale has really gone. The talk has died down, no one seems particularly interested. The seller's also a bit pissed off, because they think they missed out on getting fifteen thousand euros. The valuation has now slipped way back, much closer to what it had been originally. Which, by the way, is part of the reason it ends up on a plane to the States, in the hope of giving it another boost.'

'We know who the seller is?'

'The estate of a man named Anton Steiner. And, you'll be shocked to discover, it's his estate that's the seller because Mr Steiner himself died in a car accident three years ago.'

'Convenient.'

'His brakes failed.'

'Jesus,' muttered Buchan, and as he did so, he automatically pressed the brake pedal to make sure they were working. 'Any chance there was an investigation?'

'Doesn't look like it. It's just down as an accident.'

'Damn it.' A pause, and then, 'K, thanks, Agnes. Keep digging.'

'Boss.'

She hung up. Buchan, the phone on his knee, glanced quickly down, called Kane.

'How are you getting on?'

'I don't know, sir. We keep going back to the ops room, and we keep coming up with a list of things to do, and things are kind of falling into place, and yet... Ultimately, I'm not sure we're getting anywhere. We've got a dead guy, we know Claire Avercamp's still alive at least, though we've no more idea where she is, and we've got this massive escalation with the book shop raids. And...'

'Yep,' said Buchan. 'Lots of noise and smoke, no clear route through the tumult to the other side.'

Kane was also driving, and together, in their separate cars, they drove in silence for a few moments. The buck might have been stopping at Buchan, but they both felt the pressure of it. The fear that they were missing something obvious, or the need to create a breakthrough from what they had. The stroke of genius, the random thought from nowhere.

'You hungry?' said Buchan.

'God, aye. Was just thinking that. Want me to grab some food for everyone and meet back at base?'

'Let's give ourselves half an hour. Call the team, we'll meet at Jerry's on Stevenson Road. I'll call ahead, get some pizza lined up. Half an hour, get back to work, give it another two or three hours. If nothing else comes up this evening we can head about midnight.'

'Shall I include the chief?'

'I'll call her. See you shortly.'

44

Buchan, Kane, Houston, Liddell, Cherry, Dawkins and Roth at a large round table in a booth at the back of the pizza place. Seven pizzas, four waters, two Coke Zeros, one elderflower, and seven phones sitting beside seven plates. There were so many people who could potentially call at any moment, and none of the phones were ringing.

'So, what've you been up to?' said Dawkins to Roth, picking a lull in the conversation. The question sounded upbeat. Buchan didn't glance at Roth, in case she glanced at him. He didn't want caught in what would be interpreted as a significant look across the table.

'Playing a lot of online chess,' said Roth, smiling self-consciously. 'That's a bit geeky.'

'Are you any good?'

'Nope. But… you know, my dad taught me when I was a kid. I think he had this idea he could train me to be a chess genius. So, that never happened.' She laughed, Dawkins laughed along with her. Really, this was a conversation between the two of them, but the work chat had died down, and the others were all interested to hear how she was. 'And then… Dad passed when I was like fifteen, and I always thought, you know, I wish I'd played more chess, I wish I'd played against him more. It was kind of all we had.'

She was taken by the memory for a moment. No one else knew what to do with it, Buchan realising that everyone was still walking on eggshells around her, but it wasn't as though he knew any better than anyone else how to handle it.

Roth shrugged.

'There were all these times, you know, when he'd say, fancy a game of chess, and I'd be like, it's OK, maybe tomorrow, I've got to do whatever. I mean, what the hell was I even doing when I was fifteen?'

Buchan felt the glance from Kane, but he didn't return it. Instead, he bit into a slice of capricciosa, staring at the table.

'Yeah, that's tough,' said Dawkins.

'You know, it's thirteen years ago. Time passes,' said Roth, and she made a fluttering gesture. 'And I always kind of liked chess, but never really gave it the time since then. But this year, well I've had that time on my hands.'

'Take it you're not reading three crime novels a week anymore?'

Roth sort of winced, shaking her head.

'Haven't read any, to be honest. Chess is equally absorbing, and no one dies.'

'I could give you a game some time,' said Cherry from across the table, and Roth smiled and said, 'That'd be cool. I might not be able to give you much of one, but I'll try,' and Cherry laughed, lightening the mood, saying, 'Well, I know which way the horse moves, so you're in trouble,' and Roth laughed with him, and Buchan allowed himself a glance at her now because he liked her smile, and he looked quickly away without looking at Kane.

Houston's phone rang, he lifted it, and instantly a tension returned to the table. Now there were six people eating pizza, waiting for the one person on the phone, a lot of weight instantly being placed on the call, as it was the first one to come in since they'd arrived.

'Not sure this is really panning out the way you hoped, inspector,' said Liddell, her voice low.

'Good to get away from the office, regardless,' said Buchan.

'That's the conceit, certainly,' said Liddell, drily.

'And you've no idea where any of them have gone?' asked Houston, followed shortly by, 'And no addresses presumably?' and then another couple of nods down the phone, and then, 'OK, thanks, Andy. Yeah, I'll be in touch,' and he hung up.

He took a moment, couldn't stop himself taking a bite of pizza, and then talked through it, his hand hovering over his mouth.

'More information to slot into the narrative, but nothing that drives us anywhere nearer the conclusion,' he said. 'That was Andy Turner at UK Borders. They've been dealing with an issue the last couple of days. There's a building firm in Ayrshire. The last few years, whenever they get a big job, they bring in the same crew of guys from Poland. Around thirty of them, occasionally there's a minor change of personnel, but you're looking at the same core crew every time. Brexit hasn't really changed anything, apart from there being more paperwork. They've got a big contract just started, they're ramping up the workforce, the deal's done with the agency in Poland, all the usual guys are lined up, and then a week ago there's a complete change. A new list of names, every single one different. They just assumed their usual crew were working on something else. They're not delighted, but ultimately, they need thirty guys to lay bricks, or do whatever, so doesn't matter who they are. They have accommodation for them set up in the area, the bus was due to arrive on Sunday afternoon. It got off a late night ferry in Dover on Saturday night, and then...' He snapped his fingers. 'Nothing. No word, no sign of the men or the bus.'

'I think we know they're in Glasgow,' said Liddell. 'I wonder how they think they're going to get off this wretched island, though.'

'Sadly,' said Buchan, 'they sound like they have more than enough resources to stay here unnoticed, followed by a return to Poland at a time of their choosing on thirty fake passports.'

'Or they already arrived on the fake ones,' said Houston, 'and they leave on the real. Or other fakes. We're dealing with an operation here.'

Silence fell upon them again, and they all started eating. There was only one other occupied table, a quiet night at Jerry's Pizza Place. Four men in shirts and ties chatting loudly about football, getting ready to leave. Dean Martin was singing. Dean Martin, thought Buchan, was this place's Sinatra, except unlike Janey and her Sinatra misery albums, the restaurant liked Martin in *Volare* mood.

Nowadays, Buchan still found himself at the Winter Moon, but while it had used to be most nights, it was now two, maybe three times a week, on its way, he knew, to some nights, eventually becoming occasionally. Perhaps, finally, it would be never. The spell had been broken. Indeed, if he was to be honest, he recognised that he sometimes now went to the Winter Moon to stop himself spending an entire evening with Roth, and if he was allowing himself the brutal honesty of a long, hard look in the mirror, he would avoid the long evening with Roth because he really wanted to have it.

The door opened, the four men left, two of them throwing a *thank-you* over their shoulders, and then there was a young waitress putting the empty coffee cups on a brown, oval tray, and then she was gone, walking backwards through the swing door to the kitchen, and now there was just the seven of them, eating in silence to the sounds of Dean Martin singing *Dream A Little Dream of Me*.

Outside, the early dark of evening had arrived, exacerbated by the streetlights covering the last vestige of grey in the sky. Buchan hadn't left work in the dark in a month, but tonight felt like one of those where he'd be going home at four a.m. to catch an hour's sleep.

Dammit, he thought. This wasn't working. Liddell was right. They were going through the motions, eating pizza, drinking whatever, aware all the time that the clock was ticking, and that there was work to be done back at the office. It hadn't taken long for him to rationalise with himself, to decide that this was a better idea than getting the pizza delivered to the work place, but it had been a mistake.

'Time we were wrapping it up, folks,' said Buchan. 'Let's give it that other couple of hours back at the ranch.'

A few nods, a last piece of crammed pizza, a last gulp from the glass, a shuffling of shoes, the putting on of a light, summer jacket.

Dean Martin finished, the next song did not immediately start up.

Silence.

Buchan stared at the window, from nowhere senses suddenly heightened, a strange fear gripping his stomach.

From outside the sound of a motorbike. They'd been listening to traffic the entire time they were here, but this particular bike seemed, for reasons they couldn't explain, to stand out. As though they were watching a film, and the so-far unseen bike had been made the centre of attention.

They sat for a moment, the seven now all suddenly drawn to the same noise, Buchan feeling the unease growing in his guts, a hand wrapping itself around them.

The bike stopped outside. A figure in a helmet, pulling into the side of the road. Head down, not paying any attention to the restaurant. Cherry, who'd turned round to look at it, was the first to turn away. Just a guy on a bike. Buchan lowered his glass, pushed his plate a little away as the first act of getting ready to leave. The grip on his stomach was not loosening, however.

'Come on,' said Liddell, the first to get to her feet.

The motorcyclist turned quickly, a sudden whirl of movement. Threw something at the front of the restaurant, the glass smashed. A cacophony of sound. The motorbike gunning off, the growl of the engine loud through the broken window. A brick landed on the floor, bouncing towards them.

A second, then an ejaculation of, 'Oh, fuck!' from Houston.

He dived out of his seat. He lifted the brick, shouting, 'Get down!' as he did so, running towards the window, ready to throw it back outside.

There was nowhere to throw it. Passers-by in the street, looking fearfully into the window. The traffic lights had changed, several cars beginning to pick up pace on the road outside. Houston hesitated. A frantic stare at the device in his hands.

Tick-tock.

He tucked it into his stomach, kept his back on the others, and crouched down beside the front wall. At the last, he glanced over his shoulder and caught Roth's terrified eye.

The small explosive detonated.

45

Buchan, Kane and Sgt Meyers, head of the SOCO team were standing together. The road was closed, the area a swarm of officers. The ambulances that had been in attendance had already left.

Buchan felt sick. Kane had thrown up, and now the nausea and shock and fear had been replaced by anger. Meyers hadn't spoken yet, having come to stand with them, and view from across the road the scene at which she'd just been working. She wanted to give Kane a hug – maybe she just wanted a hug herself – but this wasn't the place. For now, for the rest of the evening, until such times as they were able to walk back into their own homes and collapse into someone's arms, or to collapse onto the sofa, they had to be seen to be keeping it together. To be doing the job demanded of them. They had their colleagues to think about, and they had the press on the periphery of the crime scene, long-angled cameras pointed in the direction of every member of the emergency services.

Buchan and Kane, along with Cherry and Liddell, had been unharmed. Roth had taken a piece of flying debris on the chin. Dawkins, at the end of the table, had been thrown back in a way that none of the others had. A bang to the head, a bruise, a sore arm; when she got up she found she was limping.

Liddell, Cherry, Roth and Dawkins had gone back to SCU headquarters. Buchan and Kane knew they should be back there already, but they couldn't bring themselves to leave. Buchan had never had one of his officers killed in the line of duty before. This was the last place Houston would ever be.

The device had never been intended to cause huge damage. It had obviously had the capacity to kill anyone in its proximity, but it had never been going to take down the entire front of the restaurant, or to collapse the building. Houston had managed to smother the blast, but of course, had had no chance of surviving it.

His body had been split in half, the two parts blown yards apart. Blood and flesh had flown. Both Buchan and Liddell had got some of it on their clothes, their faces. At some point Buchan had taken off his light coat, emptied the pockets, and thrown it to the side on the ground, to be swept up with all the other detritus. It was a coat he would never wear again.

There wasn't a police officer in the city who hadn't been called back on duty. The city itself, beyond the crime scene, was quiet, as though people had decided everyone had to lie low. There was something major playing out, there was too much chance of being caught in the crossfire. Every now and again a distant siren would cut through the silence, but there wasn't much traffic around, not much need for a siren.

Tony, the owner of the restaurant – there hadn't been a Jerry in over twenty years – was sitting to the side, against the stone window ledge of a shop across the road, chain smoking. Buchan had told him he could go, and Tony had gestured towards the shattered glass of his diner, cigarette between his fingers, and said nothing. He was as devastated as any of Buchan's crew.

The instruction had already come through to get the scene cleaned up by the following morning. A busy road in the middle of Glasgow, if it was still closed by eight a.m. on a Wednesday, the place would be gridlocked. There was no reason for the team not to comply. Houston was gone, dead, blown in pieces, and keeping the road closed wasn't going to do him any good.

'Did you manage to get Ian's body?' asked Buchan. He had no idea how long they'd been standing like this. Time was lost. Time no longer existed. He wouldn't be going home tonight or tomorrow, he wouldn't be going home until he'd found the man who'd killed his sergeant.

And that was all he had. The person on the motorbike, dressed in black biking leathers, wearing a dark helmet, had the build of a man.

Meyers shook her head, though first answered in the affirmative.

'I think so, but... God, I don't know. A few hours from now this place is going to have to be washed down, and...'

She shook her head again, she left the thought there. None of the three of them needed to think any more about that image.

'I should get back to the lab,' said Meyers. 'Hopefully we'll be able to identify the explosive, and that'll give you a lead to its origins.' A pause, and then, 'Sorry, that's all I've got.'

Buchan nodded, said, 'Thanks, Ruth,' and Meyers started to

turn away. She stopped, she looked at Kane, they shared their pain for a moment, and then Meyers left quickly without reaching out.

'I'm just going to have another quick word with Tony, then head back,' said Buchan to Kane. 'If you want to stay here a little longer, I don't mind.'

'No, I was just about to go. I'll join you, if that's OK.'

'Course.'

They turned away from the damaged front of the restaurant, and the last thing that Detective Sergeant Houston would ever do, Kane unable to stop herself looking over her shoulder, and approached Tony Bonucci.

He was leaning forward, staring at the ground, cigarette burning down between his fingers.

'Tony,' said Buchan, and he lifted his eyes.

'How are you doing?' asked Tony. 'I've seen you two looking a lot better.'

His voice was flat. Tony played the part of the Italian pizza parlour owner for everything it had, but his accent was pure Glasgow, having lived here all his life.

'We're OK. Your people went home?'

There had been three others in the kitchen, including the waitress. Bonucci had already told Buchan that Tuesdays were quiet, and he staffed accordingly.

'Aye. They spoke to one of they, one of the constables over there. Said their bit. None of them had anything to say, anyway.' He swallowed, he gestured towards the restaurant. 'Bloody lucky Susie wasn't in the, you know, Susie wasn't in the restaurant at the time. If she'd been clearing away that table those other guys were sitting at.' He ran his thumb across his throat, then seemed to regret the action. Finally he looked properly at Buchan. 'You don't think, I mean, those four guys. You don't think they had anything to do with this? Hell of a coincidence. They leave, and then boom!'

'We don't think so,' said Buchan. 'We think it more likely the perpetrator was looking to cause as little human collateral damage as possible.' He looked up and down the side of the street they were on, opposite the restaurant. 'This is supposition, but we think maybe there was someone over here keeping an eye out. When he saw the place only had us, he called in the motorbike.'

'But how'd he know youse lot would even be here in the

first place? You says yourself, it was a last-minute decision. Youse lot wouldn't normally all be working at this time on a Tuesday.'

Buchan shrugged, although he already had the answer. This was a big organisation, be it the Baltazars or anyone else. The police could have no idea how many different plans they might have in place, which they could be ready to unleash at a moment's notice. Big enough, agile enough, complex enough, to think on their feet, to take advantage of whatever situations presented themselves.

'You OK?' he asked instead.

Bonucci held his gaze for a moment, and then sort of shrugged and once again indicated across the road.

'We'll get it repaired, I suppose,' he said. 'Fuck knows what it'll do to the place once we're back up and running. I mean... someone died over there. Your man died... on the premises. Who's going to want to come and have their dinner on the spot where that poor bastard got blown up? Aye, I know, there'll be some weird fucker somewhere, there's always one, who'd get a kick out of it. But you know what, I don't want to serve a sick bastard like that his dinner.' Another pause, another shrug. 'I don't know what I'll do,' he said eventually.

Buchan put his hand on Bonucci's shoulder. That was all he had. He turned away.

46

The team was in the open-plan, but Buchan and Liddell had come upstairs to her office to discuss the direction of the case.

They were in a familiar position, Buchan standing at the window looking out on the night, Liddell at her desk, the unlit cigarette back between her fingers.

Buchan had only just arrived, having stopped off at the open-plan to make sure Dawkins and Roth were doing OK after their injuries, he'd nodded at Liddell and then made his way straight to the window. As though he needed to keep a watch over the city, as though by standing here he might be able to see the next outrage coming on this damnable day, as though he might be able to stop it. The room was illuminated by the small lamp on Liddell's desk, and only the absence of cigarette smoke separated the scene from a dark and tense moment in a nineteen-forties Bogart drama.

Buchan's thoughts could not be so flippant. In any case, they rarely were, but now they might never be again. He recognised the day for what it was. Awful and life-changing in equal measure, a plummet into an abyss from which there might never be an escape. At the very least, this was a day that none of them would ever forget.

'We've been relegated,' said Liddell, finally getting to it. 'Again. I just took the call from Dalmarnock.'

Buchan didn't turn. It was hardly unexpected. The day had been building to it, but after what had happened to Houston, and the size of the force that had been deployed on the investigation, there was no way it was going to be left in the hands of a detective inspector.

'Who's taken over?' said Buchan. It was barely a question, as though he wasn't really interested.

'Reynolds,' said Liddell.

Again Buchan didn't turn. He'd thought it through, the process of little more than a couple of minutes, and Reynolds was obvious.

'Can we trust him?' he said, his voice cold and dead.

Clyde Street and the Broomielaw across the river were quieter than usual. Not that he often stood here at this time in the evening, but the city had taken itself out of circulation for the night. More than likely, by tomorrow morning everything would be back to normal, the explosion at Jerry's, the death of Houston, just a thing that had happened the previous day, the water cooler topic of the morning. Tonight, however, there was still fear. If not fear, at least guardedness.

'It would be glib to say that we have to,' said Liddell, 'but we do. Nevertheless, while he's never been my favourite officer, I think we're some way short of thinking he's in league with any of these clowns involved in this game. He'll do a good job, and while it might not be the job that I would do under the same circumstances, that doesn't make him untrustworthy.'

'Where does it leave us?' asked Buchan.

'For the moment, we are unchanged. We run our investigation, but we're no longer the central point of contact. Everything will get passed through Reynolds' office. I don't know yet who he's actually going to have running the ops room, who his principal lieutenants are going to be on this. For now, we can do what we're going to do, but we have to be careful we don't overlap with someone else, and we don't step on anyone's toes. Everything we learn has to be passed to the centre, and at some stage, maybe not tonight, but soon enough, they're going to be telling us what to do.'

Buchan gritted his teeth.

'And we're going to listen, inspector,' said Liddell, and finally he turned and looked at her.

His face was grim and dark in the night, his eyes distant.

'You'll need to appoint one of your staff to be the liaison with the centre,' said Liddell, and when Buchan still didn't speak, she added, 'Who will that be?'

'Agnes,' said Buchan. 'She'll be here, so it makes sense.'

'Is she all right? Given where she's coming at mentally today, having that happen in front of her might be ev –'

'I've spoken to her. She's got her head down, she's working, she doesn't want to be anywhere else.'

Liddell was tapping the cigarette harshly on the table. The end of it buckled, and she scowled at it, as though it had been the fault of the cigarette, and tossed it into the bin.

'Keep an eye on her,' she said, then, head shaking, she added, 'Scrub that. Ask Sgt Kane to keep an eye on her.'

47

From nowhere, a whirlwind of noise and action. The motorbike used in the attack on the restaurant had been identified, abandoned in an old business park about three miles from the city centre, on the same side of the river as the SCU. Kane was driving, blue light swirling through the late spring's night-time sky. Up ahead, another squad car heading in the same direction.

Buchan in the passenger seat, Cherry in the rear. Dawkins and Roth had remained back at the office, Liddell with them, having come downstairs with Buchan. 'All hands,' she'd said to him. 'Treat me as one of the team.'

With every passing minute they became aware of more vehicles heading in the same direction.

'I don't like this,' said Buchan.

The hand grabbing his stomach was back.

Kane braked hard approaching a junction, Buchan automatically activated the siren, and then turned it off again as they sped through, no other vehicles on the road bar the police cars a hundred yards ahead of them.

'Boss?'

'Them leaving the motorbike out in the open like that.'

'It's in a shitty car park, next to a couple of warehouses that haven't been used since 2008.'

'It's still been left for us to find,' said Cherry from the back. He wasn't leaning into the conversation. Sitting back, staring bleakly out of the window, his face haunted. 'It's a motorbike, not a double-decker. They could've put it in a garage, they could've changed the plates, they could've dumped it in a wood or in the Clyde, they could've got the fuck out of Dodge, riding it off into the night. Instead, they parked it for us to find. Maybe a little out of the way, but there's a reason they want us there. Why else do it this way?'

His voice sounded dead. Buchan agreed with him, didn't say anything. Kane realised he was right. She'd been concentrating on the road, on the getting there, rather than on what they would find once they'd arrived. Now the trepidation that had gripped Buchan gripped the car.

A right turn in the wake of the others, and then they were into the small, largely abandoned business park. A used car lot, still active, its stock depleted and sad, a large banner across the top of the dilapidated fence – Best Offers! A right turn, and then there were seven police cars in a car park surrounded on three sides by warehouses.

None of the warehouses looked in use. One, in particular, boarded up, windows along the top all broken. Graffito on the walls of all three. Weeds in the car park, and an overflowing, open-topped blue recycling container.

The car skidded to a halt, and then Buchan, Kane and Cherry were out and walking quickly into the midst of the crowd. A silent cacophony of swirling blue light, blending with the dull orange of the old street lights, and a single bright security light from one of the warehouses.

No one was closer than fifteen yards to the motorbike, and Buchan was relieved to realise he wasn't the only one with the thought that this could be a trap. There was a single photographer taking pictures of the bike from a distance, an engineer working with a small machine that would turn out to be a remotely-controlled device they would use to check over the bike.

As they joined the crowd, a woman at the centre of it looked up from an iPad she was being shown, and she seemed to realise just how many people were now on the scene.

'Jesus,' she muttered. The officer in charge. 'Can we all stand back, please? Everyone needs to get back!' and she waved to the other side of the plethora of police cars.

Kane and Cherry stopped where they were, Buchan made his way through the small crowd, against the tide, until he was by the officer in charge.

'DI Buchan,' he said.

'DCI Hamilton,' said the woman. A mass of unruly blonde hair, a hard-set look of determination on her face that Buchan immediately respected. A moment, and then she said, 'I'm sorry about your sergeant.'

Buchan had nothing to say to that. For now, for this evening, the only way to address it was to use it as a driving force, an accelerant to light the fire beneath the investigation.

'You're thinking it's very convenient they let us find this?' said Buchan, and as he spoke he looked around the area.

'Absolutely. Makes no sense, unless they want us here,' said Hamilton.

'Have we checked the warehouses?' asked Buchan, knowing as he asked it was unlikely.

'Next on the list. Just going to make sure this thing isn't going to pull any surprises first. I'm happy if you want to coordinate the search. Just...,' and she indicated the warehouses and stopped herself telling Buchan he should be wary of traps, as he was obviously going to have that in mind.

'OK, thanks, chief,' said Buchan, and he immediately turned away. Whatever was going on here, whatever the set-up, they needed to find out what it was as quickly as possible. He was sure there were no answers here. This was just part of the game that had to be undertaken, a move played by their unseen opponents, before the police could decide what had to be done next.

'We need two people at each of the entrances to these warehouses,' he said, approaching the small crowd of officers that had drifted back. At a vague look on one or two faces, he produced his ID, held it up and said, 'DI Buchan,' and could immediately recognise more acceptance from the small crowd.

'Two each at the main unit door, two at the side doors. Anyone left, fan out, encircle the buildings as you can, see if there's anything lurking on the other side. I really don't think we're going to find anyone active in here, but be wary just in case. How many weapons do we have?'

Three of the officers made a small acknowledgement, and Buchan said, 'One of each of you to the three warehouses, please. And be mindful, people, before attempting to gain entry, look for signs of recent activity, and any hint there might be a booby-trap. You find anything, be loud, make it known.' A pause, and then, aware there were more sirens in the night, Buchan picked out one of the small crowd, said, 'Constable, I need you to stand out there, out on the road. Stop anyone else coming in here for the moment, unless they have direct business with the DCI. We don't need anyone else here until we know what we're dealing with.'

'Sir.' And she turned quickly, through the crowd, and out on to the road, arm raised as the next police car in the parade arrived on scene.

'Let's go,' said Buchan.

Affirmatives were thrown into the warm night air, and then

---

the crowd split seamlessly, each knowing instinctively to which task they'd been individually assigned.

Leaving Kane and Cherry to another part of the search, Buchan and an armed constable he didn't know, walked quickly to the warehouse on the left. They passed Hamilton and the team of two engineers who were getting ready to check the motorbike. Hamilton looked as though she was about to object to their approach, and their proximity, then realised it was Buchan heading to the warehouse, and she turned away.

At the front of this warehouse, two large, broad doors in the middle of the side of the building, the one on the right containing its own narrow door that would be used by staff if the double door didn't need to be opened. The double door had a thick chain across, wrapped several times through handles on either door and then sealed with a massive padlock. The smaller door within the right-hand door had a Yale and a mortice lock.

'Constable?' said Buchan, studying the door, asking the constable's name.

'Niamh Connor, sir.'

'Niamh,' said Buchan. 'Trip-wire check first,' followed by the unnecessary, but unavoidable, 'Be careful.'

Torches on, they checked over the door. The locks, the chain, the partition between the two doors, the ground around it. There was nothing to suggest there'd been any recent disturbances, but they were obviously dealing with professionals, and they couldn't be too careful. Indeed, Buchan already thought, if these people wanted to kill twenty police officers, they more than likely would be able to do it.

There were shouts behind them, but nothing urgent. Confirmations, requests, assurances. 'You got that bolt cutter, Alan?' loud and clear in the night.

'We good?' said Buchan, looking along the front of the building, torch aimed at the ground.

'Clear,' said Connor. 'You want me to get hold of metal cutters from the –'

'I should be able to do the locks on the small door,' said Buchan.

He took the old, faithful Lishi lockpick out of his coat pocket, and got to work on the mortice lock, Connor coming alongside and shining a torch on the door.

Behind them the loud crack of metal, another couple of shouts, and then the sound of the large roller door of the middle warehouse being raised. Buchan felt the tension of it, of the sound of the rising door, fearing it could be booby-trapped. He let out a low curse, as his lockpick missed its grip again, and he took a second.

'We're good, sir,' said Connor, and then, 'Relax.'

The young woman reminded Buchan of Roth. Nevertheless, there was another curse on his lips, but he kept it to himself. Accepted she was right. There was too much tension in his hands for such an intricate task, no matter how easy he usually found it.

Behind them, the roller door had reached the top, clanging loudly into place, there were another couple of shouts, and then silence.

Buchan finally turned the lower lock, took a deep breath, then moved to the Yale lock at the top.

'Sir.'

Buchan could usually pick a Yale lock in under twenty seconds, and he didn't want this evening to be any different. Around him, the evening settling into a strange quiet.

'Sir!'

He turned, not yet able to make the pick catch, annoyance on his face.

'What?'

Connor was turned away from him, looking over at the main warehouse door. Buchan stared at her face for a moment, and then looked over his shoulder. The intended quick glance became a slow straightening of his body, then he was standing beside Connor, looking at the hangar.

Inside held a deep darkness, the forefront illuminated by the torches of the few staff who had entered the warehouse, and whatever light entered the building from the street.

Nothing inside was immediately obvious, but what had drawn Connor was the look of everyone else within the vicinity. All standing stock still, staring in shock inside.

Buchan and Connor moved a little closer, just as Hamilton started advancing quickly. Round the cars, and then stepping through the few scattered officers. In the distance the howl of an approaching siren.

Buchan and Connor moved into view. They could now see more clearly what everyone else could see, and they stopped.

'Jesus,' in awe and fear softly escaped Connor's lips.

Having stepped into the warehouse, Hamilton now stood,

her neck bent, her eyes trained upwards.

A few more seconds passed, the upturned faces caught in perfect horror in the blue light, as though Joseph Wright of Derby had arrived to capture the scene.

Buchan was first to react, walking forward, hands clapping, approaching the horror of the fourteen corpses left hanging on meat hooks in a row as though they were cuts of pork in an abattoir.

'All right, people, let's pull back until we've got some lights on in here. Meantime, don't touch *anything*! Careful in here. We've got to assume the perpetrators are gone, but you never know. Make the call, get searchlights brought over. Until then, line the cars up at the door, headlights on full beam. We need this place flooded with light. Don't touch any electrics inside the building. Watch for trip wires.' He paused, the team already reacting to his instructions, and then, 'We're going to need more people, we're going to need everyone Scenes of Crime can spare. Let's go!'

48

They knew them all. All fourteen. Eleven men, three women. Operatives for the Bancroft gang. The ones they'd spent the afternoon looking for, Davie Bancroft himself amongst them. Also present, Lenny McLeod, the man who'd been with Malky Seymour when Buchan had interviewed him six or seven hours ago, or perhaps it had been a hundred hours ago. The day had grown long and awful and desperate and never-ending. Lenny McLeod, honest by the terms of his own code, loyal henchman to Seymour, his throat slit, then his corpse suspended from a metal beam – running the length of the hangar – by a meat hook thrust into the nape of the neck, and up beneath the skull. Just the same as the other thirteen.

Eddie Harmon was there too. Eddie Harmon, who Buchan had sent away, to be protected by a police tail. Since then, and Buchan couldn't think how long ago it had been, Buchan had completely forgotten about him. He hadn't checked up on the tail, he hadn't thought to ask if there was any information forthcoming. As it was, Harmon had chosen to go it alone, slipping the tail within ten minutes, quickly paying the price.

Eddie Harmon had sought out the protection of the police, Buchan had turned him loose for his own ends, and now he was dead. Another name, another face, to join the procession of guilt that paraded through Buchan's dreams at night.

Malky Seymour, however, was not amongst the dead. The missing name, thought Buchan, far more significant than those who were there.

The bodies still hung where they'd been found. Time had passed. Now, well into the depths of evening, the team of SOCOs all over the hangar, collecting everything they could before the authorisation was given to lower the corpses.

Word was out, of course, and now the warehouse door was closed again, the place illuminated inside by huge searchlights. There was no clear view of the warehouse frontage from anywhere the public could access, but they didn't want this picture taken and published online, shown to the world.

Buchan was outside, leaning against the car in which he and Kane and Cherry had arrived. He'd already dispatched those two back to the office, taking a lift from a squad car heading hurriedly back into town.

Hands in his pockets, Buchan was staring dead-eyed across the small business park. There was nothing to see other than the side of buildings and the great mass of emergency vehicles that had been brought on site.

It was three minutes after midnight.

Hamilton approached, thinking Buchan looked like a haunted, unreal figure. Perhaps he needed a cigarette, or maybe just a cup of coffee, to humanise him.

'You've had a long day, inspector,' said Hamilton.

Buchan nodded. Didn't look at her. No longer than any of his staff, he thought.

'Looks like you've been in the wars,' she said, indicating his face, something which she hadn't bothered to say when he'd first arrived.

Buchan had no reply. Didn't even have a shrug in him.

'Perhaps it's time you went home and got some sleep.'

'No,' said Buchan, bluntly.

Hamilton nodded, then settled beside Buchan, looking around the same scene.

'You knew all the people in there?' she asked.

'Yes.' He was in no rush to talk.

He wanted to be. He wanted to have this conversation, he wanted to get on with it, he wanted to get back to the office, he wanted to arrive there with a nailed-down plan to get to the bottom of this Hell. But he had nothing. Empty tank, empty mind, and Hamilton was right. He did need to go home and get some sleep.

'Anyone significant missing?'

'Malky Seymour,' said Buchan. 'Davie Bancroft's number two. I spoke to him and Lenny at some time this afternoon, then we brought Malky in for questioning.'

'Why?'

'He gave us the address of a safe house belonging to the Polish mob we're assuming is responsible for that,' and he made a small gesture towards the warehouse. 'When we got there, we found a body, gunshot wound to the head. Don't know the guy. We're assuming he's one of the Baltazar mob, we haven't ID'd the body yet.' He paused, he corrected himself. 'Maybe we have.

I haven't heard, and I haven't thought to check recently. We then identified the weapon used as a gun thought to belong to Davie Bancroft's mob, used on the murder of two of William Lansdowne's lot last year.'

'That was Jones and Kilbride?'

'Aye. So, now we have Seymour pointing us in the direction of a house with a corpse in it, and it turns out the corpse was murdered by a gun we believe belongs to Bancroft's people.'

'So you brought Malky Seymour in.'

'Yep. He didn't talk, of course, though he perhaps unsurprisingly sent us in the direction of William Lansdowne. It being about time we spoke to Lansdowne anyway, I left Seymour in the cell, and went to have a word. By the time I got back...'

He left it there. Could feel her looking at him.

'By the time you got back?'

'Seymour's release had been authorised.'

'By whom?'

Buchan finally turned and looked at her, accompanying the look with a slow shrug.

'You're fucking kidding me?' said Hamilton.

Buchan didn't reply. He turned away. Somewhere there was a thought germinating at the back of his head, but he couldn't quite catch it yet.

'We have someone among us who's working for the Bancrofts?'

'I don't know anymore,' said Buchan. 'That was what I thought, but look at that in there. That's the Bancroft boys, one 'n all, and Malky Seymour isn't amongst them.'

'Jesus,' said Hamilton.

A head shake, a long, exhaled breath, then she added, 'God, this is a fucking nightmare.'

'Who'd you think Seymour might be working for?' she asked, when Buchan didn't respond.

'Genuinely don't know,' said Buchan. 'Could be the Poles. I mean, that would make sense. That would explain that in there. He would've been able to help the Poles get hold of all his people, then he himself wouldn't be amongst the dead. Then again, maybe he's jumped ship and he's working for Lansdowne. Maybe he's setting up shop on his own.'

'You think?'

'Well, no, I don't. I think he'd have taken Lenny along with him, if that was the case. Lenny was loyal to Seymour, not to Bancroft. So, it's not much to go on, but I just don't think it's that.

'Nevertheless, it does always leave the potential for the other thing. The fourth thing. The unidentified player. The unknown unknown, as someone somewhere would call it, coming out of nowhere. We thought the presence of the Baltazars was explaining everything, as they're so unknown to us, but perhaps it's the someone else, someone we can't even look up on the Internet and in Europol files.'

'I think we can stick with the Baltazars,' said Hamilton. 'You've uncovered enough to not have to worry about imaginary gangs created out of nothing.'

Buchan nodded, head dropping, looking at the dry ground, illuminated still by blue light. How long had he been standing here? How much time had he wasted?

'You got any leads on this Baltazar lot and their movements in Scotland?'

Buchan shook his head. It was time to move. Puffed out cheeks, he let out a long breath, turned to look at her.

That was it. That was the thought that was lurking somewhere in the dark recesses, needing to be dragged out. They needed to identify the corpse in the Baltazar house. If it turned out to be one of Baltazars own men – and certainly he wasn't anyone they'd come across in Glasgow before – they could possibly track his movements and pick up one or more of his companions.

'I need to get back, see how we're doing with identifying the victim at the Baltazar safe house,' he said.

'If you get him, you might get the others?'

'Yep.'

He straightened, finally, stretched his neck and shoulders, feeling a sense of purpose that hadn't been there for quite some time. There would be no rush of enthusiasm though, no burst of energy. The day had been too long, too bitter, and, with the death of Sgt Houston, too bloody sad for that.

'Go, inspector,' said Hamilton. 'Stay in touch.'

49

'How are we doing?' asked Buchan, walking into the open-plan.

Liddell, Kane, Cherry and Dawkins looked blankly back at him. Dawkins, in particular, looked drained and pale and thin and tired.

'I think, unless you have some other instruction for the team, we should go home,' said Liddell. 'Resume in the morning. Everyone needs some sleep, and that includes you.'

'No,' said Buchan, 'not yet. I'm not going to introduce any false drama or deadlines, nothing like *this finishes tonight*, but I'm not done yet. None of us are getting any decent sleep when we get home, not with this hanging over us. Have we identified the man we found dead at the Baltazar safe house yet?'

Three blank faces, and then Dawkins finally shook her head, an act of waking up, and she said, 'Yes, sorry, I saw that in the last hour. Sorry, there's been so much.'

'That's OK,' said Buchan. 'If we have a name, that's great.'

She typed quickly, her back straight, the room now waiting for her.

'Łukasz Kamiński,' she said, then she turned to face Buchan again. 'Known associate of the Baltazar gang for the last seven years.'

'OK, good,' said Buchan. 'We need to start scouring Europol databases, whatever access we've been given to the Baltazar files. Anything from the last seven years that implicates this guy and anyone he might have worked with. At any point in the last seven years, it doesn't matter. If we get names, and if we get faces, then we can start searching for their presence in Glasgow in the last few days.'

'Is this something that's going to get done best at one in the morning?' said Liddell.

'We can get started now,' said Buchan. 'We've had access to all sorts of databases today as we've run around after these people. We still have that access. Let's use it, the time of night is immaterial.'

'On it, boss,' said Kane, and Cherry nodded along with her.

Buchan and Liddell exchanged a look, Liddell nodding appreciatively at the efforts of the team.

'Leave us with it, inspector,' she said.

'Agnes is in the ops room?' asked Buchan, and Kane nodded.

'She's not great,' said Kane. 'I thought she should sit in here, but…'

'I'll have a word,' said Buchan, and he turned away.

*

He wondered if she might be sleeping, and that was why she'd wanted to be alone. Instead, wide awake, but trance-like, staring straight ahead at the wall over an opened laptop, the screen of which had long since shut down.

There was a small bandage on her chin, where she'd been struck by flying debris from the explosion that had killed Houston. Seeing the bandage reminded Buchan of Houston's death, much more than walking into the open-plan and not seeing him there, and he took a moment as the grief of it hit him squarely in the stomach. A silent gasp escaped the back of his throat, and he caught himself, stopped it happening again.

Took another moment. A clenching of the fists, a deep breath, a resetting of the narrative of the next five minutes.

There would be time for grief, and possibly there would time for tears if he still knew how to let them come, but not now.

Roth had not noticed his arrival.

'Hey,' he said.

He hesitated, he closed the door. When was it, how many hundreds of hours ago had it been that he'd been deciding to leave that door open when he'd been in here with Roth?

She turned, she half-smiled, but the smile was never making it all the way to her lips.

'How are you doing?' he asked.

She looked away, her eyes back on the same spot on the wall. She shook her head. Her hand drifted to her chin. Her face said she didn't know what to say. There were no words.

Buchan had a familiar moment of helplessness, and then he pulled out the seat next to her and sat down. He was the leader of the team, and this was as much a part of his job as the logistics and the organisation and the divvying up of tasks and the investigations. This, however, more than any other, would have previously been something he'd have handed on to one of the sergeants. And, more than likely, it would have been Houston, the more empathetic of the two. But here, even if Houston had still been with them, Buchan would have had to do this himself. He'd taken responsibility for Roth three months earlier, and was a long way from being able to relinquish it.

'You heard about the warehouse?' he said.

He wasn't sure whether he had compassion in him, but he made the judgement that talking about work at this stage was the best course. This is who Roth was. Or, at least, this was who Roth used to be.

She nodded.

'Nothing coming out of that investigation yet,' said Buchan. 'These people have been so thorough, I'm not sure anything will.'

'Sarge said it was horrible,' said Roth, finally speaking. Her voice sounded small.

'Yes.'

'You ever see anything like that before?'

This time Buchan's turn to answer without speaking. It was up to him to make sure they didn't wallow, however, that the conversation remained positive, moving forward rather than stagnating in discomfort and self-pity.

'We've got a name for the Polish guy we found shot in the head earlier in the day. We're trying to track down some more detail on him, see if we can identify any of his known associates within the gang, and by extension, if any of them have been registered, caught on camera, however it is, in Glasgow in the last few days.'

She nodded, managing to say, 'That's good.'

'Have you been able to find any more on *Incarnate*?' he asked, when silence threatened to return.

'No,' she said. 'When I filled you in earlier, I really had… you know, I'd extracted pretty much everything I could dig up from various records in Poland.' A pause, and then, 'Have you found out anything more? You said that Lansdowne had a copy?'

'He claims to,' said Buchan. 'I mean, he definitely has a book by that writer, and I meant to check the name to see if it translated…' He paused, he tried to remember, he tried to visualise the word, but there was nothing there. 'The book was in Polish. I'm presuming, without taking it for granted, that it's

---

167

at least a copy of the book we're looking for. Could it be *the* book? God knows. The whole thing smells kind of fishy, but it's hardly the weirdest thing to have happened today.' Looked at his watch, the day long since having ticked over into Wednesday. He didn't bother correcting himself.

'It is fishy,' she said, her voice gaining a little more strength. 'We work out the book we're looking for and, hey presto, the first guy you speak to has a copy.' She smiled weakly, and shook her head, dismissing the thought.

'What?' said Buchan, his voice softer, more encouraging than usual.

'I just thought, it's like that Python scene in the *Holy Grail*. '*He's already got one.*' We think this is all about this lost book, and Lansdowne's like, what, this? Just something I keep lying around.'

Buchan smiled.

'Monty Python is exactly what it's like.'

The smiles faded, the awfulness of the long day returned.

'I need to do something with this, with Lansdowne having the book, but I'm not sure what.'

'You've got to use it to lure people out,' she said. 'Maybe it's the real thing, maybe it's not. Maybe, in fact, everyone else knows Lansdowne has this blatant fake. But we should let them know.'

Buchan looked at his watch again, then cursed himself for caring about the time. It didn't matter. Everyone, regardless of who they were, was awake at the moment. All the players. No one was stopping for eight hours' sleep, because no one had the time for it.

'Make me a list of people, numbers, whatever, that we can call,' he said. 'Anyone you can think of in the entire damned city.'

'Then you post someone outside Lansdowne's place, and see who shows up? I don't suppose anyone's going to ring the doorbell.'

Buchan nodded.

Silence returned. He had nothing else to say. A moment, while they sat staring at each other from a couple of feet apart. His next movement was automatic, coming out of nowhere. He reached forward, he took hold of her hand, gently squeezed her cool fingers, then quickly withdrew.

'I can't say it'll be all right. It's already not all right, no matter how this plays out from here on in. But we need to work, we need to bring this thing to a close, we need to find Claire Avercamp, and we need to find whoever killed Ian. Then...'

Then they could face the awfulness of having watched their colleague die. Then Roth could face that, on top of not having recovered from her previous trauma.

He didn't say it.

She nodded. He stopped himself touching her hand again. He got to his feet and went to the door.

'Sir.'

He turned.

She swallowed. She gathered her words, forced them out.

'You won't have read Stefan Zweig.'

Under other circumstances he might have laughed at the question. Of course he'd never heard of Stefan Zweig, just as Roth would know.

'He wrote a novel called *Beware of Pity*.' A pause, and then she kind of smiled. 'Terrible name for a book, but... I thought I should mention it. Just, don't pity me, sir. I'll be fine. I'll sort myself out... I'll get there.'

Buchan had grown so that he wasn't so sure, even before today.

'I know you will,' he said, though it felt like lying.

He turned away, opened the door, left it open, and was gone.

———

50

'However this plays out, the landscape of the city, the crime landscape, is completely altered after tonight.'

Buchan and Kane were standing at the window of the open-plan, looking out on the night. The night, like the day, like all days, was coming in fits and starts. It seemed, however, that unlike most other days, this one was a month of investigation and drama poured into twenty-four hours. Or, at least, they could hope it was twenty-four hours. The thought of this lasting longer, that this day would be followed by something similar, was unthinkable. They were already braced for what the morning would bring politically. A police officer killed in a targeted attack, accompanied by the elimination of almost an entire gang, was going to have everyone from the First Minister down, dropping everything and demanding instant results.

There would be many, of course, celebrating the death of the crime gang. There would be little pity. However, Buchan knew, as did the rest of the police force, and anyone else who cared to give it more than surface analysis, that one gang being eliminated by another, just meant that the conquerors would take over the territory of the old. Nothing would change except, perhaps, for the worse.

Buchan took a drink of tea. Behind them, Cherry at his computer, Dawkins and Liddell on the phone. Outside, nothing was stirring. The river a flat calm, the lights of the opposite bank perfectly reflected in the smooth surface. Neither traffic nor pedestrians on the bridges, no cars on Clyde Street. The dead of night, the city asleep.

Except, they knew. Not everyone was asleep. The forces driving this evening forward were likely still at work.

'Can't think about that,' said Buchan, taking another drink. 'All we can do is play it as it lays, as the card sharps say.'

'One game at a time?' said Kane.

'Yes,' said Buchan. 'Let's deal with tonight, before we think about how bloody awful this is going to be tomorrow.'

He turned, and looked over the open-plan in the low light.

If this had been five p.m. in January and dark outside, all the lights would have been on, the place would have been bright, and buzzing with it. But this was a horror day, and no one wanted the overhead lights. The lighting was low, coming from the in-built desk lights of the partitions. It was enough, matching the sombre mood of the night.

Roth entered, looking a little more switched on than Buchan had seen her previously.

'I have a list of numbers, names, people we can notify about this copy of *Incarnate*. Players from all sides throughout the day. Not sure if you want to call them at this stage, or text, or…'

Liddell had hung up, said, 'Lansdowne's expecting you, inspector.'

'Thanks, boss,' said Buchan. 'Agnes, speak to the chief, the two of you work out how best to contact these people. You've included Reynolds and Savage?'

It felt odd, alien even, including the names of police colleagues, as though they might be suspects.

But they *were* suspects.

'Yep.'

'OK, thanks. Get to it,' he said, looking at Liddell with raised eyebrows, and she nodded.

'We'll do it now,' she said. 'And I believe we will call everyone on the list. As you suggest, not many players in this drama are going to be asleep tonight, and certainly none of those who are interested in this damned book will be.'

'Sergeant,' said Buchan, 'you're with me,' then he looked at Dawkins and Cherry who were working on contacts of Łukasz Kamiński and said, 'You'll let me know?' and they both answered in the affirmative, and then Buchan and Kane were on their way back out.

51

'Didn't you use to smoke?' said Lansdowne.

He had an amused, garrulous look about him, a glass of brandy in his hand, sitting in the same seat as previously, in the same elegant room of books and conspiracy. This was a room that spoke of late night meetings to plot crime and revenge, not police interrogation. This would be conducted entirely on Lansdowne's terms, but it was where Buchan needed to be.

Did he really suppose someone, having been alerted to Lansdowne's possession of a copy of *Incarnate*, would turn up here in the middle of the night? It seemed such an absurd leap, forcing the issue, trying to make something happen, trying to make something fall into place. He knew it rarely worked. Nevertheless, Baltazar and his people had proven themselves capable of anything. Breaking in to a family home at one-thirty a.m. would barely get a mention in the top five acts of the day's outrages.

'I quit five years ago,' said Kane, little time for the casual conversation, the faux civility.

'You heard about Davie and his gang?' said Buchan.

He'd taken the seat directly across from Lansdowne, Kane had stayed on her feet. Her intention was to wander around the room, studying the contents of the library, giving Lansdowne something to be distracted by. Maybe it would unsettle him, maybe it would be utterly meaningless. The chances of him having anything else of interest to a police officer in this room were slim to non-existent.

'There's talk. All dead, are they?'

It hadn't been on the news yet, though it was coming, and it certainly would be by the morning TV shows.

'Mostly,' said Buchan.

'Mostly, eh? Someone escaped the bloodbath? Who was that?'

'How did you get to hear about it?' asked Buchan.

'Word's going around,' said Lansdowne. He smiled, he took another drink. He cast a glance at Kane, who had turned

---

away and was looking at the spines of books. 'Couldn't possibly reveal my sources.'

'You any idea who might be responsible?'

'This Polish mob, I presume. I mean, Davie mostly ran the joint around here, didn't he? No big admission from me there. There was a time we could compete on level terms, but after the, what-d'you-call-it, the Parkland raid, that was... man, that was a raid. You lot never did manage to pin it on him, did you? That was like getting a cash injection from the Saudis. That was like Newcastle or Man City getting transformed from a bunch of spanners. And then, of course....' And he finished the thought with a laugh, the smirk at the end of it not leaving his face.

'Of course, what?' said Buchan.

'I think it's pretty well known around these parts that they have someone *on the inside*.' Another laugh. 'Maybe it's one of you two.'

'It's not,' said Kane, turning. 'You any idea who it is?'

The smirk was still there.

'I wish,' said Lansdowne. 'I mean, far as I'm aware all you coppers are straight as a die. Barely a bent one amongst you, just this one rogue individual, who unfortunately fell into the clutches of Davie Boy. Of course, as we've discussed, Davie had the resources. Maybe now we'll be able to get this character on our team. He'll have to take a pay cut, but if we're the only show in town.'

'I don't think you're going to be the only show in town,' said Buchan. Then, quickly, 'Tell us about *Incarnate*.'

Lansdowne wasn't for responding to quick questions. He wasn't going to let Buchan control the pace of the discussion. Another drink, another laugh to himself.

'Sounds like a wonderful book, inspector,' he said after the laugh had died away. 'Too bad I can't read it. Might get it translated sometime, we'll see. But it's not top of the list, let's put it that way.'

'How did you get it?'

'How did I get what?'

'Your copy of *Incarnate*.'

'Ah, that. Not sure. I thought I said that earlier. Anyway, it's not here now.'

'Why?'

Another drink, another toying of the conversation.

'Here's the thing. I'm the outsider here. I'm the, what

would you say, the spectator. The innocent bystander even, since I don't really care to watch that much. This whole shitshow is between you and this Polish mob and Davie Bancroft. Seems to me, by the way, that you lot are getting just as much of an arse handing as Davie, so I wouldn't be booking anywhere for breakfast, you know what I'm saying? I wouldn't be planning ahead.'

'Where's the book?'

'Right, the book, the book. I have zero idea what's going on here. I've got nothing. And you keep turning up here with your news and your views and your questions, and I'm like, I don't want dragged into this. This is a riot in a turd factory. I don't want anything to do with this crap. And then, from nowhere, you pull this book out your arse, like it means something. And the only thing it can mean, is that people are looking for it, and the trouble is, I've got it. Time to lay low. Time to keep my head down, and keep the book out of the way. We want nothing to do with this.'

'Your innocence is heartwarming.'

'Thanks.'

'Where's the book?'

'By the way, I'm hoping here that you've no' told anyone I've got it. Because, to be honest, outside of my lot, you're the only one who knew. So if anything should happen, well that would mean you'd thrown us under the bus. It'd mean you'd called up the dogs and said, you don't know where to look for this book? Let me point you in the right direction.

'Would that be the kind of thing you'd say, inspector? I mean, maybe you're the insider after all. Maybe this would be some sort of quid pro quo for you. He scratches your back, you land me in the shit with my competitors.' A pause, and then another barked laugh, 'Of course, my competitors are now dead.'

'You seem very unconcerned about the Baltazar gang,' said Buchan. 'They may now consider themselves your competitors.'

'We'll deal when we need to deal, inspector. And unless you've called up everyone and their granny to let them know where they might find a copy of *Incarnate*, that can wait for another day.'

Lansdowne was the person Buchan had known he would be. With the exception of this rogue copy of *Incarnate* – real or fake, at this stage it barely mattered – nothing had been revealed by their three conversations so far. They could have another three, or another three hundred, and nothing would likely be revealed.

So why was he here?

'Too bad about Sgt Houston, by the way,' said Lansdowne. 'Seemed like a decent enough copper. Bit soft maybe, a bit too compassionate for a polis I often thought. Wondered if he was gay, sometimes, you know. Presumably, though, at least we can say he wasn't Bancroft's inside operative. Unless that was why he was killed, of course.'

Kane moved swiftly, unable to stop herself. A small room, one step, and she hit Lansdowne violently across the face with an open hand, the slap loud and sharp in the night.

Buchan winced. Kane stood back, gritting her teeth, cursing herself and her lack of discipline.

Lansdowne, however, continued to dictate the narrative. He lifted his drink, he took a sip, he rubbed the side of his face.

'I asked for that, sergeant,' he said. 'I apologise.'

'We told everyone who's still alive that you have the book,' said Buchan, doing what he could to exercise any control of the conversation. 'And now that I'm sitting here, I realise that you played us, and that that was exactly what you intended us to do.'

'Oh, surely not,' said Lansdowne. 'You asked about a book, I happened to have a copy, that was all. Didn't realise at the time that all this, all these deaths, all this mayhem, was going to be related to it. If I had, to be honest, I might just have let you take it after all. Too bad it's not here now, though.'

'Where is it?'

'I'd need to speak to Brendan.'

'Get hold of Brendan, then.'

'Very heavy sleeper, Brendan. And with all the shenanigans, I told him he could have the day off. Reckon he might have popped a couple of sleeping tabs, likely won't emerge from his bed until two tomorrow afternoon. I'd say he's earned his rest.'

'You think anyone's going to come here tonight looking for this book?' said Kane.

'Now that the word's out? Interesting...'

He stroked his chin, took another drink, sub-consciously rubbed the side of his face. There was a red mark where Kane had struck him.

'That's a decent question,' said Lansdowne, his words, his

actions, still performative. It would be nice, thought Buchan, to be able to break through the bullshit, but he didn't know how to do it. 'Depends who you told, I suppose. Who did you tell, Inspector Buchan? I mean, I expect if you informed Sky News and the Daily Record, they'll be here any minute.'

Buchan had another *Dammit, Bill*, on the tip of his tongue, but he didn't bother. Looked at his watch, looked at Kane, rubbed an imaginary itch on his chin.

'I think I'll take that cup of tea,' said Buchan.

'I never offered you a cup of tea.'

'You did when I came earlier.'

'I don't remember.'

'Well, then I appreciate you making it even more. Tea, sergeant?' he asked, and Kane nodded.

Lansdowne, unhappy perhaps at having his performance matched by the officers, allowed the first scowl of the night to cross his face, and then he pushed himself up off his seat.

'Fine. I'll put the kettle on. I won't pretend to know where to find the teabags.'

'We'll help you look.'

'I'm not sure you will. Come on, I'm not leaving you two in here.'

Lansdowne tightened the chord on the dressing gown, then led them down a corridor, past paintings of nineteenth-century winter maritime scenes, into a large kitchen.

There was a woman there, dressed mostly in black. Obvious bulge beneath her thin, dark coat. Night security.

'This is Tania,' said Lansdowne. 'Say hello to the inspector and the sergeant.'

'Seems late,' said Tania.

She was at a small table at the back of the large kitchen, looking at a laptop, the cold light illuminating her face. She was the most attractive security guard either Kane or Buchan had ever seen. Nothing about her face or her demeanour suggested it was two a.m.

'A hero's work is never done,' said Lansdowne, and he barked another laugh.

Tania watched the two officers for a moment, allowed herself a nod at Kane, and then turned back to the screen.

'I've got green, I've got regular, I've got regular decaf, I've got Earl Grey, I've got jasmine, I've got some sort of Christmas spiced thing my daughter-in-law gave us. Fucking terrible by the way, but some people like it. Got this other thing, but I can never remember how to pronounce it.'

'Builders is fine,' said Kane, and Buchan said, 'Same,' and Lansdowne put out four mugs, a teabag inside each one.

Having done that, he leant on the counter, took a moment, then turned. Now his focus was on Buchan, and Buchan could tell in the act of stopping and thinking and turning, Lansdowne had made the decision to properly engage. It didn't mean he'd be any more forthcoming, but at least it would likely be less irritating.

'Tell me about the warehouse,' said Lansdowne.

Well, it was something, Buchan supposed. It was positive engagement, and it wasn't like the story wasn't going to be all over the news in the morning. A few specific names aside, there was little to hide.

'The victims were all suspended from the same central beam. It wasn't an ex-meat factory or anything, it wasn't designed for it, but the internal structure of the roof contained this thick, metal beam running the length of the building. Chains had been slung around it, at the end of the chains a meat hook, which was thrust into the base of the neck at the back of each victim.'

The kettle started to rumble slowly. Lansdowne grimaced. Five minutes earlier he would have flippantly said, 'Sounds nasty,' but the show was over, the facetiousness gone from his voice.

'They'd all had their throats slit,' continued Buchan. 'They were all dead before they were suspended. We turned up, wary in case the whole thing had been booby-trapped...'

'How'd you find it?'

'They led us there.'

'Shit.'

'Yeah,' said Buchan. 'Shit.'

The kettle continued to rumble, getting louder, then the quiet ring of Buchan's phone. He was regarding Lansdowne warily the whole time. Took his phone from his pocket, checked the caller. Constable Harkness, currently sitting in a vehicle seventy yards up the road.

'Incoming, sir,' said Harkness.

'How many?'

'Just the one.'

'K, thanks.'

Buchan hung up.

The kettle clicked off, the rumble and spit and bubble of boiling water died away.

'You have a visitor,' said Buchan.

'It's a popular house,' said Lansdowne, his tone still dry and wary. Nevertheless, in an act that at first seemed as flippant as his previous tone, he lifted another mug down from the cupboard, popped the teabag in, and then poured five cups.

'Should just've made a pot,' said Lansdowne. 'Moira'll be mad if she gets up.'

There was a noise at the front door, it opened, footsteps entering the hallway, the door closed. Lansdowne did not react. Tania, the security for the night, continued to look at her laptop.

Buchan and Kane shared a gaze, then Buchan couldn't help the eye roll as he turned back to Lansdowne, and said, 'What are we missing?'

The door to the kitchen opened. Malky Seymour walked in. He stopped for a minute, he looked around the room. Dark circles around his eyes that hadn't been there seven hours previously, his face strained and tired.

He nodded at Buchan and Kane, acknowledged Tania, said, 'Boss,' to Lansdowne, then he turned back to Buchan and jerked his thumb in the direction of the door.

'You might want to have a word with your Baker Street Irregular out there, Buchan,' he said. 'Can see him a mile off. One of Baltazar's lot turns up here, the kid'll have a bullet in the back of the head before he knows what's hit him.'

52

They were sitting round the table, two minutes later, Buchan with a constant eye on his watch. There was some explanation coming, if it could be trusted, but it was unlikely to tell them where Baltazar was, and where they'd find Claire Avercamp.

'So, what d'you want to know?' asked Seymour.

He took a slurp of tea, set it back down.

'First of all, tell us how you come to be here,' said Buchan.

He wanted Cherry or Dawkins to call, he wanted sight of Polish operatives in Glasgow in the last few days.

Seymour glanced at Lansdowne, who nodded an understated green light.

'I was stagnating at Davie's. Davie was a control freak, never let anyone else do anything. And then there's that nasty little son of his. You believe the little bastard's at Gordonstoun at the moment? I mean, Jesus H Christ, man. You're a two-bit gangster in Parkheid, there's no need to send your flippin' kid to private school. What a dickhead. Anyway, that was the plan. Long-term. Davie runs the ship until little Quentin's ready to take over. And the likes of me, experience coming out my arse, and total oversight and command of the entire operation, fuck all. Know your place. You're not family, you've got no more rungs on the ladder to climb. But you know too much, so don't think for a second about leaving.'

He snorted. There was no trace of humour or lightness of tone. Regardless of any bitterness he'd felt towards Davie Bancroft, it was still his work colleagues of the past few years who'd ended up dead. Seymour was as hollowed out as any of them after what had happened.

'So you offered your services to Mr Lansdowne?'

'Aye. Everyone could see he'd no succession plan in place. Those boys of his…'

Head shake, which Lansdowne joined, adding, 'Fucking useless the pair of them.'

'I thought, come over, make myself useful. Might be able to inveigle my way in, see how I get on.'

'You're on the shortlist at least,' said Lansdowne, 'which is better than you were over there.'

'You never worried Davie would find out?' asked Kane. 'Must've been a tough secret to keep.'

'Davie knew.'

No reaction from Lansdowne. He was staring darkly at the table, tea travelling intermittently between table top and his lips.

'He supported you infiltrating the Lansdownes, thinking you'd be an undercover agent, when, in fact, you were a double agent.'

'Exactly,' said Seymour. 'Just like you get in the movies.'

'How could William here be sure you weren't a triple agent, ultimately answerable to Davie? Or to the Baltazars for that matter.'

'Never trust a crook, eh?'

'Something like that.'

'You'll have to ask him.'

Buchan looked at Lansdowne, Lansdowne, whose mood appeared to be sinking the entire time, grunted, 'We had someone else in there keeping an eye on him.'

'The fuck was that?' asked Seymour.

'Doesn't matter. Dead now.'

'How'd you manage to avoid the round-up today then?' asked Kane.

'You lot had taken me into custody. So the Baltazars made a coordinated swoop, just like the antique shops. Took all our crew off the board in one go, right at the moment youse lot were demonstrating to me, by your shitty questions, that you had absolutely no clue what was going on.' A beat, and then, 'Well, they took them all off the board at that point except Davie, as obviously they'd got him this morning.'

'And Lenny Harmon,' said Buchan.

'What about him?'

'He handed himself in to us some time after we released you. So he wasn't picked up the same time as everyone else.'

'Little Lenny, eh? He was always pretty under the wire, because that's where Davie wanted him. Out of the way. Didn't trust him. So how come I heard he ended up dead?'

'We let him go.'

Seymour and Lansdowne stared grimly across the table. No more needed to be said. They understood.

'So, you were released from police custody, you start

making calls, there's nobody around?' said Buchan.

'Aye.'

Seymour took another long drink.

'I went round to my place, but I took a cab. Got him to stop a block away, nipped through a couple of gardens. Oh aye, got a right eyeful in one of them, by the way. Sun was out, cannae blame the lassie, out there, butt naked in her back garden. She probably called you lot to complain, but good luck to her getting hold of one of youse on a day like this, eh?'

'Nice tits?' said Lansdowne.

'God, aye.' He made the appropriate gesture. 'Massive.'

'Can we stay on point, please?' said Buchan.

'What happened at your house?' asked Kane.

'There were some guys there. Didn't recognise them. I'm assuming it's some of this mob Baltazar brought in.' He looked between Buchan and Kane, glanced at Lansdowne, got nothing in return. 'This is some serious escalation, by the way,' he said.

'Thanks, Malky,' said Kane, 'we wouldn't have worked that out otherwise.'

'Chippy one, this,' said Lansdowne, with a nod in Kane's direction.

'That's when I realised. I mean, I thought you guys had just decided to release me, which seemed a bit odd.'

'We didn't,' said Buchan.

'Aye, I get that now. Didn't make sense.'

'We thought you had someone on the inside,' said Kane.

'On your inside? That Davie had a contact with the police?'

'Yes.'

'God, no. He'd have loved that shit. Been trying for ages, never could find anyone bent enough.' A bitter, dry laugh, and then, 'Strange though it sounds.'

Buchan looked at Lansdowne, who caught his eye and shrugged.

'I was wrong,' muttered Lansdowne.

Buchan held the look for a moment, but that was all he was getting, then he turned back to Seymour.

'D'you know if the police had someone on your inside, inside the Bancroft gang?'

Seymour stared intently across the table, but the eyes said that he was thinking about it, running through the possibilities.

'I doubt it,' he said. 'I mean, look at me, no one had any idea I was answering back to the big man here, so who knows?

But I can't think of anyone. And if there was… they're dead.'

'So, when you got released…?' said Kane, her eyes narrowing. 'It wasn't us, and it wasn't from within your gang.'

Seymour shrugged.

'That's what I realised. Presumably this Baltazar lot have someone on the inside, someone in Police ruddy Scotland, and they got me released so I could be rounded up with all the others.' A pause, and then he added, 'These are serious people.'

'How many of them at your house?' asked Buchan.

'I didn't go inside to count. Three that I could see. No pretence about it, by the way. They were practically standing around with AK-47s under their arms. Looked almost paramilitary. That was some scary shit, by the way. I thought then, if they've taken Davie, and now they've rounded up our crew, we are completely fucked.'

'What did you do?'

'Got on a train to Dumbarton.'

'You got on a train to Dumbarton?'

'Aye.'

'Why?'

'Out of the way. Knew I'd get a bit of dinner, keep my head down, wait and see how this was going to play out. Plus, up until eleven-forty-eight, there was a train back into town.'

'What brought you back?'

'The last fucking train, man. Called William, he said I could come here. Nae cunt wants to spend the night in Dumbarton unless they absolutely have to.'

Buchan looked at his watch. Wished the phone would ring. Felt like they were trapped here, needing to hear this, needing to find out what it was Seymour could tell them, but knowing it would unlikely take them anywhere nearer Baltazar.

'OK, the rest,' said Buchan.

'The rest?'

'This whole thing is about *Incarnate*?'

'You know about that now, eh? How'd you work that out?'

Lansdowne grunted.

'I have staff who know what they're doing,' said Buchan. 'This is about *Incarnate*?'

'Aye.'

Seymour nodded, took a long drink, shook his head at the thought of how it had started.

'This guy, this Jan Baltazar character, wants a book. That's it. He wants some shitty little book, that literally no one else wants. But the guy who has it wants him to pay for it, and Jan insists he shouldn't have to. Anyway, to cut a lot of years short, it ends up in Scotland. This Baltazar mob have no operation here. He subcontracts it to Davie. We do the job, a couple of their guys come over. At this point, Davie should've given the Polish guys the book and said, there you go, thanks very much, nice doing business with you, we'll look you up next time we need to steal something in Warsaw.'

'But Davie was an idiot.'

'Oh, aye. I says to him, don't do it. He says, ach, it'll be fine. I'm on top of it, let's just milk the situation for a bit.'

'Why'd it take so long for the whole thing to play out?' asked Kane.

Seymour breathed out heavily, took another drink of tea, settled the mug back on the table. Buchan noticed the glance cast between Lansdowne and Tania, his security. Couldn't read anything into it. Maybe that had just been Lansdowne telling her he needed to go to bed. Maybe he was telling her she needed to go with him.

'One of Davie's brilliant plans. The two guys who come over, they don't actually know what they're coming for. Our man Jan paying for his decision to make sure no one knows too much. But he doesn't want to risk moving the entire stash of stolen goods back across the continent, so he's had to trust Davie with the name of the book out of the haul that's most important to him. Davie, in a stroke of fucking genius, sends the two guys back to Poland *with the wrong book*. He then alerts immigration in Poland to these two notorious gangsters passing through the airport with stolen goods. They get picked up, the books get impounded. Baltazar thinks his precious book is now in a lock-up at police HQ at Warsaw fucking airport. Davie's laughing.'

'But what good does it do him?' asked Buchan. 'Davie didn't want the book, no one else wants the book, so there's no market for it, other than this one guy, who's obviously going to be pissed off when he finds out Davie still has it.'

Seymour was nodding by the time Buchan had finished. 'I know. Every eejit knew. I can play him, says Davie.' Seymour made a small gesture at the futility of the plan. 'I think Davie genuinely thought he'd come up with something brilliant, some amazing plan the likes of which you'd be lucky to find in a Guy Ritchie film, man, and you know what? He never thought of anything. And then…'

'And then Jan Baltazar found out,' said Kane.

'Exactly. A couple of weeks back. And he called up and says, I'd like my book back, please, and Davie, the daft bastard, says, let's talk. Jan hangs up on him, and there's been no more talking. Until today. Jan, it turns out, has got a pretty fucking loud voice.'

'You had no idea it was coming?'

Seymour let out a long sigh from puffed up cheeks, head shaking. He looked at Lansdowne, Lansdowne gave him a glance, something that said, you're on your own, keep talking if you want, and looked back at the table.

'Everyone knew something was coming. Everyone. It was like some fucking war movie, or zombie film or something. Every fucker holed up, protecting the vulnerable points as best they can, but they don't know where the attack's coming from. Davie was a fucking monster. Knew he'd fucked up, man. Just waiting for it. Tried to get hold of this Baltazar guy. Not a chance. Stupid prick was lashing out all over the place, taking it out on every fucker. Pretty ugly.'

'You didn't seem so worried when we were talking to you earlier today,' said Kane.

Seymour shook his head, stared at the table. A movement of the shoulders, lifted the tea, put it to his lips, didn't take a drink, set it back down again.

'I genuinely thought they'd come for Davie, then they'd deal with whoever's left. I was waiting to hear from them.' He swallowed, finally looked up. Eyes on Buchan. 'I guess I did, right?'

'You seem loquacious,' said Buchan, unwilling to be sucked into Seymour's grim introspection. 'Malky Seymour never talks. The Malky Seymour we interviewed earlier had nothing to say. Now, here you are, spilling the beans.'

Seymour shook his head, a brief, rueful look flitted across his face before the haunted expression returned.

'Whatever. I'll likely wake up in the morning, if I get to wake up in the morning, and think I should've kept my mouth shut. But this is me. Thought we were in the game, thought we had a chance to play it, maybe get something from it. Turns out we're the ball, and all we're getting is a kicking.'

Again Lansdowne grunted.

'Where does Claire Avercamp fit in?' asked Kane.

'She still alive?'

'We don't know.'

'She was sniffing around, making some shitty movie about the book heist. She was making inroads. Investigative journalist. Ha. What a joke. But Davie was getting worried she'd find out what had happened. Put two and two together 'n all that.'

'Why would she have been able to do it if Baltazar couldn't?'

He looked between the two of them, Kane to Buchan, back to Kane.

'She had smarts,' said Seymour, tapping the side of his head. 'Then she had someone on the inside feeding her info.'

'Starbuck?'

Seymour smiled stupidly, then quickly wiped it from his face.

'Was wondering if it was you,' said Buchan, and Seymour laughed bitterly.

'Aye, whatever. Starbuck. Stupid name. She thought she was using me, I was playing her, really. Just having a laugh, poor bitch.'

'You told her it was all about a Chopin manuscript?'

'Aye. I was doing that thing, you know. Feeding her truths, half-truths and downright lies, whatever suited me and/or Davie best at any given moment.'

'That was a complex web you were spinning,' said Kane.

'Aye, hen, it was.'

'Did you have complete control of it?'

'Ha.'

'You killed the Pole at the Baltazar safe house, then sent us to find him? That was all part of the web?'

He smirked again, and again the smile quickly vanished, and he made a gesture to dismiss the conversation so far.

'Sounds like you're accusing me of murder,' he says.

'What happened with Avercamp?' said Buchan.

'Davie decided to take her out the game, and we just had to go along with it. Set her up, make it look like she'd just gone off on a massive bender. He hadn't decided what to do with her. Some of the guys were saying, might as well just slit her throat, dispose of her body, but he was like that... Hadn't made up his mind yet. I don't know, think he fancied her. Maybe he wanted a shag. Maybe he got one. Or took one. You can ask her, if she's no' deid.'

185

'Some of the guys in that sentence meaning you?' said Kane.

'There we go with the whole murder thing again,' said Seymour.

'You're telling a story, while admitting nothing?'

Another small shrug, then he took a drink, and set the cup back down on the table.

Silence returned. Buchan and Kane kept their eyes on Seymour, Seymour kept his eyes on the table. He wasn't avoiding their stares, he genuinely looked shell-shocked with what had happened. Finally, he lifted his head.

'You get names for everyone in that warehouse?'

Buchan nodded.

'We knew them all.'

'Andy Summers? Caroline? Wee Malcolm?'

'All of them,' said Buchan.

'Fuck me.'

And his head dropped.

'You know where it is now?' asked Kane.

Seymour didn't respond, then finally raised his eyes.

'Where what is?'

'*Incarnate.*'

Seymour held his gaze for a moment, then glanced at Lansdowne, then sort of shrugged in Buchan's direction.

The tale was in the wordless reply. He'd taken it, he'd given it to Lansdowne, it wasn't in his power to give that information, and he obviously didn't know that Lansdowne had shown Buchan the book earlier.

Buchan glanced at Lansdowne, who was also keeping his head down. Buchan thought he recognised the smirk on his lips. Then he took a quick glance at Tania. Tania was sitting at the end of the table, silent throughout. Sometimes the silent ones were the ones to worry about. Sometimes they just didn't have anything to say.

She caught Buchan's eye, holding his gaze until he looked away.

The phone vibrated in Buchan's pocket. A call rather than a text.

'What about this guy Maplethorpe?' he asked.

Nothing. Seymour looked like he had drifted off, thoughts receding into darkness. The phone continued to vibrate.

'What about Maplethorpe?' repeated Buchan, and finally

Seymour lifted his head.

'I don't know who that is,' he said.

Buchan glanced at Lansdowne, who shook his head, then Buchan turned to Tania. Tania stared dead-eyed back at him. The phone still vibrated.

Buchan reached into his pocket, checked the caller, answered the phone as he rose from the table, aiming to take the call out in the corridor. Said, 'Just a second,' then to Seymour, 'I'll need you to tell us where they were holding Avercamp,' and Seymour stared blankly back, 'And the addresses of all your other houses.'

Seymour looked unimpressed, gave a sideways glance in the direction of Lansdowne, who shook his head.

'Avercamp at least,' said Kane, and at this Lansdowne made a small gesture to indicate it was OK, then Seymour said, 'Sure, whatever. It's no' like she'll still be there,' and Buchan glanced at Kane to indicate she should take the address, then he walked out into the corridor and said, 'What have you got?'

53

This house looked a little more lived in than the other safe houses they'd visited that day. An ex-council house in the middle of Springburn, an average looking place in an average looking estate, just like all the safe houses. That was the point of them, of course. Their safety came from their anonymity.

The room she'd been kept in was obvious. Blinds drawn. A single bed, iron bed posts, handcuffs left dangling. Some signs of blood, but nothing that suggested a mortal wound. Innumerable stains on the old, faded sheets, but impossible to tell from first look how recent any of them were. On the floor next to the bed, a single plate, cleared of food. An empty bottle of wine. Off the room, a toilet and a basin.

'Nice of Bancroft's boys to feed her habit,' said Kane, indicating the bottle.

'Without wishing to give them any credit,' said Buchan, 'under the circumstances, it wasn't the dumbest thing they could have done.'

'Low bar, given everything else,' said Kane, and Buchan smiled grimly.

The smile went, they walked back through to the sitting room. There was nothing in this room to indicate this was anything other than a normal family home. A sofa, a single armchair, a large television on a long, low cabinet. Bland pictures on the wall of the type hanging on walls everywhere. A beige carpet, a blue rug. On a side table, two wine glasses, one stained red. A coat dumped on the single chair. Kane had already been through the pockets.

There was nothing to find here, nothing in the main bedroom or the kitchen or the bathroom or in any of the cupboards that one would not expect to find, that would help them in their quest.

They hadn't really expected to find anything, anyway. This was checking because, of course, it had to be checked. They couldn't risk missing the obvious. They couldn't spend the night scouring the city for the missing Avercamp, if it was going to turn out that a bullet had been put in her head and her body dumped where it had been kept. Now, at least, they knew Baltazar's people had elected to take her with them, and if they'd done that, there was a reasonable chance she was still alive. It had, after all, only been a few hours, despite the avalanche of catastrophic events enveloping the city.

'We should get back,' said Buchan. He looked at his watch. Two-thirty was becoming three o'clock, the night passing by, daylight only a couple of hours away. Buchan felt no tiredness, driven on by a restless fear, a need to see the working day end with something positive to cling to.

Cherry had called when they were with Seymour and Lansdowne. No breakthrough yet, no CCTV leading them straight to wherever the Baltazars had set up camp on arrival in Scotland. Nevertheless, progress. They had identified seven men with whom Łukasz Kamiński had previously worked, and they had established that at least three of them were currently in Scotland. Now they were running facial recognition software on every piece of CCTV footage they could get hold of from the previous week. Concentrating on Glasgow, but allowing themselves to go further afield. It wasn't as though the crew wouldn't have been able to base themselves elsewhere, and then move in and out of the city. 'In fact,' Cherry had said to Buchan, 'that might've made more sense for them.'

'Give Danny a call, please,' said Buchan, as they closed the door of the house, and walked down the short path, 'see what progress they've made. If there's somewhere else we can go on the way back to the office…'

Kane called. There was nowhere else for them to go.

Feeling the same tortuous crawl of fear, the same grip on his stomach that he'd felt most of the day, Buchan drove back into the centre of town.

54

The slight hope they'd allowed themselves with the identification of confederates of Łukasz Kamiński had evaporated. Software being run, checks being made, nothing positive having yet come of it. A couple of the men had been caught on camera, but one was in Glasgow Central station, another walking along the banks of the Clyde, on the opposite side but not far from SCU HQ. The latter might have been because he'd been checking the place out. The lay of the land, the movement of the staff in and out of the building. They had nothing of him on this side of the river, or too close to the building, so they couldn't be sure.

Buchan was in his spot. They were leaving him alone, hoping perhaps that the silence would be enough for him to think of a way out of the quagmire. They all still thought him capable, and likely, to come up with a breakthrough, though Buchan himself had long since given up such self-belief.

Liddell exchanged a silent glance with Kane, and then got up and stood beside Buchan. He acknowledged her with the most imperceptible of nods, and they stood in silence together for a minute, that became two and then three.

Finally.

'I know,' he said. 'I'm not leaving though, but everyone else should. Get a few hours' sleep.'

'You don't need sleep all of a sudden?'

'I'm not tired.'

'You're also not functioning properly. Not thinking properly at any rate,' she added, in response to his raised eyebrow. 'We all need to stand down for the evening. We all –'

'Fine,' said Buchan sharply, 'I'm fine with that. All of you, go. You should go.'

He turned and looked at the few others in the room, his tone still sharp.

'Really, you don't have to do what I do,' he said. 'You should get some sleep. Ellie, maybe you could take Agnes back to your place if she's not comfortable going home or going back to mine.'

'Inspector,' said Liddell quietly, insistently, 'we will all go, and I'll speak to Agnes, but you need to go home too. You're tired, and this is an order.' He stared harshly at her, and she returned the look. 'And if you talk to me in that tone again, I'll have you up on a charge of insubordination.'

Buchan gritted his teeth, thought of something glib and stupid and superficial, an inane line about how she was working for him this evening, which he could deliver like he was in some godawful US cop show, but the line wouldn't formulate, and he tried to relax his jaw, expel the tension he knew was evident in his face, and said, 'OK, OK, you're right,' thinking all the time that fine, he could go home, but he was going to work when he got there, and if he discovered anything new, he would act on it there and then.

'Thank you.' A moment, Buchan did not move, and then Liddell indicated the three others in the room. 'You can give the order now, inspector.'

The door opened, and Constable Roth entered, holding a laptop.

'Got something useful,' she said, oblivious to the tension of the moment. For what it was worth, the tension vanished with her entrance.

She came round, and set the laptop down on an empty desk. Kane leaned across, Cherry and Dawkins got up and stood behind Roth, as did Liddell and Buchan.

On screen, a CCTV image of Piotr Kuczyński, one of the Poles Cherry and Dawkins had been searching for.

'Nice job, Agnes,' said Cherry.

'Where'd you get him?' asked Buchan.

'I was thinking about what you were saying about William Lansdowne,' said Roth. 'His attitude just sounded a little off, the way you were describing it. I just had a hunch. What if Baltazar and Lansdowne are working together? I mean, it might make sense for this Baltazar fellow, right? He doesn't know Glasgow, it's why he got Bancroft involved in the first place. Now, he wants to make a quick, fast strike in the city.'

They nodded along with her.

'The enemy of my enemy is my friend,' said Cherry.

'So, we've just been ignoring Lansdowne most of the day. At least, we've been ignoring his people. I ran checks on the four different places around town where he has known warehouse facilities. This one's outside the city, but it's handily not far from the old Silverwood plant. That's no longer in operation, of course, but there's still heavy machinery in that building, so they still have CCTV all over the outside of the place. More, in fact, than people realise because everyone just thinks it's more or less derelict.'

'It's half a mile away from the Lansdowne warehouse though,' said Cherry.

'It is, but here, in this image,' and she indicated the one on the left, two figures sitting in a car, 'we have Kuczyński, right?'

Cherry and Dawkins nodded.

'And this, on the left, is the same car, thirty seconds or so later, turning into the Lansdowne place.'

'Bingo,' said Buchan.

Mind racing, all of a sudden. The surliness of two minutes earlier now gone, replaced by a renewed burst of urgency.

'Too simple?' he said, looking around at the others.

'I don't think so,' said Cherry.

'Nope,' said Kane. 'This is exactly what we've been looking for. Let's get out there.'

'Two cars, in case we need them on the other side. Sam, with me. Danny, Ellie, you OK?'

'Sure, we'll take the Ford,' said Cherry.

'Boss?' said Buchan, thinking at the last he should run it by her before he disappeared into the night once again.

Liddell looked unsure. Held Buchan's gaze, a measured look to counter his urgency.

'Boss?' he repeated.

'Every officer in Scotland is on this,' said Liddell. 'Perhaps we should get one of the locals to take it, they can report back. We can continue to work on this, see what else we can dig up.'

'There are people playing more than one side,' said Buchan, his voice edgy, then he stopped, controlled his tone, making sure he sounded less melodramatic. 'It's not just Malky Seymour. The Baltazars, as far as we're aware, have someone on the inside. *Our* inside. We can't afford to bring anyone else in on this.'

They held the look, a short, silent exchange, broken by Roth.

'It's fine, ma'am,' she said. 'I can keep looking. I've got seven different programs running at the moment as it is. There's no need for six of us to be doing it. They can go, you and I can stay here doing this. We find anything, we call. Meanwhile, we can be sure this raid won't be compromised.'

'Boss?' said Buchan, insistent, as soon as Roth had finished.

'Inspector, can I remind you how many people the Baltazars have killed today? How many individual operatives they had on the bookshops operation? How many people it must have taken to exterminate the Bancroft gang? And now, it would seem, they have joined forces with William Lansdowne. That is a large facility up there. There could be a lot of resistance.'

'We can't afford for them to know we're coming,' said Buchan. 'But you're right, I shouldn't knowingly put the others in danger. We need to –'

'I'm coming too, boss,' said Dawkins, quickly presaging agreement from Cherry and Kane.

'We can't risk it,' said Buchan to Liddell. 'We call it in, doesn't matter how quickly the locals get there, by the time they arrive, the Baltazars, or whoever's there, are gone.'

'And are you going to arm yourself before you go?'

They had been there before. And they all remembered that it was Houston who had discharged his weapon the last time.

'As soon as we get sight of people, as soon as we know they're there, we call it in,' said Buchan. 'In fact, we call you, and you can call whoever you think it best to call at that stage. Whoever it's safest to call. We're not going to walk into a warehouse, unarmed, and tell thirty armed men and women they're under arrest.'

Another long, cold stare, and then Liddell nodded and said, 'OK, go. And I want to know when you've arrived, and before you've made any move.'

Buchan nodded, the others followed, and then they were gone, quickly out of the open-plan, their sense of urgency not allowing them to stand in the lift, taking the stairs two at a time.

*

The door of the open-plan closed, and then Liddell and Roth were left in silence. Suddenly, awkwardly, Roth felt uncomfortable, alone with the boss. That part of her which felt like she'd been betraying the office, staying away so long, that part of her which felt she should have fought this better, overcome her fears better, made more effort to get back to work, came rushing to the fore. Buchan, she knew, was soft on her. Too understanding, too willing to forgive, because he hadn't really known how to handle her struggle. He had enabled her to burrow down into a ball, and hide herself away. Not for his own ends, but because he hadn't known what else to do. And because he'd pitied her.

'Would you be more comfortable back in the ops room, Agnes?' asked Liddell.

Roth wasn't sure how to reply. She wanted to stay where she was. At least, she felt she *ought* to stay where she was. But she desperately wanted to return to the ops room, as though the bleak sanctum of the windowless inner office would shield her from evil.

'It's OK,' said Liddell, 'on you go. I need to make some calls. I'll stay here, man the phones.'

Roth nodded. Found she couldn't look at Liddell, and then lifted the laptop and walked quickly from the open-plan, down the short corridor, into the ops room. A moment, a hesitation, and then she closed the door.

She sat down in the seat in which she'd spent most of the day since Buchan had said she had to come in. She stared at the computer screen. Nothing registered.

The programs were still running, although so far they had given up no further useful information. If they had, she very possibly wouldn't have seen it.

Her mind wasn't blank, however. She was seeing Houston. Houston, who they'd all been fond of. Houston, the empathetic one. Houston, who had called her at least once a week for the past few months, not realising she was at Buchan's apartment every time they'd spoken. Houston, who had been so understanding. Houston, who earlier that day had squeezed her hand and given her the sweetest smile when he'd thought none of the others were looking. Houston, who had literally saved her life three months earlier when he'd killed her abductor. Houston, who had saved them all, by jumping on top of a small IED. Whose final act had been to find her, a last, desperate, hopeless glance, that had felt like a look of doomed love.

Houston, whose body had been blown apart. Whose blood had flown. Whose flesh had been scattered. Whose bloody eyes had stared into the bottomless depths from his battered face, as they'd all picked their way out of Jerry's. Houston, now in a mortuary somewhere, just another entry in a day that had turned into a catalogue of death.

Detective Sergeant Ian Houston, killed in the line of duty.

She held off the tears as long as she could. In fact, she hadn't cried at all in all this time. Not since she'd been rescued in January. Not since she'd been about twelve. And she didn't think she was going to cry now either.

When the tears came they arrived on the back of a great sob, heaving from her throat, and then she was leaning forward on the desk, tears on her face and in her hands, her nose running, unable to contain the flood of grief.

55

'Bad time to bring up that Agnes has daddy issues?' said Kane.

Sitting in the car. Middle of the night, tension upon them. She kicked herself as soon as she spoke.

Buchan, face set hard, said, 'Seriously, sergeant? Anything else you want to discuss at the moment?'

'Sorry.' Then she couldn't help adding, 'Just saying.'

'She misses her father,' said Buchan, hating his own defensiveness. 'He's dead. Virtually everyone with a dead father wishes their father wasn't dead. I may seem like a soulless oaf with a heart of burnt toast, but even I miss my dad and he's been gone thirty years. That's not having issues. It's... life.'

Silence returned to the car. Buchan checked his rear-view mirror, making sure the others were still with him. Kane silently accepted the rebuke, told herself to keep her mouth shut.

*

They approached on a parallel road, parking half a mile away, in between dimly-illuminated street lights.

They got out of the cars, and met in the shadows by a high wall. Here they were, about to raid another warehouse, this time with much more trepidation. The previous warehouse raid had almost been one of curiosity. Why had the Baltazars left their motorbike at this particular point? If there was a reason, perhaps it was in one of the warehouses. That was all. No one had thought they were going to find fourteen corpses.

Now though, they felt the fear of it. For the first time in this long, unending horror of a day, they had something they could call a breakthrough, and the people who had carried out the slaughter of the Bancroft gang might well have been based in this facility. Heavily armed, and more than happy to use the weapons at their disposal.

Buchan showed the Lishi tool to Dawkins and Cherry.

'Should have checked,' he said. 'Leaving in haste,' he added with a head shake. 'You have one of these?'

'Sir,' said Dawkins, nodding and indicating her pocket, as Cherry shook his head.

'Good. We'll stay in twos. You managed to study the layout of the place on your way over?'

'Sir,' she repeated, with another nod.

'OK. I think we might well have to jump the fence. We circle, we find the two least illuminated spots. If they have major security round the place, then we're possibly busted right from the off. Just have to take our chances. We approach along here, split as we get to the first side road. Sam and I go to the far side, you take this side. If, by some chance, there's an open gate... we don't take it. Once inside the fence, we'll take the single door on Parkfield street, you take the door on Renton. We good?'

Cherry and Dawkins nodded.

'Phones on silent, set to a single vibrate. Let us know as soon as you're aware of anything.'

'Boss,' said Cherry, and then the four of them turned and began walking quickly along the road in the direction of the warehouse, with the large red and white sign stating Lyon International, which, as far as they knew, housed many of the goods from William Lansdowne's legitimate operations.

They separated as Cherry and Dawkins turned away, and then Buchan and Kane were running alongside a high, grey railing, constantly looking into the warehouse facility to see if they were being watched. There were bound to be cameras, and they had no idea how closely they'd be getting monitored. Nevertheless, they'd not been fed this information, it was something they'd worked out for themselves. They could at least be confident they weren't walking into a trap.

Round the far side of the fence, and then running down the road into a shadowed area between street lights, in the lee of the long, high wall of the warehouse. They stopped, they lay low, they listened.

Dawkins and Cherry were long since lost to them, but at least, so far, there was no shouting, no sound of their approach having been discovered.

From his low crouch, Buchan looked up at the height of the fence, Kane following his gaze.

'You going to make it, old man?' asked Kane, and Buchan gave her a quick sideways glance.

He scanned the side of the warehouse, picked his door, and then looked at the thirty yards between where they were and the side of the building.

'We'll aim for that large container in the first instance, in case a security light comes on. Re-assess when we're there, but we're aiming for the red door. We get busted, no messing around. We balls it out, straight to showing our ID and demanding entry to the warehouse.'

'Boss,' said Kane.

A quick look, and then Buchan reached up, hands gripping two railings near the top, and hauled himself up. A moment when he thought his momentum wouldn't carry him, and then he'd established his grip, a foot solidly on the top of the railing, another anxious moment, and then he was over and down onto the other side, landing clumsily, a slight turning of the ankle, and then stepping away.

Two yards to his left, Kane had come at the same time, landing just after him. The security light came on, as they ran the short distance to the container, Buchan feeling his ankle the whole way. Then, backs against the container, looking at the service area now flooded with light, they stood still, peculiarly out of breath, as so often happens in the tension of the moment, after little more than a few seconds of action.

'We wait until the light goes off?' said Kane.

'Give it thirty seconds,' said Buchan, and he made a small gesture to indicate listening out for any reaction, for anyone who might have become aware of the light.

Silence, then a sound, but in the moment something that suggested no threat, and then a rat scurried across the edge of the light, and back into the shadows.

'Feels a little like we're in a Bond film,' said Kane. Nervous chatter.

Buchan didn't respond. Listening to the night. Waiting.

'You all right?' he asked, after a few moments.

She nodded in the night.

The light went out.

'Come on,' he said, and then they were along the side of the container, then back out into the open and quickly to the side door of the warehouse, the security light back on as soon as they emerged.

Lockpick already in hand, he got to work on the Yale lock, it took less than twenty seconds, and then they were inside. In the light of the beam from outside, they could see a large space, mostly empty, concrete floor, double doors at either end, another single door on the other side, rows of packaging to the right, and then they'd closed the door behind them, and they were plunged instantly into darkness.

Phones out, their torches coming on simultaneously, shining them behind and around.

'Don't like the look of that,' said Kane, and she indicated the deadbolts at the top and bottom of the inside of the door. Buchan knew what she meant. Had the bolts not been used because there had never been any need for them, or had they been left undone as an invitation? Someone was expected. Perhaps even Buchan and his team were expected.

'Any ideas,' said Buchan, starting to move quickly across the empty space.

'Nothing brilliant,' said Kane. 'I think we aim for the single door, and take it from there.'

They were already heading towards it, and Buchan continued quickly in its direction. Once there he hesitated, put his ear to the door. Silence in the large room while he listened, he and Kane with their eyes on each other.

'Anything?' she asked, more in the movement of her lips than in sound, and he gave her a small nod in reply.

'Voices,' he said softly.

She waited, thought of pressing herself next to him and trying to listen, but decided against it.

'Doesn't make sense, though,' he said, after a few moments. 'Think it's a TV.'

Someone was watching a show, he thought, or else this might possibly be how it looked on the surface. A ghost town. The building hollowed-out of people. No one on the other side, a TV left playing to confuse them and taunt them, as though Lansdowne and Baltazar or whoever was behind all of this knew that Buchan and his team were going to arrive at some point.

He glanced at Kane, and together they looked down at the lock, Kane indicating it was time for him to work his magic.

Buchan hesitated. It might well have been that it wasn't even locked in the first place, but trying the handle would instantly alert whoever was inside to their presence. The sound of the pick in the lock, no matter how quiet he tried to be, would do the same. Kane nodded as he went through the thought process, indicating she was thinking the same thing, and she made a gesture with her shoulder.

Buchan thought about it, considered the standard mortice

lock and handle, at the mid-point of the door, then, his face set grim and hard, nodded and took a step back. He hated doing this, but it suddenly seemed the only way. There was a strong possibility that the people inside had guns, and the only way they'd manage to give themselves any advantage at all was by surprise.

They, of course, had no idea if they had that. And there was barely a guarantee that the door would give way, no matter how much weight and force he managed to put against it.

Kane pointed to herself and indicated the door. Buchan decided that he likely would have more chance, and shook his head.

Took a step back, tensed, braced himself, his phone buzzed, he ignored it, muttered a quick 'Dammit' under his breath, and then he leant into the kick, the sole of his shoe against the door next to the lock, and the door gave way instantly, and he fell forwards behind it, Kane rushing in next to him, nearly tripping on his stumbling rear leg.

They straightened, they stopped, they stared.

'Shit,' said Kane.

They were too late.

56

There was a television playing. An American cop show Buchan didn't recognise. Dawkins and Cherry had beaten them to it, and were already in the room. Cherry still had his phone in his hand from having messaged Buchan. They were standing over the couch, where Claire Avercamp's body had been left, sitting upright, unbound, as though watching the TV. Like the first corpse of the day, the body of Łukasz Kamiński who they'd found in the Baltazar safe house, she'd died from a single gunshot wound to the forehead.

'Crap,' muttered Buchan.

Cherry approached, a note in his hand.

'This was left on the corpse,' he said, holding it forward.

Buchan took the note, held it so that Kane, standing next to him, also had sight of it.

Too late, Inspector. Some people just know too much. Until the next time.

Buchan read it a second time. A third. Felt the mockery of it seep through his bones.

'How'd they know you'd be the one to come across the body?' asked Kane. 'Maybe they're still on the premises.'

Buchan didn't feel it. Suddenly he didn't want to talk, words seeming useless. The note could have been found by anyone, he thought, and sure, he was no longer the only detective inspector working on the case, but everyone would've known who they'd meant, and this would have got back to him.

'Fair enough,' he said. 'Flood the place with light, Danny. You and I'll make a quick search. Ellie, call it in, please. Sam, we need someone round at Lansdowne's house, right now. I want eyes on him, and I don't want him going anywhere until we're speaking to him.'

'Boss,' they said together, then Buchan, as he followed Cherry from the room, perhaps far less careful than he ought to have been, took out his phone and called Liddell.

'How is it?'

'They've cleared out already,' he said, following Cherry

through to the main part of the warehouse. Cavernous, made all the more so by being completely empty. 'The only thing they left behind is Claire Avercamp's corpse.'

There was a heavy sigh from the other end of the phone.

'Dammit,' said Liddell.

'They left a note. Too late, inspector, some people just know too much.'

'Goddammit.'

'Until the next time.'

'That was also part of the note?'

'Yes.'

'Goddammit.'

'I asked Sam to call, get someone round to Lansdowne's place. Make sure he's not going anywhere tonight. We have no proof who did this, but it's on his property, we know that much.'

'It's not.'

Buchan had walked around an internal side wall, looking down a well-lit corridor. This was the way Cherry and Dawkins would have come. There was nothing to see.

'What?' he said.

He stopped, his heart sinking, this day, this night, lurching from one disaster, one horror, to the next.

'It was sold last week,' said Liddell.

'To Baltazar?'

'Not so that we can prove. Agnes is still digging. But it looks like one of those murky international deals where the paperwork has been constructed in such a way as to make the actual current owners of the property almost impossible to establish.'

'Fuck's sake,' spat Buchan, his voice low, then he straightened his shoulders, took a deep breath, trying to expel the demons of self-loathing and hopelessness. 'Sorry, sorry,' he said, head shaking.

'Once again, said exactly the same thing myself,' said Liddell.

Cherry walked back towards Buchan, head shaking, just as Buchan was walking through to see Kane. He caught her still on the phone, and made a small throat cutting gesture.

'Boss?'

'Leave it for now,' he said, his voice dead. 'Lansdowne sold this place last week. He's up to his eyes in this, but… we'll leave it for tonight.'

'He what?'

'Agnes has been digging.'

'This is no longer a Lansdowne property?'

'Correct.'

'Fuck me,' said Kane, gritting her teeth.

She turned away, took a moment to compose herself, and then resumed her call, this time to call off the latest early morning visit to Lansdowne's home.

'Sorry, boss,' said Buchan, putting the phone to his ear again.

'That's OK. You've called in Avercamp's murder?'

'Ellie's on that at the moment.'

'Wait for Ruth and her team to get there, or whoever's still standing at Scenes of Crime, then get back here. We need to wrap this up for the day.' A pause, her voice was heavy. 'We're done for now, inspector.'

The phone clicked off. From nowhere, in the near distance, the sound of a police siren.

Buchan stood for a moment looking at the empty warehouse. Everyone gone. Everything gone. Silent, bar the footsteps of Dawkins and Cherry, intermittently echoing through the large space.

His mind was still working. What Liddell had said, we need to wrap this up for the day, were the words of a leader. They made sense, thought Buchan. She was looking after her staff, she was looking after the investigation. Everyone needed to get some rest before attacking this again. And yet, for all their worth, the words were pointless. There was no way any of them were just dropping a day like this, going to bed, and falling asleep in a couple of minutes. There was no way anyone was waking in a few hours, refreshed, bright, full of ideas that weren't coming to them at the moment.

There had to be something. Some element of closure, or else no sleep would come. Not for him. Not when one of his staff had been murdered. Not when the woman they'd spent the day trying to find had been killed at the last.

'What are you thinking?' asked Kane.

Her voice was flat. Tired. Defeated.

'I'm thinking that they didn't need to tunnel out of here.'

They stood in silence for a moment. Buchan's arms were folded, as he stared at the large double doors at the far end of the warehouse.

'Sorry, I'm not sure what you mean,' said Kane.

'They've had a crew here,' said Buchan. 'It's possible, of course, they were using other places around town, they've obviously brought resources to the party, but for the moment all we have is this place. We know they were using this place. And if they had a crew operating out of here today, they've all gone very recently. Tonight. They brought Claire Avercamp here, and they left again.'

Kane was nodding by the time he finished.

'And they didn't tunnel out,' she said.

'Let's get the footage from the CCTV along the road. Let's get number plates. Let's get what we can.'

'First thing in the morning, or…?'

'We need to do it right now,' said Buchan. 'perhaps they're splitting up, and blending happily into society. But it could be they've moved out en masse, heading south, heading somewhere, and they're already halfway to Dover.' He looked at his watch. 'Middle of the night, dammit, could be more than that. South coast in eight hours from here at this time of day, they could be on a ferry by seven a.m.'

'Boss,' said Kane. 'We should get back, but I'll call ahead. Get Agnes on it.'

57

'Bingo,' said Buchan, and the buzz of it, of actually honing in on something that might be of use to them, meant that he barely heard the flippancy of the word as it crossed his lips.

Standing at Liddell's shoulder as they looked at footage taken from around the warehouse facility.

They'd been disappointed at first. There was so little movement at the front of the building that they'd begun to think the gang had become aware of the CCTV cameras along the road. Spotting them, and avoiding them, would hardly have been an act of astonishing clear-sightedness. A basic job on the first day of operations. The fact that the police had spotted anyone at all in and out of the place, albeit a couple of days previously, was the surprise.

So they'd checked a lot of footage, with nothing more to show for it. Finally, a minibus parked at the far side of the compound, the front of the bus marginally in view.

It was enough.

Liddell had closed in on the front of the van, she had quickly cleaned up the blurred and indistinct image. The details had become discernible.

An electric blue, Ford Transit. Registration SJ17VBH.

Kane had joined them, Liddell indicating the number plate on the screen.

'Make the call, sergeant, please,' said Liddell, and Kane turned away, buoyed by the same enthusiasm that had just gripped Buchan.

*

Half an hour later. They were all standing in or around Buchan's spot at the window, albeit not in a straight line.

Buchan, Liddell, Kane, Cherry, and Dawkins. The moment had passed. It had been a stroke of good fortune, it had been a lead to be followed, a piece of information to be disseminated. There had been a buzz to it, but it wasn't as though it had ever been going to achieve instantaneous results. No port authority, no airport, no local police force anywhere in the country, was going to be able to immediately respond with a positive identification.

Under different circumstances, it would have been a positive moment to drive them forward. But it was the early morning, after a long, dreadful day, and the buzz had quickly died. Now the day, that had drifted into a long and even more dreadful night, was coming to an end. The sky was lightening, cloudless and fair, the first hint of a low sun etched on the buildings to their right.

They had not brought Lansdowne in, they had not brought in any of his people. But they had sight of them. None of them had fled, none of them were dead. They had stayed where they were, protected by the blanket of apparent innocence. However suspicious Lansdowne and his people looked, they knew that Buchan and his team had nothing on them.

No one had spoken for several minutes. Both Buchan and Liddell knew they had to leave so that the others would follow, but the day was beginning with a crushing sense of unfinished business. They had to get some sleep at least. Go home, three hours perhaps, back in the office and ready to go by nine.

But the feeling of it was overwhelming. Baltazar was gone. The unseen, invisible presence had swept through, flexed his muscles, he had wiped out one gang, done a deal with the other – who he could easily have eradicated if he'd chosen to – he had killed a police officer, and had again not killed any more through choice rather than opportunity, and then he had disappeared. In the process he had possessed complete command and control of the city.

Perhaps, of course, Baltazar himself had not even come to town. More questions for Lansdowne, but if Baltazar was as much a player as he appeared to be, and as careful as he'd been so far, more than likely Lansdowne would be unable to answer.

'The horror of losing Ian aside, there's a lot about this that sticks in the throat,' said Liddell, her voice soft and unexpected, coming out of nowhere. 'But nothing as bad as the fact that someone, Bancroft or Lansdowne or Baltazar, or God knows who, but one of these people, these players, has someone on the inside of our force, and we have no idea who that is.'

She grimaced when she'd finished talking. A couple of the others nodded.

'We're going to have to root them out,' said Buchan, after a few moments. And then, after another couple of nods, he added, 'But not at five in the morning.'

'It's going to be tough knowing where to start,' said Liddell. 'Who to trust.'

Buchan thought of something to say, but it was just words, just pointless, stupid, hopeless words. He kept them to himself. He forgot them.

'I feel like the presence of a police insider,' said Kane, 'might just be a poor second to the fact that thirty Polish hoods walked in here, took over the city for the day, and then just waltzed back out of the country, undetected.'

Her hopelessness was initially greeted by silence, and then Liddell said, 'We'll get them before they're gone,' though there was little optimism in her voice.

'The word is out, that van is out there somewhere,' she added after a while. 'And, if we're lucky, there'll be another one with it.'

'Regardless of whether or not they're gone now,' said Buchan, 'they'll be back. Maybe not today,' and he was going to say maybe not tomorrow, then he stopped himself going down that road. Finally, when no one else added to it, he said, 'But they'll be back.'

'We're going to need a bigger department,' said Cherry, humourlessly getting in on the act of parodying film lines.

'Yes, we are,' said Liddell.

The day was getting lighter by the minute, although it was still too early for the city to start coming to life. The water on the river was another perfect, flat calm, awaiting the first rays of the morning sun to spear between buildings.

'Everybody needs to leave,' said Liddell, suddenly. 'You're all adults, I'm not going to do that thing where I stand here like matron making sure you go. Good night, such as it is. I will see you all in a few hours. Inspector Buchan, please make sure you take Agnes with you.'

*

Everyone was exhausted and did not take any persuading. Kane, Cherry and Dawkins all stopped in on Roth to see how she was doing, to try not to patronise or pity here, to say good night, to say they hoped she'd feel better. Kane again apologised to

Buchan for her latest comment about Roth, made in the heat of the tension before what had ultimately been a damp squib of a raid on the old Lansdowne warehouse, and Buchan had again said that she didn't have to apologise.

The others had already gone by the time Buchan walked into the ops room. Roth was still sitting at her computer, head down, searching the Internet and the police databases of Europe, as though it was the middle of the working day, and she hadn't been sitting there for close on twelve hours.

The others had found her uncommunicative, and had thought her perhaps traumatised and distant rather than absorbed. As it was, she'd barely heard what any of them had said, another unpleasant feeling growing in her gut.

'Agnes,' repeated Buchan, having spoken her name when he walked into the room.

Again she didn't appear to have heard him. He approached, stood beside her, looked at the screen. A mass of information, cluttered, referencing flight manifests from private jets leaving Glasgow airport that morning.

'They're certainly ballsy,' said Buchan, 'but I don't think they're going to straight up take their thirty guys to the airport and put them on a flight, even if it is a private plane. Might be a little too obvious.'

Nothing for a few moments, then Roth finally turned and looked up at him. She had to think about what he'd said, and then she replied, 'What, sorry?'

'I don't think this gang, this gang of Poles who've swept through here today, I don't think they're getting a plane out of here. They'll be travelling on false passports, and maybe they'll fly, given we barely know who any of them are, but…'

He stopped as she was shaking her head at him again, and he said, 'What?'

'That wasn't who I was looking for. I was assuming they'll split up, use fake non-Polish passports, then fly out, or a ferry, or Eurotunnel, or whatever.'

'Who are you looking for then?' asked Buchan, studying the screen, trying to dig down into the details in amongst the jumble of information.

She turned back to the screen and indicated a single name against the second private flight of the morning, due to depart in just over an hour.

Daniel Maplethorpe.

———

'He's flying to Warsaw?' said Buchan, and Roth nodded.

Buchan looked at the departure time, then looked at his watch, making the calculation. It was significant, and it was unlikely to be a coincidence that he should be getting out of town, and out of the country, but if Buchan were to dash out there now, how exactly was he going to stop him? On what grounds could he possibly hold this man?

'I don't think there's anything we can do.'

'That's not the thing,' said Roth.

'What's the thing?'

She looked at him, her eyes exhausted, bloodshot, then turned back to the screen.

'Jan Baltazar, in his early days of low-level thuggery and crime, used several aliases. One of them was Michał Świderski. I managed to dig up a picture of Michał Świderski. Taken nearly thirty years ago, mid-nineties, way pre-EU for Poland. A police file on a charge of sexual assault.'

She changed page on her browser, and there was the picture. An old black and white photo. He had long hair and a thin face, a limp, young moustache, but the eyes, and the shape of the nose and the mouth were unmistakeable.

Jan Baltazar and Daniel Maplethorpe were the same person.

Buchan felt the thrill of it at the back of his throat.

'How on earth did that suddenly turn up?'

'Like I said, it's pre-EU. It's from the Dark Ages. There is a *lot* of information out there in the world, and eastern Europe was the wild west back then, right?'

'I need to get out there,' said Buchan, and automatically started turning away. He stopped at the door, looked back at her, suddenly remembered that she should be leaving as well. 'Good work,' he said. She had no words in reply. 'I can drop you off at the apartment, but I'll have to be quick.'

'I'll come with you,' she said.

'You sure?'

She didn't seem very sure, and didn't answer. But she got to her feet, grabbed the light coat she'd slung over the back of the chair, slipped her phone into her pocket, closed her laptop and lifted it, and then walked to the door.

'You're right,' she said, as she stopped beside him, 'we have to be quick.'

58

They didn't call ahead, fearing a change of plan, a bringing forward of the departure, or an escape from the airport. He expected Maplethorpe would be waiting in the VIP lounge at the far end of the main terminal. Coffee and early morning croissants. Perhaps he would wait until he was on his way, jetting through a clear blue morning sky, before he ate breakfast.

The phone rang as Buchan was parking the car at the airport. Liddell. He stared at the number, wasn't sure he wanted to pick up.

'The chief knows what we're doing?' said Roth, looking at the phone.

Buchan didn't respond. He didn't think Liddell could know, and what did it matter anyway?

'Boss,' he said, taking the call.

'Where are you?'

'Just got a thing to do,' he said. 'Going home shortly. What's up?'

Why wasn't he telling Liddell, now that he was literally at the airport? *She's not the insider*, a small voice said in his head.

Silence for a moment, and he could almost hear Liddell pondering whether she should badger him into telling her what was going on.

'We got them,' she said, her words, from nowhere, unexpected.

'The Transit?'

'Yes. It arrived at Felixstowe twenty minutes ago. You'd think they'd have done something smart like change vans, but maybe they're not as omnipotent as we thought.'

'Too early for names?'

'Yes.'

'Any sign of another bus?'

'Not yet. I suspect, not ever, now. But this is a start.'

Buchan stared straight ahead. Could feel Roth next to him, watching his face, waiting to see what he would do with the information.

At the moment they would have nothing that would allow them to pin any of the day's crimes on any of these people. There would be fingerprinting, and DNA samples, and blood tests; there would be interrogations, there would be the usual games of trying to play one off against the other. But yes, as Liddell had said, it was a start.

'Where are you, inspector?' she asked.

*

They showed their badges, they were viewed dimly as they walked past, through two levels of very low-key security, and then they were into the quiet, and spacious private departure lounge at Glasgow airport.

Outside the day had dawned, the sun was low, the sky a beautiful morning's pale blue. There was a woman on reception, looking fresh and awake as though she'd only just come on duty. Buchan glanced around the room, as they approached the desk, and could see Maplethorpe sitting at the back. Phone in his hand, cup of coffee on the table in front of him. He noticed Buchan and Roth as soon as they entered.

Buchan showed his card and indicated Maplethorpe.

'Just need a quick word,' he said.

'Mr Maplethorpe will be boarding in less than five minutes,' said the receptionist with a warning smile.

Buchan didn't reply, turning away, and walking through the deserted room to Maplethorpe at the back. There was no music playing, the large television in the corner was switched off.

'Inspector Buchan,' said Maplethorpe. 'How predictable.'

He glanced at Roth, giving her an obvious up and down look.

'And you've brought a new character to the drama,' said Maplethorpe. 'Who's this? We've had the chief inspector, the inspector, the sergeant... is she work experience? Is it bring your daughter to work day?'

Words were in Buchan's mouth, on his lips, and he stopped them. *This is Constable Roth who worked out you and Jan Baltazar are the same person.* But perhaps that would put Roth in the firing line. Perhaps not, but this man's approach to killing had so far been scattergun.

'We have reason to believe that you and Jan Baltazar are the same person. Baltazar is wanted in connection with a series of crimes in and around the city of Glasgow in the last twenty-four hours, including the murder of Claire Avercamp.'

'Claire's dead?'

'You know Claire's dead. You likely ordered her murder.'

Maplethorpe looked deadpan at Buchan. Roth might as well not have been there. He'd dismissed her with his glib comment on her arrival, and now, as far as he was concerned, the business was between him and Buchan.

'A very serious accusation, Inspector Buchan. Does your chief know you're here?'

'You're not getting on that plane,' said Buchan.

'You're arresting me?'

'Yes. Just as we've arrested fifteen of your men travelling in a minibus at Felixstowe in the last half hour.'

The implacability slipped for a moment, the shadow of rage flashing across his face, and then it was gone, and once again he stared blankly back at Buchan. For a moment, however, Buchan had seen behind the curtain.

Maplethorpe slipped the phone into his pocket, then his eyes drifted to the side, and Buchan was aware of the approach of the receptionist.

'Sorry to disturb you, Mr Maplethorpe, but your flight's ready for boarding.'

'Thank you,' said Maplethorpe.

The receptionist hovered for a second, but could tell she'd walked into a metaphorical gunfight, said, 'Two minutes,' and turned away.

Maplethorpe took a drink of coffee, swallowing silently, his look resigned as he faced up to something he appeared to not want to face, and then he stood up, brushed an imaginary mark from his trousers, and lifted the small case that had been propped at his feet.

'This would be a very bad career move, inspector,' he said, 'so perhaps, you might want to think again before you make it.'

'You're under arrest for the conspiracy to murder Claire Avercamp,' said Buchan. And then, his voice dropping a notch he added, 'Other charges are likely to follow.'

Maplethorpe took a deep breath as he held Buchan's gaze, then he allowed his eyes to drift to Roth, standing a pace behind Buchan.

We're going to lose, thought Buchan. I don't know how, but two minutes from now he's going to be on that plane. He felt the familiar tight constraint on his stomach, the fear of the moment. This time, though, there was no danger, but here at the last he thought they'd found something they could use. They'd learned the thing that the opposition didn't want them to know. So often that was the moment when the breakthrough came, that was the catalyst.

But not today.

'We've still not been introduced,' said Maplethorpe to Roth, his voice dismissive. 'I shall assume you are the inspector's secretarial assistant, though it was not a position I was aware existed in Police Scotland. Secretarial assistant to the detective inspector. Hmm, quite the career. The police must be far more flush with resources than we all realise.' He smiled, and she gave him nothing in return, not even contempt. He opened the case, reached inside, took out his passport and handed it to Roth. 'Perhaps you could pass the details of this on to the inspector.'

Roth waited a moment. Regardless of how she was feeling, and how run through she was, Buchan recognised the hesitation. She wanted to ignore him. Or she wanted to take the passport from him and rip it in half. Or hit him over the head with it. But she wouldn't actually have done any of those things back in the days of confidence and chutzpah and pink hair, and she certainly wasn't going to do it now.

She took the passport, she kept a dead eye on him for a moment, and then looked at the document.

Buchan had noticed the wording on the burgundy cover as soon as Maplethorpe had handed it over. *Paszport Dyplomatyczny.*

Roth looked at the cover, then opened the document to check the details. Like an agent at border control, she looked at the picture, she looked at Maplethorpe, she looked back at the picture, and then she handed it back. He nodded a thank you, and put the document back inside the case.

'Shall I spell it out for you, detective inspector?'

Buchan's face had gone into neutral. He knew this went beyond a spurious claim to diplomatic immunity. There was no diplomatic immunity for murder. But if they went through with the arrest, they would be taking someone accredited as a Polish diplomat, presumably attached to the consulate in Edinburgh in some way, and accusing them of a crime for which they had no proof. An arrest now would be on the basis of appearances. Jan

Baltazar appeared to be guilty, appeared to have his hands all over this. But, at best, they could place one or two of the men who were known to have worked for Baltazar at the heart of it, and they might well have a struggle to make a case against them, to put them at the scene, or prove a gun in a hand, to successfully bring a prosecution for a raid on an antique book shop, the explosion at Jerry's, the massacre of the Bancroft gang, or the murder of Claire Avercamp.

This would be arrest and hope. Arrest and interrogate, hoping Baltazar slipped up, or stumbled, or shot himself in the foot.

An hour or two from now the Foreign Secretary in King Charles Street would get a phone call from his Polish counterpart, or a visit from the Polish ambassador, or the British ambassador in Warsaw would be summoned to the Polish Ministry of Foreign Affairs, and words would be spoken, demands made, and soon enough Liddell would take a call, and Maplethorpe would be released and a lot of people would be very angry.

And when the dust had settled, and on the off-chance Buchan was still in a job, Maplethorpe would be even more off limits than he currently was, standing in an expensive suit, in a private airport departure lounge, with a diplomatic passport in his case.

'Mr Maplethorpe, it's time,' came the voice from somewhere behind.

Maplethorpe looked at them both, one to the other.

'Inspector Buchan,' he said. 'I'm sure there will be a next time.'

Then he looked at Roth, and she saw the shadow of malevolence flash across his eyes.

'Constable Roth,' he said. 'I should leave you to get back to the inspector's apartment, you look like you could use some sleep.'

Then he lifted something else from the case, holding it in his hands, looking at it rather than Buchan or Roth.

A book, an old-fashioned green cover, Polish writing on the spine.

'At least I'll have something to read on the flight,' he said.

He nodded, he looked at neither Buchan nor Roth again, and then he walked past them, smiling as he approached the receptionist.

59

'We'd looked this man up, though?' said Liddell. Back in the car, heading home, Buchan had called Liddell straight away, knowing she wouldn't be asleep. He could see her sitting at her kitchen table amidst a haze of cigarette smoke in the morning light, drinking several cups of black coffee. 'I mean, he wasn't listed anywhere on the website of the Polish consulate in Edinburgh?'

'No.'

'Dammit.'

After a pause, she asked the mundane question, 'Where does it leave us?'

It wasn't like Buchan hadn't been thinking it through all night, every calamity, every murder hammering a stake into the investigation, and Maplethorpe having a diplomatic passport hadn't actually changed anything.

'Avercamp is dead. Davie Bancroft, and all but one of his gang, are dead. Detective Sergeant Houston is dead.' He paused, he swallowed. 'As far as we are aware, all of these murders were carried out by people from within the Baltazar gang. However, as yet we have no evidence to support this theory. Maybe we'll be able to pin something on one of these fifteen now in custody. That's all we've got. William Lansdowne's part in all this is as yet unknown. Malky Seymour we know, at least, was aware of Claire Avercamp's kidnap. We can bring him in on that charge.'

'Very small potatoes.'

'We can hope he's willing to spill some more beans, and maybe... well, we can think about doing a deal.'

'Witness protection.'

'Aye. We'll see if he wants to play. I don't think we should be optimistic. I suspect, if Baltazar values the man, he'll throw lawyers at him and we'll be pushed to put him away for more than a couple of months. If not, he'll throw him to the dogs, and it won't matter.'

He paused. He could feel Liddell's sense of hopelessness.

'It leaves us with a Davie Bancroft-sized hole in the

Glasgow crime world,' said Buchan, 'and we wait, impotently, to see who's going to fill it.'

'If Maplethorpe and Baltazar are the same person,' said Liddell, 'what exactly was the relationship with Bancroft in the first place? Why did they need Bancroft? Not for local knowledge, surely, not if Maplethorpe has long had an office here.'

'I don't know,' said Buchan, his voice tired. 'I think we'll find Maplethorpe does not spend much time in Glasgow. Or perhaps, anywhere. He moves around. And maybe he just didn't want his own people involved up front, and only needed to get them over when Davie Bancroft raised the stakes.'

Liddell grunted at the other end of the phone.

He drove on, nearing the turn-off for the city centre. The phone on speaker, they could hear the settling of the mug back on the table, the click of the lighter, the puff of the cigarette.

'Are you there, Agnes?' asked Liddell.

'Yes, ma'am.'

'I assume you're returning to the inspector's apartment.'

It wasn't a question, but she left a gap, nevertheless. Roth didn't reply. She gave Buchan an uncomfortable glance.

'Yes,' said Buchan.

'Agnes, if you want to come into work in the morning, you are of course welcome. However, you do require to be medically signed off the sick list. If you want to come back, then I would ask that you arrange for that to be done. However, I cannot emphasise this enough, no one is expecting you to come in. You should take as long as it takes.'

Another gap.

'Thank you, ma'am,' said Roth.

'OK, inspector. There's no more news from Felixstowe. We need to let the border police do their job, and we need to get at least a couple of hours of sleep.'

'Boss,' said Buchan.

The phone went dead.

*

'Really?' said Buchan.

Back in his apartment. Tiredness had hit him at last. And the sad awfulness of it. Houston was dead. One of the good guys. A decent man. Thank God, thought Buchan, he had no family. He wasn't sure there had even been a girlfriend. But there was a mum and dad, whose doorbell in Inverness would have rung the previous night, to be told the piece of news that every parent of a police officer dreads.

'Just green tea,' said Roth.

Buchan glanced at her, then looked at the mug she'd put in his hands. There was no amusement in her, nor encouragement. She looked hollowed out.

'You should sleep for a few hours,' she said. 'Caffeine isn't going to help.'

They were standing in his other familiar spot, by the window of his apartment, looking out on the water, a mile down river from the office.

Buchan stared at the mug, took a sip of the drink, then reached behind and placed it on the table.

'I'll just have some water before I get into bed,' he said.

Silence.

They stood side-by-side, looking out on the river. Roth put the mug to her lips, automatically blowing across the top, then taking a small drink. He couldn't hear her swallow.

There was nothing on the river. No boats, no rowers. It was not yet seven a.m. and the sun was glinting off the glass of the buildings on the other bank.

'Are you all right?' asked Buchan.

There would have been other ways to put the question. He was too tired to think of them.

'No,' she said.

'You should get to bed. And, like the chief said, don't come in to work. Take your time. We'll talk tonight about what you should do.'

She took another drink. He thought he could see a shake in her hand.

'I should go,' she said. Another drink. 'This isn't doing either of us any good. I should get back to my own place. It's time.'

The words sounded automatic. Like she'd rehearsed them. Saying what she thought she should say. Saying what she thought Buchan wanted to hear.

She put the mug to her lips, then her eyes dropped for a moment, she didn't take a drink, she shook her head, she turned and laid the mug on the table behind.

She turned back, but she wasn't looking at Buchan. She

wasn't looking at the river. Eyes down, staring at nothing.

'Sorry,' she said.

'Why?'

Silence.

Finally, 'I shouldn't have... you don't need this. You don't need me here.'

'That's immaterial.'

'No, it's not,' she said, still saying what she thought needed to be said. He could hear it in her voice. No conviction, hating what she was saying, hating herself for having to say it. 'Like I said, I can't have you pity me.'

She closed her eyes, so that when he turned and looked at her, studying her face, she wasn't looking at him.

She was pale, her face drawn, her lips cold, despite the warm tea that had recently passed across them. He had words in his mouth. Words he knew he shouldn't say. Words he knew he'd likely regret. There was another voice trying to make sure he didn't say them. He thought of Kane, and what she would say if she saw the two of them standing here like this, a few inches apart, lost in the moment, like troubled lovers.

Don't speak, he thought.

A silent tear rolled down Roth's face, and she grimaced, annoyed at herself, and wiped it away. She laughed bitterly, self-consciously, and a small sob escaped the back of her throat, and she shook her head.

'Sorry,' she said again.

Finally they looked at each other. Words were easy enough to avoid. Buchan had never had any trouble not speaking. But the basic need for human contact, the touch of someone else's hand, the warmth of an embrace, particularly after such a long, godawful day, was as strong in him as it would be in anyone else.

Normally he would unthinkingly accept that it just wasn't possible. There was no such person in his life, and hadn't been since Janey had left. But here he was, alone with someone he cared about, someone who needed him.

When his fingers touched hers, it was almost as though they had acted independently.

Now he heard her swallow.

Their fingers slowly, tentatively entwined, and then Buchan drew Roth towards him and took her into his arms. She rested her head against his shoulder, relaxing into the embrace. There were no more tears. Buchan stared over her shoulder, face set hard, unable to give himself to the moment. Eventually, however, it would come.

On the sofa Edelman watched them, as indifferent to the long day and night that had ended, as to the one that was just beginning.

DI Buchan will return

in

WE WERE NOT INNOCENT

BUCHAN

(DI Buchan Book 1)

A mystery written in blood.

The head of a literary publishing house is murdered, and Detective Inspector Buchan and his team enter a world of writers and editors, of passion, jealousy and hate. Suspects are not in short supply, but before the investigation can really get going, there's a second murder, this one throwing up the existence of an unknown manuscript.

Now clues and motives and suspects abound, and the hunt is on for *Ladybird*, a book that no one knows anything about. There's a game being played, and Buchan needs to find out what it is before anyone else dies. For that is the only certainty: sooner or later, as rain sweeps across the rundown city, and the players drift in and out of suspicion, the killer will strike again.

BUCHAN is the first title in a major new Scottish detective series, featuring DI Buchan and his team from Glasgow's Serious Crime Unit.

PAINTED IN BLOOD

(DI Buchan Book 2)

Where every murder is a masterpiece.

A double murder, a public spectacle, a killer toying with the police. And then, from nowhere, a mysterious woman with a story to tell, a suspect handed to **DI Buchan** on a plate.

It's been a bad few months for Buchan and his team, little going right. They need a win. What they don't need is a murder victim, the naked corpse of the young woman posed on a park bench, erotically summoning viewers to the scene of her death. Then a week later, a second victim.

Out of nowhere, a woman finds Buchan in the Winter Moon, claiming the posing of the corpses was based on two paintings by a little known Spanish artist. And she brings ill news; there's a third painting in the series, and she herself will be the victim.

It is so unexpected, and so alien to everything they've investigated so far, suddenly it seems Buchan is carrying out an entirely new line of inquiry. However, as he gets closer to the heart of darkness, it becomes evident the two strands of the investigation are linked, the threat is imminent, and that the re-enactment of the third painting is close to being realised…